For Felicity

FINDING LIEN

R. BRUCE LOGAN

BLACK ROSE
writing™

ISBN: 978-1-61296-690-8
PUBLISHED BY BLACK ROSE WRITING
www.blackrosewriting.com

Printed in the United States of America
Suggested retail price $16.95

Finding Lien is printed in Calibri
Cover Photograph, with permission, by John Petter Klovstad

For the children whose innocence has been stolen,
the victims of human trafficking and sex slavery.

FINDING LIEN

PROLOGUE

A delivery truck stopped in front of a flophouse on Pham Ngu Lao Street in Saigon's District 1. The neon logo of the tattoo parlor next door flickered, and a metal gate secured the doorway of a pawnshop across the street, its crisscross expanse a focal point in the jumbled mosaic of signs and openings that marked the storefronts and rooms above. Two 13-year-old girls waited on the sidewalk.

The driver of the truck moved to the rear of the vehicle, pulled a canvas curtain aside and dropped the tailgate. He called his sidekick, Mau, to join him and Mau told the girls to climb in. The two girls hoisted themselves into the back of the truck.

A middle-aged woman from the hotel handed up their luggage. She reminded them of their new names — Lotus and Diamond — and wished them luck.

Lotus pushed her cardboard suitcase to the front of the cargo compartment. Diamond did the same with her bundle tied in red cloth and sat on one of the wooden seats that ran down either side of the truck box. Lotus positioned herself opposite, near the middle of the truck.

The driver, called Luong by his partner, lifted and secured the tailgate with a clang and closed the curtain, cinching it with nylon cords to the tie-down lugs on the gate. Both men walked forward and slid into their seats, slamming the doors of the cab behind them. The driver started the truck and popped the clutch prematurely, causing the truck to advance with a jerk and a shudder that jostled the girls in the rear.

Little daylight leaked through the edges of the curtain and it took a few seconds for the girls' eyes to adjust to the gloom. The cargo compartment smelled like rice straw and urine, the floor littered with food wrappers and blue and white shards from a broken rice bowl. The girls clutched the edges of their seats with vice-like grips as the truck bounced them through the twisting, bumpy streets of Saigon.

Two hours passed before the truck came to a stop and Luong opened the curtain and lowered the tailgate. Lotus and Diamond shielded their eyes from the explosion of daylight that burst into their space.

"Happy stop," Luong said, his voice little more than a growl. "We'll have something to eat here and you can go to the toilet."

The café was an open shed with a tin roof and a lean-to kitchen hanging off one corner. Several nylon-webbed hammocks hung in limp arcs between posts. There were no toilet facilities, so the girls squatted on broken ground behind the building while Luong and Mau peed against the trunk of a betel palm tree a short distance away. Lotus watched her stream of urine form a little rivulet and flow away for a few inches before the dry ground absorbed it. Tears trickled down her face.

In the café, they sat inches off the ground on blue and red plastic stools. Lotus chose a blue one like the stool she sat on at home. Her family owned three — one each for her father, her grandmother, and her — stacked out of the way during the day and positioned around a folding table at mealtime.

The proprietor of the café wore her hair pulled into a tight bun at the nape of her neck and shuffled between their table and a cauldron on a charcoal burner. Without comment, she served each of them a bowl of com ga — rice with bits of chicken — the only dish she sold.

The group spent less than ten minutes at the stop, and then drove an hour more. Now when they stopped, the truck idled for a moment before it inched forward. After five or six lurches, the driver switched off the engine.

Lotus moved to sit on the same side of the truck as Diamond. "We must be in a lineup," she said, and held Diamond's hand.

Men barked at the driver in a foreign tongue, shouting questions and snarling orders. Luong offered deferential answers in the same foreign language. Then a man in green camouflaged fatigues jerked back the curtain and peered in at the girls. He grunted, and yanked the curtain shut again.

Soon after, the engine restarted and the truck moved on, thrusting through gears as it accelerated.

The two small faces in the dim bed of the truck contorted with fear. "Troi oi," Diamond gasped. "Oh god sister, do you think we're leaving Vietnam?"

CHAPTER ONE

Pete Trutch jogged the last stretch of a six-mile run through the hilly streets of his neighborhood, until he ended up on the south-facing slope of Queen Anne Hill and turned onto his front walkway. He slowed his step as he approached the broad front porch of his Victorian home and then bounded up the flagstone steps two at a time, pleased that he could still bound at the age of 66. In the afternoon he would go for a sail, or a bike ride, and perhaps Catherine would join him.

It was a perfect late August day, the Thursday before Labor Day, with a hint of autumn in the air. Mid-morning sunlight created the illusion of glowing embers and dancing flames upon the wrap-around windows of the city's emblematic landmark, the Space Needle. To the Southeast, beyond the concrete and glass cladding of the skyscrapers, Mount Rainier stood like a Praetorian guard, its glaciated helmet standing out against the cerulean sky.

He scooped the folded morning paper from the welcome mat and lifted the lid of his postbox to collect yesterday's mail. He seldom felt a sense of urgency about examining his mail, usually a small assortment of bills and nondescript envelopes addressed to "occupant" or "resident." The third item, though, a flimsy, international airmail envelope with red and blue hachures around the edges, gripped him with foreboding. The letter was addressed by hand, in dark blue ink, to Mr. Peter J. Trutch, "Personal and Confidential." The cancelled stamp bore an image of a graceful woman in a flowing silk dress and conical hat, poling a small sampan through a stream. The denomination of the stamp was 40,000 dong. The date on the postmark had smeared and become illegible, but its origin was clear: *TP Hanoi.*

The envelope triggered an involuntary flash of images he had been trying to repress for years: bursts of white phosphorus bombs spewing tentacles of death into the air in great arcs, body bags being loaded onto choppers, red and green tracers streaking across rice paddies, wounded men moaning, others yelling instructions, his own hoarse voice shouting into a radio handset for air support and reinforcements. And for one fleeting moment, he saw the image of the young woman who had given him comfort and shelter from the insanity of war.

He tucked the newspaper under his arm and touched the three-inch scar left on his jaw, where 44 years earlier a piece of mortar shrapnel had torn into his face. It had fractured his lower mandible, destroyed three teeth and ruptured his sublingual gland.

He had been so young on his first tour of duty during the war, so scared, as an infantry platoon leader in the muck and humidity of the Mekong Delta. That was 1968. In 1970, a second tour found him in Nha Trang, where it was safer but no saner.

Shaken, Trutch took his house key from the canvas pocket laced onto his running shoe and slid it into the entrance lock, opening the heavy oak door onto the marble-tiled entry hall. He dropped the paper and the other mail onto the console table and strode into the kitchen clutching the airmail envelope. Grateful that Catherine had been called in to work, which left him alone with his apprehension, he pressed the button on his coffee maker and sat on one of the four high stools at the long counter that separated the working part of their kitchen from the small glass-encircled alcove where he and Catherine took their breakfast.

As he waited for the coffee maker to finish its interminably slow task, he eyed the envelope. A small shudder of intuition warned him, even before he opened it, that this letter was about to change his life. His hand trembled as he considered the handwriting, his mind racing to find an explanation. It might be from Dream, but my God, why now after writing nothing for 41 years? She would be 65 now, what would she look like? He stared for a moment, but then he saw that the handwriting was strong and masculine, not like hers at all.

At last, the green light on the coffee maker flashed and he poured a brimming cupful into a mug. He opened the fridge and added a dollop of soymilk, but no cream or sugar because Catherine had persuaded him that fat and sugar were just not conducive to the fitness he sought to maintain.

He slid a paring knife under the flap of the envelope and slit it open along the top edge. Carefully, he pulled the folded papers out. Three crisp, thin, blue pages emerged from their jacket and reflected beams from the ceiling pot lights upward at Trutch as he unfolded the letter and read.

Dear Mr. Trutch:

My name is Andrew Quang. I am an Australian of Vietnamese ancestry and a graduate student at the University of Sydney currently doing a stint in Vietnam with Volunteer Services Overseas. My assignment as a social worker in the city of Quy Nhon requires that I travel throughout Binh Dinh province. I have become acquainted with an Amerasian man in his early forties who is wheelchair bound, paralyzed from the waist down, and living in a small care facility in the town of An Nhon, 31 kilometers north of Quy Nhon. His name is Nguyen Le Ngoc.

Ngoc speaks conversational English fairly competently, but is not comfortable writing in this language. I am therefore writing this letter on his behalf. I will come right to the point: Mr. Ngoc believes that you are his father.

Trutch closed his eyes and saw a beautiful young Vietnamese woman standing in the nude, smiling sadly, her silhouette backlit by the glassless window behind her, in which the twin spires of Nha Trang's Roman Catholic Church dominated the view.

"You go home to the United States soon, don't you?"

"Yes," he said. "Two weeks. I'll fly out of Cam Ranh Bay."

She laced her fingers together to form a shallow bowl with her hands and held them in front of her tangle of black pubic hair. "I might have a baby in here, you know."

"If so, what would you wish that we do?" he asked, from his position on the edge of the bed. She had professed love for him, but did she mean it, or was she trolling for a ticket back to the US and a pathway to a Green Card? And if she was, who could blame her?

In broken English, Dream said, "I would take care of our baby. Someday I would tell him his father is Captain Trutch, brave American soldier who I loved."

He left Nha Trang with turbulent and mixed emotions. On the long, 20-hour flight from Vietnam to Travis AFB, in California, he wept uncharacteristically and ran through several *what ifs*. What if he admitted to Catherine that he and Dream had been together, that they had used each other, yes, but that he also cared for her and worried about her future? What if he took 30 days of leave and flew back to Vietnam to fetch her? Could he and Catherine sponsor Dream and offer her a new life in the US? Rationally, of course, he knew that none of this was remotely possible. He couldn't risk Catherine's love, and he couldn't force events into something neat and manageable, so along with

11

all the other memories he struggled to forget, he nudged thoughts of Dream aside.

He had thought about her many times during the ensuing four decades, and once, shortly after the fall of Saigon in 1975, he wrote her a letter, using his office return address. He wondered if she was well, if she was safe, if she had used the money he had left to start a business, as she had planned, or if she had been punished by the Communists for working for the Americans. His letter had been unanswered and unreturned. For a few more months he tortured himself, and then, eventually, thoughts of her receded into a suppressed compartment of memory, which he reopened only occasionally.

But now … Oh Christ, this couldn't be. This was a hoax of some kind. There was just no way that this could be real, especially after 41 years. He glanced through the glass panes into his leafy back yard, where a gray squirrel sat on a limb of the Japanese cherry tree, chittering as though to mock him. He took another gulp of the now tepid coffee and sloshed the rest back and forth in the mug.

Let me give you some background. Ngoc is a self-educated man who has always read voraciously – by the age of 15, he was reading the classics. He has recently discovered the power of the Internet. When he was six years old, his mother told him his father's name. Several years ago, he Googled "Captain Trutch, US Army, Nha Trang 1971." He got a hit on a news item describing a reunion of Vietnam veterans who had served in a headquarters in Nha Trang during 1970 and 1971. The article included a picture of five older men standing around a hotel swimming pool, apparently somewhere in Arizona with desert mountains in the background, each man holding up a glass of beer and grinning broadly. According to the caption, the man in the middle of the portrait was Peter Trutch.

Two weeks ago, Ngoc showed me a printed page from the website and asked me if it was possible, in a country as vast as the US, to find this man. Through several of my contacts in the US, I determined that a Peter Trutch, of about the right age, lives on Prospect Street in Seattle.

Mr. Trutch, I'm sure this is a bolt out of the blue for you, but Ngoc has asked me to tell you that he wishes to connect with you and hopes that you will come to Vietnam to meet with him. His mother's name was Nguyen Thi Tuyet. The Americans called her Dream.

Dream!

The 1970 monsoon season in Nha Trang had begun in October. He had driven a jeep through the gate of the US Army's 8th Field Hospital in blinding rain, wipers racing in a feeble attempt to clear enough of the windscreen so he could see to avoid the muddy potholes. In the emergency room, a Quonset hut connected to others by a series of breezeways, he complained of pain in his lower jaw, just below the gum line.

The corpsman on duty seated him on an examining table, gave the inside of his mouth a cursory glance, and said, "I'll see if I can get one of the docs to look at that, but at the moment they're pretty busy with casualties choppered in from Tuy Hoa. Meanwhile, let's walk over to radiology and have that jaw x-rayed."

Trutch returned to the examination room carrying the film of his x-rays. He sat in a folded chair and amused himself by reading backdated issues of *Stars and Stripes* for an hour.

Finally, an army major in blood-spattered scrubs entered the examination room with a lithe and smiling Vietnamese assistant. "Good morning, I'm Dr. Frederick. Let's have a look in your mouth." The major examined the x-rays without comment, glanced at the tools laid out on a small table, and then with a syringe injected anesthesia into Trutch's jaw. Moments later, he made a small incision into Trutch's gum. When he found what he was looking for, he grunted.

Trutch had felt a slight pressure as the doctor sliced into his anesthetized jaw, but the sound of the blade against flesh crackled in his ears until it changed to that of metal on metal. The army surgeon in Dong Tam had missed this piece of fragmentation three years earlier. When his dentist discovered it in subsequent x-rays, she had advised that he leave it alone until it moved toward the surface. Which it had, and from the sound of things, he would soon be relieved of it.

"Hold his lower lip down, please," the doctor said to the assistant.

Trutch felt his lip held gently as she moved in closer. He tried to swallow the saliva and blood that had accumulated in his throat, but he gagged.

She waved the suction wand around the back of his throat until he could breathe again. Her black silk trousers and white tunic fit snugly in some places and draped enticingly in others. She had pulled her hair back into a severe but stylish ponytail. The plastic nametag over her right breast read "Dream."

When the major finished with him, Trutch caught her eye and said, "Dream, that can't be your real name."

"No. My name is Tuyet. Doctors and nurses have a hard time saying that so they call me Dream."

"Why Dream?"

She blushed, "They say I'm so helpful I am like a 'dream come true.'"

Trutch left the letter unfinished on the table and walked to the sink with his coffee cup. He pulled a frosted can of Budweiser from the fridge, popped the tab, and took a long swig before he returned to his stool.

There is further news of which you should be aware. Ngoc's mother was sent to a re-education camp after the Communists took over and he was sent to live with his aunt in Quy Nhon. The aunt treated him with indifference, more or less merely warehousing him. She fed him minimally and did not allow him to attend school. When Ngoc was ten, he became disabled, under circumstances that sound to me like the result of extreme abuse. But he is a survivor and now at the age of 41, he is fairly well adjusted and mentally healthy, although he lives with constant sadness over what I am about to describe next.

Mr. Trutch, if in fact you are Ngoc's father, and it seems likely to me, then you also need to know that you have a granddaughter. Ngoc married in 1996. He and his wife had a baby girl in 2000. His wife died of dengue fever in 2009. Without his wife's income as a seamstress, he struggled on for several years doing the best he could at single parenting by growing flowers and living in his mother-in-law's modest house. But two months ago, his daughter, Lien, now aged 13, disappeared. Ngoc tells me she was lured to Ho Chi Minh City with the promise of work to help support the family. He has not heard from her since she left, some eight weeks ago. Ngoc is hopeful that, since you are her grandfather, you will help find her.

If you wish to contact me by e-mail, you may do so at andyaussie89@yahoo.aus.com.

I would be pleased to act as intermediary for any questions you may have for Ngoc.

Sincerely,

Andrew

***

Trutch made his way upstairs, where he removed his sweaty running clothes and flung them at the hamper in the bathroom. He stepped into the shower and let the steaming hot water beat on him. The letter from Andrew seemed genuine. Why would anyone make that up, and who would know enough about the events of 41 years ago to try? So unless this was an elaborate masquerade, Ngoc really could be his son. If the information in the letter was accurate, Dream had been incarcerated in a Vietnamese Communist gulag, with thousands of other South Vietnamese who had worked for, or consorted with, Americans during the war. But the letter never indicated whether she was eventually released or had died in the camps. If alive, where was she?

He turned off the water and grabbed a thick gray towel to dry off. He attended to his toiletries on autopilot, then dressed casually in chinos and a black polo shirt. Across the hall in his home office, he plunked into his desk chair and stared pensively at what he called his memory wall, which Catherine sardonically referred to as his *ego* wall.

The plaques, framed photos and certificates reflected a 22-year army career. Among them was his army commission as a Second Lieutenant and his certificate of retirement as a Lieutenant Colonel, signed 22 years later. Encased in a glass-fronted frame, his medals hung in three rows, topped by the blue and silver metallic likeness of a Springfield rifle surrounded by an elliptical wreath of silver laurel — the Combat Infantryman Badge. He had been awarded the Silver Star for valor, and the Purple Heart, which signified that he had been wounded in combat. A picture of him shaking hands with General William C. Westmoreland, both of them in combat fatigues, a parked helicopter in the background, hung next to the medals.

On the credenza behind his desk, his framed bachelor's degree in Business Administration sat propped alongside a wedding photo of Catherine and him. Catherine looked like a model, tall and slender with wavy auburn hair, her radiant smile showing through the white veil. He, then a 22-year-old Second Lieutenant, wore the army Class A green uniform.

Catherine. He loved her intelligence and incisive wit. During a rainy-day game of Scrabble two years ago, he had looked up in frustration from his rack of tiles to ask if she would accept "voik" as a word. Without so much as a second of hesitancy she replied, "Only in the bedroom. You wanna go upstairs and voik?" She had been his close companion, soul mate and best friend for over 40 years, and she had an edge. She brooked no fools. This would be one tricky minefield, with plenty of fireworks, exacerbated by the fact that he had concealed the affair for all these years.

But Andrew Quang's letter and Ngoc's claim were credible. He owed it to himself, and to Ngoc, to look more closely at the possibility they were father and son, and if so, to help. He knew he risked losing Catherine's trust, but would he lose their easy, chummy times together as well?

She claimed to admire his strongly held determination to always do right — even when it required tough decisions and difficult choices, and she often called him her "knight in shining armor." He doubted there would be much shine left when he admitted that he had violated her trust by failing to disclose the one time he had wandered from the straight and narrow.

He had wanted to confess to her shortly after he returned from his assignment in Nha Trang, but always found a reason to put the telling off to a more appropriate moment. Eventually, he realized there never would be a perfect moment, so he lived with his unhappy conscience and continued to let the disclosure slide. There had always been a strong possibility that somehow, someday, he would push smack up against a moment of truth.

Someday had arrived.

CHAPTER TWO

Catherine's day began with a blow to her ego at 6:30 a.m., when she opened an e-mail from the chairman of the Seattle Art Museum. He chastised her for a stance she had taken at their board meeting the previous evening, when she had defended another trustee's diatribe against waste and abuse in executive expense claims. By 7:30, she had calmed down and was looking forward to her yoga class when she received a call from the Substitutes Office of Seattle Public Schools, asking her to pitch the day's lesson for a summer course on Contemporary American Literature at Ballard High School. The three-hour class started at 9:00, and the regular teacher had left no lesson plan. She would have to wing it, relying on her years in the classroom and her wits. If only she could get through the morning with a sense of humor, she'd count her time a success.

She addressed the group of teenagers. "Okay class. I understand you've been reading Pat Conroy. Which of his books are you dealing with?"

A girl in the second row answered, "*The Water is Wide*. Most of us have finished it."

"Good. Now what do you think was Conroy's intent in writing it?" She looked around the room. No hands went up. Her eyes fell on a gangly-looking 16- or 17-year-old slouched in his seat, wearing a backwards baseball cap. She consulted the seating chart on the lectern and said, "Larry?"

Larry jerked his head up. He fumbled to get his smartphone into his pocket and then lowered his head again to mumble, "Uh, I think it was like … autobiographical or something."

"Larry. I would like you to sit up straight and project your voice so that it can be heard. Speak to me and to the entire class."

A girl decorated in red glasses, two seats behind Larry, quipped, "Yeah, Larry. It's sort of like texting, only you use your tongue and your lips."

Subdued laughter rippled through the classroom.

Larry sat up. "Well," he said with excessive volume, "I think Conroy wanted our generation to like … understand about how ignorant and poor the, uh, blacks of South Carolina were at that time."

"I doubt if we were the target audience," asserted the bespectacled girl. "The book was published in 1969. You weren't even a gleam in your Daddy's eye yet, dork."

Again, titters of laughter.

"Alright," said Catherine. "Thank you Larry. Now, who would like to describe the theme?"

Several hands went up and Catherine gestured to a boy near the back of the classroom, so tall and thin and blond that he resembled a lone stalk of wheat waving in the wind.

"The theme is about racism and segregation. It tells about the resulting oppression, ignorance and poverty."

"Does everyone agree?"

Two and a half hours later, Catherine felt a little like Pat Conroy, unsure that she'd helped the students much, but confident they might at least move forward as a result of her presence. She thanked the class for their interest and participation, strapped her briefcase over her shoulder and headed out the door, bound for the comforts of home.

***

At home, the blue coffee mug and an empty Budweiser can still sat on the countertop.

"Are you home Pete?" she shouted. "I see you've been mixing your drugs of choice. Kinda early in the day for the brewski, isn't it?"

"I'll be right down," Trutch called, from the second floor.

Catherine sat in one of a pair of ivory-colored chairs and was just kicking off her stylish but sensible Keens when Trutch entered the living room. "Have you had lunch?" she asked.

"Uh, no. Have you?"

Hearing a dissonant note in his voice, Catherine looked up to search his face and noticed his grim mouth, the tension around his eyes. "No. The morning's been too frenetic. On top of that, the Ballard bridge opened for a couple of very slow ships and I sat waiting for half an hour. So let's eat something. But first, what's troubling you?"

"I'll whip up an omelet while you change clothes, then we'll talk about it."

"For heaven's sake, you're leaking anxiety through your pores. This must be more than just a decline in the Dow-Jones. I'll be back down in a few minutes and then I want you to spill it."

When they sat for lunch, Catherine, now dewy from a quick shower, ate ravenously, stopping long enough to say, "Come on. Out with it. What's eating you? You're pushing your food from side to side on your plate. "

"I have something to tell you, but it won't be easy."

"Let me guess. You're leaving me for a 25-year-old. Okay, I want the house, my car, 75 percent of all our assets and the goldfish. You and your bimbo can live on your sailboat."

"Catherine. This is serious."

She reached out and touched his arm. "Okay, I'm all ears, Pete."

"You should finish eating first."

She set her fork and knife on her plate and wiped her mouth with the napkin Trutch had slapped down beside her plate. She couldn't remember ever seeing him so hesitant. "You're scaring me. I can't eat with this knot in my stomach. Out with it."

"I've never told you this, and I wish I knew a way to soften it." He busied himself with his own napkin and then set it back in his lap. "I had a ... liaison during my second tour in Vietnam. A young local woman. It was brief, two ... three months. I got a letter today. It's possible I have a 40-year-old son in Vietnam. He's disabled. A paraplegic."

The muscles of Catherine's face rearranged themselves like particles in a kaleidoscope, shifting from an expression of humorous cynicism to one of quizzical confusion. She stared at Trutch, suddenly a repugnant stranger.

He fidgeted, rubbed the scar on his left cheek with his thumb and looked down at his plate, taking a great interest in the virtually untouched lumps of egg and cheese.

After a long silence, Catherine said, "Do you mean to tell me that during our third year of marriage you boinked some Vietnamese ... What was she? A bar girl? Christ, Pete." She went silent, then a moment later erupted as if she had only been gathering steam. "What was her name? You must remember that, even though you forgot to tell me about it four decades ago, when I may have brushed it off as, I don't know, one of those things that happen in war when healthy, horny young men are confronted with temptation."

"She was a medical assistant, working for the army's 8th Field Hospital. Her nickname was Dream."

"Dream. Oh give me a break. Was she the girl of your dreams?"

"Of course not."

She raised one hand. "Say no more. Don't talk. Don't even breathe. I need to process this a bit." She sat motionless for a few seconds and then pushed her chair back so hard it fell over. She stepped around it and stomped across the living room to retrieve her shoes. "I'm going for a walk."

"Catherine, wait. There's a granddaughter. This man who claims to be my son has a daughter who's disappeared."

The front door slammed.

***

Through the window, Trutch watched her tramp down the stairs and stride briskly up Prospect Street until she disappeared around the corner of 5th Avenue West. He considered jumping into his car to follow her. She was distraught and could blunder into traffic. But she had also left for a reason and needed time alone. He took a deep breath in an attempt to calm his racing heart, and then slumped into an easy chair.

He had been a senior at the University of Washington when they'd met in March of 1967, a few months away from him receiving his bachelor's degree, as well as his army commission through the four-year ROTC program on campus. Catherine, a freshman at the time, had approached him in the Husky Union Building, the HUB, where he was drinking a cup of bitter *U-Dub* coffee.

"Excuse me General, sir, do you mind if I take your picture?"

He looked up at the sound of her throaty voice and saw an attractive young woman with a crown of reddish-brown hair to her shoulders, a Nikon camera on a strap around her neck. "Are you speaking to me?"

"Yes. I saw you leaving Clark Hall this morning. You were wearing your army suit and looked a little silly walking through that ring of scruffy anti-war protesters. But not nearly as silly as you do in that absurd sweatshirt."

He looked down at the image of Donald Duck adorning the front of his kelly-green sweatshirt. Donald held a steaming cup of coffee and wore a military-style campaign hat. The quip beneath the picture read *Up at the Quack of Dawn — US Army.*

Recovering from his surprise, he smiled into her sparkling eyes. "Why do you want my picture?"

"I'm a photographer for the UW Daily. I'm thinking that a picture of an ROTC cadet, one with the *cojones* to wear his uniform outside of the ROTC building, will make for an interesting image in the paper later this week. Especially one who walked across a radicalized campus smack into a crowd of Vietnam War protesters."

"Then why didn't you snap the picture when you saw me this morning, while I was still *in* uniform?"

"I couldn't get the right camera angle, given the shoving and jostling of the crowd. I was right in the middle of them."

He liked her irreverent, cavalier attitude. "Let's go over to the Red Robin and have a beer together," he said, "then you can take the shot with me lifting a schooner of frothy ale."

"Sorry General, sir. I can't get into the Red Robin. I'm only 19."

"Then let's go to my room and have one."

"Do you live in a dorm?"

"I share the upper floor of a house at 39th and University Way with four other guys."

"Fine, then. As long as there's someone else there."

By May, they were engaged. They married in June and after a short honeymoon at a waterfront resort on Lake Chelan, Trutch left for the Infantry Officer's Basic Course at Fort Benning, Georgia. Married co-eds couldn't live in the Alpha Gamma Delta house, so Catherine moved into a two-room apartment in the basement of her parent's house on Brooklyn Avenue Northeast. For nearly 50 years, he had loved her profoundly.

Trutch paced the house for 15 minutes, then he went up to his office and sat at the computer. He booted up Skype and entered Andrew Quang's e-mail address to see if he had a Skype account; he did, but it was 4:30 in the morning in Vietnam. He turned on the television and channel-surfed for ten minutes but felt mocked by the inane array of programs, each more ridiculous or pretentious than the last as they paraded across the 48-inch screen. He turned off the TV and resolved to sit quietly and wait.

Two hours later, he heard her steps on the front porch and leapt up as she entered.

She glared at him with puffy eyes and then stabbed the air with her index finger and said, "Okay, this is where I've gotten. The shock and surprise have subsided, I feel hurt, angry and betrayed, but I believe this was an isolated event that happened a long time ago. I don't think you ever strayed again. I don't want us to lose what we have, so I'll try to get over this, but it's going to take some time. In the meanwhile, don't even touch me."

21

"I understand, Catherine. I'm really sorry. I should have had the balls to tell you a long time ago."

"Why didn't you?"

"I didn't want to hurt you."

"Oh jeez, Pete. That's so clichéd. This is Catherine." She pointed at her chest with her thumb. "Catherine — with an IQ of around 140. Did it not occur to you back then that, yes, I would have been deeply hurt — just as I am now — but that we could have worked it through? We both have enough depth to temper our emotions. I would have been determined back then — just as I am now — to get past the problem and preserve our relationship."

"What can I say? I used poor judgment when I succumbed to temptation, and I've used poor judgment in the subsequent years by not telling you about this before now."

"You used no judgment at all. You're like so many other men. You allowed your brain to migrate south and it went into gear about four inches below your navel. I'm disappointed that you weren't the perfect gentleman I mistook you for back then. But the greatest disappointment is that you kept it to yourself all these years. I feel betrayed that you didn't have enough faith in me, and in the strength of our relationship, to share this with me years ago. I'll get over the hurt I'm feeling now, Peter Trutch — the wound will scab over and mend itself, but there'll be scar tissue on my heart for a long time."

"I'll always bear the pain of knowing that I hurt you, Catherine."

"While you're tallying up the pain, add the fact that you perhaps have a child and a grandchild. This reopens all the old regret about my own barrenness. Suddenly there is a child, but not *our* child."

Trutch cringed as if she had slapped him. How stupid and self-centered to have thought it was only the affair that would break her heart.

"I'm keeping my dinner date with Peg tonight. I'll be home when I get home," Catherine said.

When she had gone, he picked at a dinner of warmed over lasagna and went to sleep alone in their king-size bed. At 11 he woke when Catherine prodded him. "I've put some blankets on the loveseat in your office," she said.

CHAPTER THREE

At 5:30 Friday morning, Trutch connected with Andrew Quang via Skype. Bursts of static interrupted their conversation, and they endured an annoying one-second delay between words spoken and words heard, but they did manage to communicate.

"Mr. Trutch," Quang said, "I hope you will consider coming to Vietnam. The big worry here is that Ngoc's daughter, Lien, has been duped into the child sex trade — big business in many parts of Asia. Girls as young as nine or ten have been sold into prostitution. They're horribly exploited by pimps, who are in turn controlled by organized criminals. Many of the girls end up in China, Japan or Korea, where they haven't a hope of finding their way home again. They're worked until they're worn out, and then they're discarded. Often they die of AIDS."

Trutch felt a stab in his gut that was not unlike the pre-combat tension he had frequently experienced many years before. "I can't imagine how I could help."

"Maybe you couldn't, but you have legs that work and apparently the means to travel. There are a couple of NGOs working in Hanoi and Ho Chi Minh City — the locals still call it Saigon, by the way. They network with agencies in other Asian countries and work to investigate and expose child trafficking. They also attempt to rescue and rehabilitate some of these children. I think you could serve as Ngoc's liaison, for want of a better word, with one of these NGOs and attempt to interest them in getting involved in Lien's case."

"Haven't you tried that yourself? You're a social worker and apparently young and zealous. You'd have easier rapport, and probably more influence, with these do-good organizations than I would."

"I have been in touch with one of them, the STOK Foundation, for Stop Trafficking Our Kids. Their Saigon office has only four people plus a couple of local support staff, so they're overworked and underfunded, typical of non-profit social service agencies. They do have a network of investigators, informants and shelters or rehab centers. The investigators gather evidence about illicit operations and then attempt to persuade the police to conduct raids. If the police won't cooperate they will sometimes take the risk of rescuing kids from the brothels themselves. I think if I were to introduce you to the STOK people as the grandfather of a missing 13-year-old, they might investigate the whereabouts of Lien."

"What makes you think Lien has been trafficked?"

"Lien's uncle Vu is the one who suggested she could perhaps work in Saigon. He's the brother of Ngoc's late wife and a local fisherman. Ngoc was skeptical and hesitant, and Lien didn't want to go, but the uncle was persuasive, promising that Lien would only need to be in Saigon for a year. Then she would have enough money to come home and resume care-giving her father. They'd be comfortable then, he told them. He even offered to pay for Ngoc's care in the An Nhon facility while Lien was gone."

"So she went?" Trutch asked.

"Ngoc and Lien both agreed, but reluctantly. Vu took Lien to Saigon on the bus and returned a week later, reporting that he'd found her a good job as housemaid and cook for an army officer and his wife. But he was vague about where or how she could be reached, and Ngoc hasn't heard from Lien since. Uncle Vu seems to have vaporized right after he delivered Ngoc to the care facility."

"So you think she was sold into … slavery of some type?"

"Mr. Trutch, when I related this story to the director of STOK, she said this is a familiar scenario in the world of child sex trafficking. And here's what I think is the clincher — Vu showed up back in Quy Nhon wearing a $300 Seiko watch, not exactly a Rolex, but still not the average timepiece of a Vietnamese coastal fisherman."

"You've given me a lot to think about, Andrew."

"Let me know if you decide to come. I'll make the in-country arrangements for you to get from Saigon or Hanoi to Quy Nhon and meet you when you arrive. I'll be here for another three months before returning to Australia."

When Trutch signed off and looked up from his computer screen, Catherine stood in the office doorway looking calm but concerned, her hair askew from a short night of wrestling with her pillows, her eyes puffy but no longer red. Her knee-length silk dressing gown clung to and outlined her breasts. "You're going, aren't you?" she asked.

For a fleeting moment, instantly overruled by remorse, Trutch felt a surge of desire. He answered only, "I think I need to give it some serious thought."

CHAPTER FOUR

Seattle's customary weather returned on Friday, the sun's meager light filtered through a dark veil of gloom while a downpour muddied the streets, caused storm drains to overflow and gurgle and darkened the mood of the city's inhabitants. Wipers slashed uselessly at windshields awash with torrents and headlights bored into the saturated air as motorists, determined to escape their offices early for a jump-start on the Labor Day weekend, battled their way through the mid-day murk. Trutch crawled forward with all of the other vehicles as they collectively clawed along the main roadways like a vast, diverging herd of turtles.

Having finally arrived at Anthony's Homeport at the mouth of the Lake Washington Ship Canal, Trutch sat in the restaurant staring out at the melancholy day. The enormous windows, which all summer had allowed refracted, golden daylight to brighten the seating area, now acted as oversized portals into the miasma of a frothy, churning Puget Sound. It was impossible to know where the blackish waters and the dark gray sky separated, but certainly somewhere beyond the two- or three-hundred yards of visibility permitted by the weather.

While Trutch waited on Bill Anderson, his business partner, who was late and no doubt hung up in traffic, he fended off the server. Glad that he had left the Queen Anne house in plenty of time to beat the noon crowd of diners, who had cajoled and bribed their way to the best tables, Trutch had twice told the server that he would wait for his friend before ordering. No, he really did *not* need a beverage other than the glass of ice water.

He and Anderson had first met in Dong Tam, where they were both platoon leaders in a mechanized infantry company. Their friendship spanned four decades and they had been business partners for the past 20-some years. It was an easy, contented relationship, both of them having reached that place of relative comfort and confidence where they could pretty much leave the day-today routines of their business to competent underlings and show up in the office a day or two a week to make strategic decisions or extinguish serious problems.

Anderson left the military for a business career after his stint with the 9th Infantry Division, but they stayed loosely in touch with Christmas cards and the occasional beery reunion of their infantry battalion. In 1989, Trutch retired from the army at age 44 and enrolled in the executive MBA program at the University of Washington's Foster School of Business where he found Bill Anderson already enrolled. One afternoon, toward the conclusion of the two-year program, Anderson invited Trutch for a beer and asked him what he planned to do with himself when the courses wound down.

"I'll start shopping around for a job. I don't have to be in a hurry. I've got a good pension from the army and Catherine's income as a teacher is steady bread and butter with the occasional bottle of wine thrown in."

"I'd like you to consider joining me in my executive search firm. I have a good book of business projected out over the next couple of years and I could use some help. You'd be perfect. You knew how to bring out the best in soldiers back in Nam."

"Yeah," he said and laughed, "and then you selected the best to do the most difficult jobs and it often got them killed."

"It's pretty much the same in business, Pete. Many of our client companies eat their young."

"I'm not sure that headhunting would be my cup of tea, Bill."

"All the same, come around to the office next week — say, Tuesday about 10:00. I'll show you around, introduce you to some people and we'll go to lunch."

That conversation was 23 years ago.

Trutch looked up to see Anderson approaching, already apologizing: "God damn, its miserable out there." As usual, he was disheveled, his collar unbuttoned to reveal a fleshy neck, his gaudy purple necktie loosened and askew. His rain-spotted sport coat fit tightly across his corpulent girth but opened at the bottom to reveal a Texas-style belt buckle that could have doubled as a hubcap. He sat across the table from Trutch, turned and scowled at the raindrops beating against the window and then changed his expression and cheerfully enquired, "Well, what did you want to chat about? This can't be business, unless something's come up since we spoke on Wednesday."

"I want to talk about your trip back to Vietnam five years ago, with that veterans' tour. I need reminding of some of the details. Like, how did you find the people? How did they react to American veterans?"

The server, with a glance at Trutch, interrupted to ask Anderson if he would like to order a beverage.

He ordered Scotch, neat.

She looked again at Trutch and raised her eyebrows in query.

He shook his head, no. Still no.

"So then," Anderson said, as soon as he had Trutch's attention, "are you thinking about going back?"

"I'm toying with the idea. What can you tell me?"

"The people are friendly and welcoming, even among the former VC and NVA we met. I think I told you, we saw no trace of hostility, and the former enemy soldiers we met all wanted to slap us on the back and share hugs. The typical comment was, 'The war was a long time ago — we can all be brothers now.' It isn't the same Vietnam it was 40 years ago. If you can ignore garbage everywhere and the seedy side of the cities, it's not a bad place now. I replaced the ugly images I'd been carrying in my head for 40 years with a new picture of Vietnam."

"But it's a Communist country. Does the government interfere with people's lives? Did your group encounter any ... I don't know ... *difficulties* with police or customs?"

"Aw, they're pretty much like Communists everywhere. They grab power without popular support. They gobble up a disproportionate amount of the wealth through corrupt practices. And they're repressive. There's no freedom of the press and the Commies have zero tolerance for people who badmouth the system. While we were there, the local English papers made a big deal of reporting that some professor was sent to prison for 15 years for making pro-democracy statements on a website. But Western tourists aren't hassled. Tourism helps keep the economy going, the police know that, so unless you really fuck up somehow, you won't even notice the government. You do realize they're keeping tabs on you, though, because your passport and visa are always collected in hotels, and they have to register all guests with the police. But why the sudden interest?"

Trutch related the events of the past 24 hours: the airmail letter, the Skype call with Andrew Quang and Catherine's reaction.

"Oh jeez, Pete, you've got to be joking. Her name was Dream? Shit, what was her first name? Wet? How in the name of hell could some Vietnamese whore trace you after 40 years?"

"She wasn't a whore, Bill. At the time I met her I was sick and tired of the death and destruction, of the vulgar character of war. She was like a breath of fresh air. Intelligent, beautiful, soft. At first, I just took comfort in being around her and then, at some point, I crossed a line. I really fell for her."

"Yeah, but how about Catherine, will she get past this?"

"I hope so. She was furious that I kept it from her, but she has the savvy to understand the dynamics of love, loneliness and war."

"And you think going back to Vietnam to find this *alleged* son is going to help?"

"I think it's the right thing to do."

"Pete, for Christ's sake, you have no proof that this disabled dude is your son. And if he's paraplegic, how'd he ever manage to have a kid of his own? You don't know that's your granddaughter."

Trutch laughed. "Strangely, that's one of the first questions I had, though I'm not sure I would have voiced it."

"Okay, right, I'm the heel, you're the sophisticate. Whatever makes you feel good about yourself, my friend? I'm just saying."

"You sure were. So let me tell you that I did a bit of research. Even though a paraplegic typically has little or no feeling in his genitals, he's still able to ejaculate. Then, using … whatever … the semen is implanted into the woman's uterus."

"Using a turkey baster. Christ, I'm sorry I asked. But wouldn't a trip back be an awfully big emotional investment?"

"Again, my conscience tells me it's the *right thing* to do. For him not to be my son would be too big a coincidence, given what he knows about my name, rank and location during the war. Besides, I'm sure there are laboratories that will do DNA testing, if not in Vietnam, then in Singapore or Thailand if proof of my paternity is necessary."

"Okay, but let me tell you one thing. If you go over there to play detective, you'd better watch your back."

"How so? What do you mean?"

"I caught a glimpse of the seamy side of Vietnam — the street children, the pimps and the sleaze of back alleys. If you start poking around in Saigon for this supposed granddaughter, you're biting off way more than you can chew, my friend."

The waitress delivered Anderson's drink and asked if they were ready to order. Anderson ordered grilled salmon and Pete asked for the seafood chowder.

"Pete, what I'm saying is that you could be putting yourself in harm's way again. After the veterans' tour, I stayed another five days in Saigon to get a feel for what it's like now. I wanted to know how much Vietnamese I'd recall from the ten-week crash course the army gave me before I went the first time. I may have wanted to relive my brief experience in Saigon as a 24-year-old. I popped into a few bars, even a karaoke joint, where as a 62-year-old American I probably had no business. I formed the distinct impression, even a bit sloshed, that there are places in Saigon where people tend to look the other way and ask no questions. We're talkin' pimps, thugs, mean-looking bouncers and cops blind to whatever nefarious activity is raging around them. Stay away from the night spots. And if you can't, at least watch your ass."

***

Ten days later, at 11:50 in the evening, Trutch settled back into his Elite Class seat on the EVA Airlines 747-400ER that would deliver him from Seattle to Taipei. The smiling flight attendant placed a glass of sparkling mineral water with a wedge of lime onto his wide armrest and asked if he would like a pillow and blanket. He declined both and briefly entertained the inane notion that the lime matched the color of her smartly tailored uniform, then dismissed the thought and watched as she and her stately and efficient colleagues went about their pre-flight pampering of other, mostly Asian, passengers in this privileged cabin.

Conversation with Catherine on the way to the airport had been amicable, even to the point of approaching tenderness, as she assured him that this was in fact the right thing to do. "I'm proud of you for stepping up to the plate and grappling with this responsibly," she'd said. "But then I would expect no less of the man I married during the turbulent 60s." The words had come from her heart, even as her overall demeanor showed that she was still smarting, not only from his betrayal, but also at the realization that another woman may have borne him the child that she couldn't.

She had parked curbside on the departures level at Sea-Tac, and then came around to the sidewalk to say goodbye as a porter took Trutch's luggage. "Please be careful over there, soldier," she voiced softly as she clung to him. "I love you."

He stood blocking the doorway to watch her pull away from the curb. I'm one lucky son-of-a-bitch, he thought. Then he turned and walked resolutely into the terminal and toward the nightmare awaiting him on the other side of the Pacific.

CHAPTER FIVE

Three months earlier...

At 12:30 p.m. on a Saturday afternoon, a mile-wide smile on her face as she rode rhythmically and with carefree abandon, side-by-side with Ha, her friend who lived across the rice field from Grandmother's house, Lien pedaled her bicycle home from school. In white uniform blouses, with red neck-scarves, Lien and Ha resembled scarlet-throated egrets as they floated past the emerald green paddies. On Saturdays, they and their classmates were tested on how much they had learned during the week. This week, Lien's responses had earned high praise from her teacher, Co Loan.

At 13, Lien was slender. Her breasts had just begun to bud, but she had not yet had her first period and was scarcely aware of such things. Apart from the five hours each day spent in the village school, she had little time, or inclination, to socialize with other children. Like many of her friends, who also lived with one parent or grandparents or aunties and uncles, she lived with her beloved father, Ngoc, and with her maternal grandmother, Quy, whose modest house they now shared at the edge of the village of Tuy Phuoc. They subsisted by growing their own vegetables and rice, and while Grandmother Quy worked the garden plot and a small rice paddy, Ngoc produced a modest sum of cash by growing ornamental ochna trees, popular during the New Year festivities of Tet, and a stunning array of lilies, daisies and carnations. Lien cut and arranged a few each morning, and then sold them in the market before school.

To celebrate Lien's achievement this week, her mother, Kinh, were she still alive, would have clapped her hands at the news and made *banh khot*, Lien's favorite crispy pancakes, drizzled with extra coconut milk. Sometimes, mostly lying in bed before sleep, Lien thought of her mother, and of how she had gently braided her hair every morning, and the coolness of her fingers when she touched her face, or bent to kiss her forehead at night. She had often smelled of lemongrass and mint, and somehow her tea always tasted better than Grandmother's. During an outbreak of dengue fever, three years earlier, she had been sick and had recovered, and then she had died suddenly, without warning. Secretly, Lien still ached for her. But deep in the eyes of her Papa and Grandmother Quy, she recognized pain that equaled her own, and the tragedy had bound them that much tighter. To share her good news, she rushed home to them now.

Ha peeled off from her and bumped across a paddy berm, toward her own house, while Lien glided up to the lean-to porch where her father sat in his wheelchair smoking, staring out at the undulating green fields.

"Papa, Co Loan said I am number one student," she boasted. "I remembered everything that we learned in mathematics and history this week."

The darkness in her father's eyes lightened a little as he turned his attention to her. "I'm so proud of you, my peach blossom."

"I want to tell Grandmother Quy. Where is she?"

"I'm sorry, my daughter, Grandmother is sick. When she woke this morning, she couldn't move her right leg, and she had no feeling up her side to her arm. I called the *bac si,* and he sent men who took her to the hospital in a cyclo. I've been waiting for you, we need to go into Quy Nhon and see her."

Lien felt the familiar ache in her chest return, a pain she had not known before her mother's death, but she said only, "Let's go then, Papa. We should go right now. It may take me an hour to get us there."

As Lien pushed her father's wheelchair along the rutted and traffic-clotted Tran Hung Dao Street toward the General Hospital, large gray and black clouds loomed over the city of Quy Nhon. The rain started first as a patter, leaving little dimples in the dust along the road, but soon pelted so fiercely that it bounced a foot up off the now steaming pavement, and each drop struck Lien's forearms with the sting of a sharp needle. Her tattered yellow slicker and bucket hat, pulled low over her ears, offered scant protection from the elements, and each time a bus, motorbike, car or bicycle passed, she was drenched in a muddy wash. As always, the surge was rapacious, with all manner of vehicles stampeding and bawling like cattle, making a great fuss while doing so, with some cars and light trucks swerving onto the verge in order to pass slow movers, scattering dogs and chickens, splashing mud everywhere in their haste. Horns blared and bleated while headlights pierced the dim light. Ngoc, covered by a clear plastic poncho, flimsy and torn in several places, was fully exposed to the downpour from the thighs down. Wet and muddy, his pants clung to his bony legs.

Lien trudged onward, her thoughts focused on her grandmother, her achievements in school temporarily forgotten. "Papa, will Grandmother come home from hospital?"

"I don't know. When the men took her away, they couldn't say what was wrong with her."

A clap of thunder reverberated off the surrounding hills with a low rumble and swallowed his voice at the same time that one wheel of his chair slipped off the asphalt into the muck and gravel at the verge.

Lien struggled to push the chair back onto the surface of the roadway, only to be forced off onto the muddy shoulder again when a lorry loaded with bellowing water buffalo careened toward her along the lip of the pavement. Undaunted, she swiped a blast of muddy water off her father's poncho and said, "Sorry Papa. Don't worry, I'll get us there."

At the gateway to the hospital, under the meager shelter of a corrugated metal panel that jutted out from the brick wall, a disheveled security guard hovered, also shrouded in a poncho. With a desultory hand gesture and little interest, as if he often saw young girls pushing middle-aged men through mud in a rainstorm, the guard waved her through.

Lien pushed the wheelchair across the muddy courtyard and up the cement ramp to the main entrance. Her arms and legs burned from the effort of pushing, and her chest heaved. She stopped and draped herself over her father's head to catch her breath.

Ngoc pecked her muddy cheek. "You did well, little one. Just a few feet farther."

At the reception desk, a young woman, incongruously clad in a silken *ao dai* and a quilted winter jacket, sat reading a magazine. When Ngoc identified himself, she gave them Grandmother Quy's room number and returned to her magazine.

Down a long tiled corridor, Lien and Ngoc made their way, past pots and bowls of uneaten food. Chicken bones, fish bones and rice littered the floor next to the open doors of small wards on the right. On the left side of the hallway, heavy rain seeped through green louvered shutters, over unglazed window openings, and pooled on the floor.

"Be careful you don't slip and fall on the wet tiles," Ngoc said.

"It's okay, Papa. I'll get us to Grandmother's room."

They found Grandmother Quy in a room with six beds, all occupied by

34

elderly women. Emaciated, pale and waxy, two of the women looked moribund. Grandmother, sitting up in her bed, appeared fairly alert but could not speak.

A nurse, as she spooned rice porridge between Grandmother's slightly parted lips and watched a little stream of it drool back out, told them that the entire right side of Grandmother Quy's body was paralyzed.

The doctor, when he arrived, patiently explained to Ngoc and Lien that he wanted to keep her in the hospital for at least a week to watch her, but after that she could probably go home. In all likelihood she would remain severely impaired from the stroke.

"What does that mean?" Lien asked.

"She'll be partly paralyzed, like me," Ngoc replied. "I don't know what we'll do, Peach Blossom. If Grandmother is in a wheelchair, who will cook? Who will tend the rice and the vegetable garden?"

"I'll do those things, Papa."

"No, you have to stay in school. We'll find a way."

They sat with Grandmother Quy a few minutes more, during which they prayed, and apologized for not staying longer, and cried, and then Lien pushed her father's wheelchair back through the door, ready to begin the long trek home.

***

A week later, when Grandmother Quy was discharged from the hospital, Uncle Vu provided the solution by taking his mother to the care center in An Nhon. "The three of you can't possibly manage in the house alone," he said to Ngoc. "I'll come by to help Lien manage the household chores, and to help care for you."

For the next three weeks, Ngoc cared for his flowers and plants and took over some of the laundry. Lien rose daily at five to prepare a breakfast of *pho* for the two of them and then picked flowers and pedaled to the market to sell her bundles. On a good day in the market, she could generate 20,000 dong. Often she earned as little as 5,000.

Between 7:30 and 1:00, she attended school and then rode home to tend to the vegetable garden, now being overtaken by weeds. Pulling unwanted plants from between neat rows of carrots and lettuce, she worked furiously until five, when she quit to prepare dinner, the dust on her face streaked by sweat and deposits of reddish-brown dirt crammed under each of her fingernails.

35

She dipped a bucket of water from the well, washed up beside the lean-to porch and then prepared dinner, a bowl of steamed rice each, along with a few vegetables from the garden. There was no money for meat, and they saw no sign of Vu.

***

On Sunday of the fourth week, Lien pedaled her bike into Quy Nhon and found Uncle Vu at Ghenh Rang Beach sitting on the edge of his round basket boat mending nets, the stub of an unfiltered cigarette hanging from his lips. "Uncle," she said, "Papa and I are having a hard time. You said you'd help us."

Vu stopped his work, laid the needle in the bottom of the boat and took a long drag from the cigarette before flicking it off into the sand. He stared at her. "I'm too busy trying to make my own living. But I've come up with a better idea. A friend in Saigon can get you a job there." He stared out at the sea. "You can make lots of money in one year. While you're there, your papa can live in the same care center in An Nhon as your grandmother. I can arrange everything."

Lien shook her head and lowered her eyes. "No, Uncle. I don't want to leave Papa. I want to go to school."

But that evening, Uncle Vu came to the house, conveniently after the gardening and household chores had already been done.

"Everything will be fine," he assured Ngoc and Lien. "She will have a job as a domestic helper in the house of a person with great wealth."

"She's too young," Ngoc said, "and we only have each other. There must be another way."

A sorrowful expression elongated Lien's face and she pressed a hand to the middle of her chest. "I can't leave Papa alone."

"It won't be for long. At the end of this year, you can return to Tuy Phuoc with 20 million dong. You and your father can get by for a long time on that much money."

"What about school? I want to be a teacher someday."

"I think you will be given time to attend school each day at one of the better schools in Ho Chi Minh City."

For almost two hours they listened to Vu's persuasive arguments, until finally Ngoc turned to Lien. "Maybe it's a good thing, Peach Blossom, we'll talk with the fortune teller tomorrow."

***

The next afternoon, an old man pedaled up to the little house on a rusted white bicycle, his wispy beard yellowed with nicotine stains. He wore blue peasant pajamas, and atop his gnarled brow, a brown fedora.

From under the lean-to roof, Ngoc and Lien watched him dismount and approach. When he reached them, he steepled his hands at throat height and bowed slightly toward each of them. *"Xin chao Anh, chao Chou."*

"Xin chao, Ong," Ngoc and Lien each said politely in unison, returning the shallow bow.

Lien served tea and then sat off to the side, as if to be as unobtrusive as possible, while Ngoc and the elder smoked and sipped tea and talked about the family dilemma.

The old man produced a small bag from his pocket and poured five worn, cast copper coins into his hand. Each coin, about the diameter of an American nickel, had a round hole in the center. One side was blank and on the other Chinese-like symbols stood out in low relief. From another pocket he pulled several joss sticks and asked Lien to fetch a bowl with earth or sand in it so that he could stand the incense upright.

He lit the sticks with a disposable lighter, shook the coins with two hands, passed them over the smoking joss sticks five times and then tossed the coins on the tabletop. Three of the coins landed face up, revealing symbols; the other two fell face down.

"Ahhh." He looked directly at Lien. "Yes, you must go to Saigon to work. You and your father will be rewarded for your efforts."

Lien's eyes teared up. Her face as blank as one side of the coins, she wrapped her arms around herself and said nothing.

Ngoc, too, looked pensive and unhappy. "Are you sure that's what the coins say?" he asked.

"I'm certain. And you will both be blessed by the Buddha." He produced a bottle of rice vodka from the folds of his clothing and instructed Lien to bring two cups. When she complied, he poured three fingers worth for both himself and Ngoc. "To your future and that of your daughter," he said, raising his glass in a toast. Then he swilled the strong drink down in three gulps, a broad smile showing his satisfaction with himself.

Ngoc seemed to inhale his vodka, as if he hoped it would numb the pain in his heart.

Still grinning, the fortuneteller extended his palm for his fee of 20,000 dong.

***

Lien, normally ebullient and quick to smile, was subdued in school over the next two days, unsure why she should do something that would help her father but hurt both of them. After school, she plodded through her afternoon chores in the garden and kitchen. As a Vietnamese girl of the countryside, duty demanded that she obey her father and provide care for him. He had agreed that she must go to Saigon to work, so she must, but how could she care for him from more than 600 kilometers away? She spoke little as they ate their meager supper of rice and garden vegetables.

Ngoc lay down his chopsticks and reached across the table to pat her hand. "It will be okay, Peach Blossom. I'll be fine in An Nhon, and I can look after Grandmother. We can write each other letters and maybe even speak on the phone while you're in Saigon."

"Yes, Papa," she said without enthusiasm, and from the corner of her eye a tear escaped.

She washed the supper dishes and then joined her father on the porch where he sat smoking and listening to the crickets chirp. "Papa, I am sad and afraid to go far away from you to Saigon. I can't imagine not seeing you every day. Is this how you felt as a young boy without your papa and mama near? Were you lonely?"

"I never knew my father, Little One. But my mother told me he was an American soldier, handsome, brave and intelligent. One day I would like to meet him."

"What was your mother like?"

"Her name was Tuyet. She was beautiful and kind and loving. We lived in Nha Trang, where she had a difficult life after the Americans left, because of me. I was *con lai*, the dust of life, and people scorned my mother for that. Our culture didn't approve of Vietnamese who fell in love with foreigners and had their babies during the war."

"What happened to her? Why did I never know her?"

"Shortly after the Communists took over, they sent your grandmother to a place called Camp Z-30 near Xuan Loc. I was sent to live with your mother's sister, my Aunt Thuy, here in Quy Nhon."

Lien looked forlorn. "Did you ever see your mother again?"

"One time, when I was six, my uncle took me on a long bus ride to Xuan Loc to visit her. The other passengers gave me dirty looks because they knew I was a half-breed. A big boy slapped me on the back of the head as he walked up the aisle and called me 'dirt.' Then we arrived and so many people crowded into that place where they kept my mother. We all had food to give our relatives. The guards stood close by in green uniforms, and we spoke in whispers.

"My mother was skinny and pale, her hair, which I remembered as shiny and beautiful, was tangled and matted. Some of it had gone gray. We both cried, and just before the scowling soldiers led all the prisoners away, she told me about my father. That's my last memory of her. As she drifted into the throng, she looked over her shoulder at me with the saddest expression I've ever seen. That was the last time I saw my mother."

Lien remained silent for a long moment. Finally she asked, "Do you have a picture of her, Papa?"

"No. At the same time the Communist soldiers took my mother, they took over our house in Nha Trang and everything in it. We lost everything we had with the house. I was three years old. My aunt took me to Quy Nhon just two days before the soldiers came and seized our house."

Lien flung herself at her father's feet and placed her head on his knees. "I don't want to go, Papa. I don't want us to be apart."

Ngoc stroked her hair. "It's the best thing, Lien. I know a year seems like a long time to you, but it's hardly a blink. We'll be back together very soon."

***

After 13 bumpy hours, the bus from Quy Nhon arrived in Ho Chi Minh City and Uncle Vu spoke his first words in many kilometers when he told Lien to follow him. He led her down a narrow alley busy with the undulating rhythms of traffic and commerce. At the end of the lane, on Pham Ngu Lao Street, he pulled her into a doorway under a sign reading Outback Hotel.

He grunted a greeting to the older woman at the reception desk and released Lien's hand. "You'll stay here with Mrs. Nguyen for a day or two, and then she'll get you to your job."

"Where will you be?" Lien asked.

"I have work to do. I have to go home." He accepted a fat envelope from

Mrs. Nguyen and stuffed it down the back of his jeans. "Now you do as you're told." He turned without saying goodbye and was gone.

Lien stared after him and then at the woman behind the desk.

"Come on," Mrs. Nguyen said. "I'll show you to your room."

Lien followed, eager to be taken to her room and left alone. Mrs. Nguyen reminded her of the nurse who had weighed her on the first day of school — not unkind, but strictly business. No time for chit chat.

Up two flights of narrow stairs, they entered a room halfway down a shabby corridor, furnished with a bed and a wooden chair. Off in a nook, a dipper floated in a plastic bucket of water beside a porcelain squat toilet. Another girl about Lien's age sat huddled on the bed.

Mrs. Nguyen said, "This is Diamond. Your new name is Lotus."

Lien blinked. But before she could ask why she needed a new name, Mrs. Nguyen had left the room, shutting the door behind her. Lien heard the door lock from the outside.

CHAPTER SIX

Muddled thoughts tumbled through Trutch's mind as the huge airliner lifted off the tarmac at Sea-Tac. He had hurt Catherine, perhaps unforgivably, and he wondered whether she would ever recover completely from his betrayal. The jolt of elation he had felt on the airport sidewalk, when she had kissed him and told him she loved him, already felt distant. She was a complex woman. Often, she harbored moods and feelings hidden beneath the surface until, twisting, turning and changing shape, they erupted like the breath of a Chinese New Year dragon. He was an idiot, first for his indiscreet behavior four decades earlier and secondly for the clumsy manner in which he had blurted out his confession ten days ago. His sudden revelation made him, in part, a stranger to the person who loved him most. If only he had known how to adequately express his remorse. And this trip to Vietnam — he hoped he had made the right decision.

He had dredged up a plethora of information about child trafficking at the Seattle Public Library and on the Internet. His backpack brimmed with notes and printed articles from websites about kidnapping, rape, child prostitution and the horrible conditions under which many trafficked children were held captive, crammed together in tiny rooms, beaten, drugged, abused in every way. Although governments and NGOs around the world tried to combat the problem, it seemed impossible to extinguish, owing partly to corrupt officials and enforcement agencies in many of the countries where human trafficking flourished. As long as there remained a global demand from pedophiles and sex tourists for children, underworld businessmen would exist, willing to supply the inventory. Ensconced in the pampered salon of business class, Trutch felt close to nausea as he brooded over the possibility that he could have a granddaughter caught up in this seamy side of life.

A chime sounded, and the accented voice of the chief purser came over the PA system. "Ladies and Gentlemen, the captain has extinguished the seat belt sign. It is now safe to get up and move about the cabin. We recommend for those still seated to keep your seat belt fastened loosely around you." The announcement was repeated in Mandarin, and then the same flight attendant who had greeted him appeared at his seat and asked, "Mr. Trutch, can I bring you a beverage?"

He returned her smile and held her gaze for perhaps a fraction of a second too long. With her silken skin and luxuriant black hair, she reminded him of Dream.

"Scotch on ice, please."

When she returned with the drink, he smiled his thanks and watched her move down the aisle. He sipped the drink and rested it on the arm of his seat. For the thousandth time, he wondered what could have happened to Dream. In which re-ed camp had she been incarcerated at the end of the war? Could she possibly still be alive?

After their brief meeting at the 8th Field Hospital, as Trutch half raced through the rain back to his jeep, she caught up with him.

"Captain Trutch," she asked, "Do you ever go to the beach?"

"Sometimes," he said, "On Sundays, when I have a half-day off."

"Do you want to meet me there on Sunday afternoon and go for a walk?"

He barely hesitated. "I think that would be pleasant."

***

The ao dai, one of the most elegant symbols of femininity on earth, is an ankle-length silken shirt fitted on the top and slit up the sides to the waist to form two flowing panels worn over ankle-length silk pantaloons. It gives its wearer the appearance of graceful fluidity while emphasizing modesty and caution. Dream met Trutch on the beach in a mint green version, its panels fluttering in the ocean breeze. His heart stopped, and then flipped over. For two hours they walked and talked on Nha Trang's palm-lined crescent beach.

They had ended up in Dream's flat near the Catholic church, where with slow and graceful hands, she pushed each of his shirt buttons through its buttonhole. From then on, for the remaining two months of his tour of duty, Trutch saw Dream every moment he could manage.

He emptied the glass of Scotch and ordered a second. He had read about the disdain with which children of American soldiers were treated, and about how unwanted they felt in the homeland of their ancestors. How had Ngoc managed to survive into adulthood, particularly with a profound disability, in a country whose citizens treated him as little more than dirt?

42

Trutch slept fitfully, these thoughts eddying though his subconscious for much of the 13-hour flight to Taipei.

**

On his second flight, bound for Ho Chi Minh City, he sipped coffee and breakfasted on an Asian meal of cold fish, rice and fresh fruit. Minutes before landing, the plane swerved south and west on the approach path into Ho Chi Minh City's busy Tan Son Nhat International Airport, affording him a fragmentary view of the Mekong Delta. He spotted a sizeable town, many of whose buildings had red tile roofs, and where big leafy trees lined some streets. Could that be My Tho? If so, it was a darn sight bigger than he remembered.

Below the wing tip, Trutch spotted a muddy river, which he reckoned was the Vam Co, a distributary of the Mekong. In a terrible flash, he recalled a firefight in a village near the banks of the river. His platoon had been passing through the area when sniper fire, originating in a small grove just outside the village, pinned them down. His soldiers hit the dirt and returned the fire, but one of his men, a machine gunner named Butters, rose to one knee and swung around 90 degrees to direct his fire into the village itself.

When he ignored Trutch's shouted order to cease firing, Trutch rose and ran over to him. He knocked the machine gun from his arms and wrestled Butters to the ground. "That's a village, you idiot. There are women and children in those hootches."

"They're just Gooks, sir. And that's a fuckin' Gook shooting at us from over there. Hell, his fuckin' wife and kids are probably cheering him on from their house in the ville."

"It doesn't matter Butters, they're women and children. Non-combatants. We don't shoot civilians."

Just then, a mortar round exploded within ten feet of them and Trutch felt a piece of shrapnel rip into the left side of his jaw. Curiously, he had felt no pain, but his own warm, sticky blood had run down his neck and across his chest. Butters lay dead, a gaping hole in his chest.

By the time the purser made the landing announcements in three languages, Trutch was bathed in sweat. He put his seatback up and mopped his face with the warm towel provided by the flight attendant. He couldn't quite shake off the effects of the flashback to the fuck-up with Butters, and as the plane touched down in what had once been familiar territory, he wondered how many of these scenes might plague him.

The modern terminal, clean and air-conditioned, did not resemble in the least the old stucco building that had served both military and commercial aircraft in the 60s, and the formalities of immigration, luggage claim and customs all happened fast and efficiently. But another round of déjà vu engulfed him as he stepped out of the terminal into oppressive heat and humidity that smacked him like a wet blanket, heavy with the diesel exhaust fumes of trucks and buses.

Amid the sea of greeters, chauffeurs and taxi drivers, he spotted his name, "Mr. Trutch," neatly printed on a cardboard sign held aloft by a handsome young man. "I'm Trutch," he said to the man.

"Andrew Quang. Nice to meet you, sir." Quang wore lightweight outdoor sporting clothes topped off with a gray baseball cap. The words *Seattle Mariners* were emblazoned across the front of the crown in teal blue. He led Trutch to a waiting taxi. "I've arranged for us to stay overnight at the Continental Hotel. Tomorrow afternoon we'll fly up to Quy Nhon if that suits you."

"Suits me just fine, as long as I can Skype my wife from the Continental?"

"Of course."

***

Trutch had just fired up his iPad and was preparing to call home via Skype when the warbling noise of an incoming call sounded. He clicked on the answer icon and up popped a video image of Catherine sitting at their kitchen counter, dressed in a blue sweatshirt, a mug of coffee at her elbow. They greeted each other and established that they were both safe and well.

Then Catherine said, "Listen, I've had an idea. It's pretty wild. Are you ready to hear this?"

"Well, a minute ago I was frazzled with jet lag, but now you have my full attention. Shoot."

"You know there's a sizeable community of former South Viets in the US, 189,000 in Orange County alone. And Little Saigons all over California, the Southwest and the Gulf Coast. There's even an enclave of Vietnamese here in Seattle." She paused and studied Trutch's face on the screen to gauge his reaction so far.

His eyebrows shot up.

"I've been thinking about Dream. What if I were to place some personal ads

44

in their media? Maybe someone will have heard of her or know what eventually became of her. It's a long shot, but you never know. Of course it would help if I knew her real name."

A flash of incredulity crossed Trutch's face. "You'd do that? I thought you were still angry about the whole thing."

"I am. But it dawned on me that if she was once part of your life, and apparently is again, dead or alive, then she is also part of my life. And if she bore your child, then the son you are going to see is, by extension, my stepson, his daughter my step-granddaughter. I think it would be good for us both to know what became of Dream."

"You're an amazing woman, Catherine. If anything were to come of it, we could be in for a hugely emotional sleigh-ride."

"You've always known that I have a strong need to get to the bottom of things."

"All right. I plan to probe a little on this end about what ultimately became of her, but Andrew has already warned me not to even entertain the notion of asking the government, at any level. So maybe your idea's a good one."

"Of course it is. What have we to lose?"

"Her full name was Nguyen Thi Tuyet. Hang on a second, please. I'll write it out for you." He fumbled in his backpack for a three-by-five notecard, on which he wrote her name with a broad felt tip pen, then held it up to the web cam. "I just learned from Andrew on the ride in from the airport that she was sent to a re-education camp called Camp Z-30, in a place called Xuan Loc." He pronounced it Soon Lop. "That was in Long Khanh Province. Here, I'll write that out for you too."

"Good, maybe that tidbit will help."

They spoke for another ten minutes before signing off, and then Trutch tossed fitfully between the sheets for several hours before he finally dozed. He couldn't shake a feeling of foreboding that crept over him, as though a sinister creature were sharing the bed with him. By 4 a.m. Saigon time, he was fully awake, and aware that this sinister creature — a deeply disconsolate feeling — had been lurking around since he first read Andrew Quang's letter two weeks ago.

CHAPTER SEVEN

Lotus saw by looking through a tear in the canvas flap that the vehicle had stopped on a rutted dirt street. She turned to Diamond, who sat on the opposite bench seat. "We're in a strange place. I don't like it. I'm scared."

In the fading afternoon light, the driver, Luong, ripped the canvas curtain aside and told the girls to get out.

As they dismounted the truck, Lotus looked around and noted several shanty buildings and one of grimy concrete. Directly in front of them a high grilled gate in a gritty brick wall scraped open.

Mau, unlike Luong, had shown a bit of humanity to the two girls during their lunch stop, but now his tone turned brusque. "Welcome to Svay Pak. This is my house. You'll work for me."

Mau gripped both girls by their upper arms.

He smelled like cigarettes, and Lotus shriveled at his touch.

"Come this way," growled Mau in Vietnamese. "Six girls already work here. One died last week."

Lotus and Diamond looked at each other with one shared expression of terror.

Mau half dragged and half pushed them across a small courtyard where moss grew between the brick tiles and felt incongruously soft underfoot. He released his grip on them as he pushed them into the house.

The spartan room had a concrete floor and several pieces of cheap vinyl-covered furniture. Overhead, two bare light bulbs hung from the ceiling. A half-sized refrigerator, with a small Bose sound system resting on top, hunched in a corner. In another corner a metal spiral staircase led to the second floor and just beside it, a long corridor, with a half dozen doors opening on each side, led toward the rear of the building. A grim looking woman stood squarely in front of the entry to the corridor.

In a curt voice she said, "You follow me," and led them down the dimly lit hallway. A curtain of beads, rather than a door, covered each of the doorways.

"Working rooms," the woman announced. At the end of the hallway, an exit had been cemented up from top to bottom. The last doorway on the right, uncurtained, revealed a set of steep wooden stairs leading up. The woman led them up the stairs, speaking over her shoulder.

"My name is Nakry. I am the boss."

Mau, limping heavily, followed the girls up.

At the top of the stairs, Nakry pulled a key from her jeans pocket and opened a sturdy wooden door on a windowless space the size of a modest bedroom, minimally illuminated by a bare bulb. Several sturdy spikes driven into the walls served as hangers, displaying a sparse variety of inexpensive clothing. A jumble of jars and cosmetic tubes overflowed from an open-fronted wooden crate.

Opposite a squat toilet and adjacent sink, five young girls slouched on bamboo pallets draped with thin blankets. Several played cards. One drew on an unlined tablet with the stub of a pencil. A forlorn-looking girl of no more than 12 stared at them, eyes swollen and badly bruised.

"You live here when not working," Nakry announced. "Dinner will come in one hour. Tonight you learn your new jobs."

Diamond whirled around and tried to bolt out the doorway, her face a mask of terror. "I want to go home," she bellowed, tears streaming down both cheeks.

Mau's slap snapped Diamond's head to the side. The sting of pain, surprise and panic registered in her expression as a drop of blood appeared at the corner of her mouth. She fell to one of the pallets, covered her head and whimpered.

Mau's hand retracted again, poised for another blow. "You do as you're told here. Nothing more," he barked.

She twisted to her side, drew her knees to her chest and coiled into a defensive ball on the filthy bed as the other girls looked down into their laps.

Lotus stood trembling next to the bed on which her friend had fallen. She closed her eyes tightly, half expecting to receive the next punch herself. When the door slammed shut, she continued to shake, but when she hesitantly opened her eyes, Mau and Nakry had both gone. She sat heavily onto the pallet next to Diamond. "I want to go home too," she whispered. "I miss my Papa."

The village of Tuy Phuoc, her Papa sitting in his wheelchair on the lean-to porch, the peaceful rice fields and the soothing sounds of Grandmother Quy's voice seemed a million kilometers away.

One of the other girls slid off her pallet and came to Diamond and Lotus.

She spoke in Vietnamese, "My name is Boupha. Always do as they say or they will beat you. The customers can beat you too, and other men who bring customers to this house will beat you if their customers aren't happy."

"But what are we supposed to do?" Lotus asked in a tremulous voice.

"You make the customers happy. Otherwise Mau will hit you and sometimes use electricity."

Confusion and fear muddled Lotus's thoughts. What was it that they were to do to "make customers happy"? How could they avoid the beatings when they had no idea what the work was? She was too afraid to ask. Instead she said, "Boupha's not a Vietnamese name."

"Nakry gave me that name, said some customers prefer girls with Khmer name."

Lotus patted Diamond's shoulder. "We'll be okay, Sister. We'll help each other, and soon we'll go home."

An old woman brought dinner to the attic, red betel nut stains circling her toothless mouth. Without speaking, she served from a battered pot thin rice gruel containing specks of diced yams and carrots.

Lotus watched the other girls swish their spoons indifferently through the thin mush, searching for the bits of carrot and yam. Without enthusiasm, she too dipped her spoon into the tin bowl and fished for the vegetables.

The girl with the purple bruises spoke for the first time. "They want to keep us skinny," she said. "Customers don't like fat girls, so there's never enough food. But sometimes they give you a pill to make you feel happy — for the customer to like us better."

Lotus managed a weak smile of acknowledgement, wondering how anyone could possibly be happy in such a place.

Soon sounds of tinny music and boisterous male voices penetrated the upstairs space from the front of the main floor. The heavy wooden door into their room opened and Nakry gestured for the girls to come downstairs, all of them except Diamond and Lotus, who she told to remain on their pallet.

They did, and sitting huddled together listened to the strange male grunting below them. They spoke little. The red mark on Diamond's face was turning a subtle black and blue.

The door opened again, on Nakry accompanied by a smarmy-looking little man in thick plastic-framed glasses. His canvas valise identified him as a doctor, and Nakry confirmed this. "He will examine you, so do as he says."

The doctor instructed them to remove their pants and underpants and lie down on their backs.

Lotus said, "No," and immediately crossed her legs defensively. Diamond curled back into a ball.

Nakry grabbed Diamond and roughly fumbled with her pants. With the doctor's assistance, Nakry managed to hold her, and despite her struggling, got her undressed from the waist down. Then, with her superior strength, she pushed Lotus onto her back and pinned her to the bed. One at a time, Nakry held them while the greasy little medic went about his examinations with an ungloved hand. Shame silenced them.

"The petals are still on the rose," the doctor told Nakry, looking pleased with his witty metaphor.

With a satisfied nod, she said, "Good. My investment is secure."

CHAPTER EIGHT

From the driveway of the An Nhon care home where he sat in his wheelchair, waiting to meet his father, Ngoc watched the rusty minivan approaching on the dirt road, reddish dust wafting from beneath its wheels like clouds of crimson soot.

Through the windshield, he could see the tall Caucasian in silhouette. He had spent part of his childhood detesting this American, unable to understand why he had left his mother and him, and why he had not returned to rescue his mother when she was taken away to the camp. She was no enemy of the new regime. Was she deemed a collaborator and incarcerated because she had worked in a US Army hospital, or because of her involvement with this man, that fact made obvious by Ngoc's existence as a mixed-blood child?

It wasn't until he was four or five that Ngoc realized his difference and understood that others saw him as non-human, a life form lower than most animals. The taunts, "half-breed, half-breed," and "filth under my shoes," echoed harshly even now, and the isolation and loneliness still cut through him like a sharp knife. In Quy Nhon, his aunt, embarrassed by his blended Oriental-Caucasian features, wouldn't be seen on the street with him. In the tiny dirt yard of his aunt's house, he spent much of his childhood attempting to entertain himself by capturing insects or counting the bicycles and cyclos that passed by. By the age of ten, his shame and self-loathing was so great he longed for the ability to peel off his skin and change the shape of his eyes.

Like most people under the new regime — except government officials, who skimmed cream from the top of every pail — Aunt was poor. Often all they had to eat were steamed cassava roots. A good day, with a good meal, was one in which they had a bit of rice and maybe a scrap of fish or chicken.

And even while his resentment grew, he yearned to know his father. Why had Trutch not come back to Vietnam to care for him? To love him, as he had loved his own child, Lien? Who was this man, Trutch? He supposed he would know in a few minutes.

Now the minivan turned into the roughly paved drive and came to a stop. When the door opened and Trutch stepped out, followed by Andrew, Ngoc's eyes widened in surprise. Trutch's skin, apart from the scar on his left cheek, was clearer and tauter than that of a Vietnamese of the same age, and his broad smile showcased a set of healthy, white teeth, also unusual in older Vietnamese men. He looked too strong and vigorous to be 66 years old.

Ngoc set his teeth in a welcoming smile and clasped his hands in his lap to still them as both men paused to size each other up.

***

Trutch knew instantly that a DNA test was unnecessary. As he took in Ngoc's face, he stared into his own hazel pupils. Ngoc's nose was not classic Vietnamese, somewhat wide and flat, but had the same aquiline contour as Trutch's. He sat proud and erect in his wheelchair, his shoulders, strong from muscling the chair, bulging beneath a clean blue shirt.

Andrew made the introductions, and Trutch and Ngoc reached across their momentary awkwardness to shake hands. As soon as politeness allowed, Trutch wanted to ask Ngoc to introduce him to Lien's grandmother, so they might learn where to look for Vu. In talking to her, maybe they would also learn a little more about each other.

But they had barely finished saying hello when another Vietnamese man walked into the breach. "I am Mr. Le," he said in English, "director of the care facility."

Protocol demanded that he welcome his foreign visitor with a tour of his facility, and as his spiel unwound over the course of the tour — facts about the institution and the good it did and the overwhelming challenges Mr. Le managed — Trutch and Ngoc openly took each other in.

"Of course we would manage better with more funding," Mr. Le said, seemingly assuming that all Westerners have deep pockets.

Trutch feigned interest with occasional responses, but it was Ngoc who held his attention. His son spoke seldom, but with confidence, and he had an air of dignity and awareness that could not be feigned. More than once during the tour, when Mr. Le said something unlikely, Ngoc's eyes met Trutch's from behind a polite but inscrutable mask. We listen, but we do not always believe, his glance said.

By Vietnamese standards, the yellow-painted cluster of three long, stucco buildings had a homey feel. The space between the buildings was paved but brightened with numerous large ceramic urns and a few concrete planters filled with lush tropical plants and small trees, creating an attractive courtyard. Inside, each of the two-story buildings contained a number of ward-like rooms opening onto open breezeways. The residents ranged in age from six to well into their 70s.

"None of these people have family to care for them," explained Mr. Le. "This is an orphanage for all ages."

The dining hall, an expansive room filled with institutional metal tables and red plastic stools, smelled of cabbage and cooking oil and had stain-streaked walls. Older residents with hungry, expectant expressions were filing in or being wheeled in.

"We're about to serve lunch," Mr. Le said, gesturing toward the only table in the hall set with a tablecloth. "We invite you to join us."

As they chose their places and sat, Trutch said to Ngoc. "Does your mother-in-law have any idea where Lien's Uncle Vu is? I think he's the place to start asking questions about Lien."

Ngoc rolled up to the only place setting at the table without a chair. "We can talk to her after lunch, but I don't know how helpful she will be, now that she's had a stroke."

Lunch was a bowl of steamed rice topped with a small piece of fried fish and a generous portion of boiled cabbage. Bottles of soy sauce and chili sauce stood at the ready on each table and beside each of their rice bowls was a ramekin of Vietnam's ubiquitous fish sauce — *nuoc mam*.

To everyone else's amusement, Trutch fumbled a bit with his chopsticks. "Is it okay to eat the rice with a spoon?" he asked. He nibbled at the rice for several minutes and then tried the chopsticks again on the fish.

Just as he got the first bite into his mouth, a wizened old man in light blue pajamas and rubber sandals ambled across the room, and thrust himself up against the table by Trutch's side.

He slammed his hand onto the table so that the rice bowls jumped, and shouted, "You kill Vietnamese." He pantomimed firing a rifle and wildly yelled, "Bang, bang, bang, bang. You kill Vietnamese people." He banged his palm upon the table again and again. "You American. You kill Vietnamese people — soldiers, old women, children." His eyes were wild and full of fire, his voice trembling in his rage.

Trutch pushed himself back from the table and sat quietly during the tirade.

The other 60 or so residents in the dining room all stared at the unfolding drama.

Mr. Le stood and gripped the old man by the shoulders, steadying him. Two attendants rushed up and helped to subdue him.

"So sorry for that," said Mr. Le, as the attendants led the distraught oldster back to his stool on the other side of the room, "Some of our residents are deranged."

Trutch wasn't sure one had to be deranged to harbor ill will toward a former enemy in an ugly war. "No problem. I understand." He glanced at Ngoc and noted that he wore an expression of pain.

After the meal, Mr. Le excused himself and Ngoc led Trutch and Andrew first to his quarters, one of six beds in a room he shared with five other men, and then to the room where his mother-in-law, who had not come to the dining room, sat slumped sideways in her wheelchair next to her bed. Her eyes were bright and alert, but she was unable to speak. She offered her left hand to Trutch and gave him a lopsided smile.

Trutch greeted her and then turned to ask Ngoc, "Do you have a picture of Lien?"

Ngoc reached into a pocket and produced a grainy, colored snapshot of a cute little girl wearing her school uniform. "Keep it," he offered. "You can help find her?"

"That's why I came to Vietnam — to help you find her. I'm no investigator, but with Andrew's help, I can make some enquiries. The first question to address, I think, is where is this Uncle Vu who took her to Saigon?" With a slight cant of his head toward the older woman he intended the question to be directed to both of them.

Ngoc responded, "None of us knows." But he turned toward Grandma Quy and carefully enunciated the question in Vietnamese, "Do you know where your son, Vu, has gone?"

A slight shake of her head indicated that either she didn't understand the question or didn't know. Ngoc rephrased the question and tried again. Again, the negative response.

Ngoc turned to Trutch and said, "I know he has several girl friends. He used to disappear from Quy Nhon for one week at a time and when he came back he was happy. He could be with one of them. But I don't know where any of them live. He likes city girls. I think they would be in Hanoi, Da Nang, Nha Trang or Saigon."

Grandma Quy made a guttural sound. They all looked toward her and she nodded slightly. She struggled and moved her lips, trying to find words that she had lost since her stroke. "S ... Sai ... gon," she rasped, in a whispery voice, her tongue and lips working together painfully.

"Do you know the woman's name?" Ngoc asked.

"Or where she lives?" fired Andrew.

Quy's head waggled from side to side and then her chin fell to her chest. She was finished with this conversation.

Andrew went off to make some phone calls while Trutch and Ngoc moved to the courtyard, where a small Tamarind tree offered a little shade. Trutch sat on a marble bench next to a potted, wide-spreading bougainvillea and Ngoc rolled up opposite him. Conversation flowed more easily between them now, and they spoke mostly of Ngoc's traumatic and demeaning childhood. Bullying was a current schoolyard concern back home in Seattle, but to be confronted by the truth of Ngoc's upbringing amid scorn and rejection from adults — adult relatives — pummeled Trutch, despite Ngoc's polite attempts to soften the details.

He asked, "How did you become disabled?"

"I was ten years old. I was depressed. My aunt said I was lazy — no good. She took me to a doctor for him to fix me. The doctor put the injection of hot water into my back. It went into my spine and I was paralyzed. I don't know if he did that on purpose."

Clutched by a surge of revulsion, Trutch supposed it didn't matter whether it was deliberate or not. Certainly, there would have been no such thing as liability in Vietnam — no malpractice insurance.

"I wished for death. I thought about killing myself. But an old man, a neighbor, also disabled and on crutches, taught me about reading and a little bit about history, and about mathematics. After a while, I thought I will not feel bad about being disabled. He taught me about — how you say in English — self-esteem. When I read about other disabled people I understood *independence*, and how it means I can make my own decisions. That is what I always try for now — to make my own decisions. My life had been like a dying tree, gray with no leafs and no sun or water. Then my tree has leafs and buds and gets strong because I find strength in my inner self."

Pride and humility in the presence of this courageous, younger man overcame the revulsion Trutch had felt a moment before. He turned his head away from Ngoc and faked scratching his brow while wiping away a tear.

"But now I feel like the tree may die again because my daughter, Lien is gone. She was like part of the sunshine for the tree." He went silent, then asked, "You will help find her, *Ba?*"

Trutch felt a surge of surprise, and pleasure, that Ngoc had called him *Dad*. "I'll do my best," he said. "I'll start by trying to find Vu in Saigon. Do you know his full name? And have a picture of him?"

"I will ask my mother-in-law." He wheeled away.

When he returned, Ngoc handed Trutch a black and white photo of a man sitting on the edge of a basket boat with the sea in the background, and a slip of paper with the name Tran Duc Vu scrawled on it. The photo was taken from too great a distance for the facial features to be sharp, but the physique was that of a short, slender man with powerful, well-built shoulders and chest.

Just before they parted company an hour later, Trutch asked about Dream. Did Ngoc know anything about what had become of her, beyond her being in a camp in Xuan Loc? Ngoc shook his head and sadly related the last time he had seen his mother at age six.

Trutch hid his disappointment and extended his hand, but Ngoc unexpectedly leaned forward in his chair and spread his arms wide. Trutch leaned down and for the first time embraced his son.

***

Trutch and Andrew Quang sat on the terrace of the Royal Resort, a three-star hotel complex in Quy Nhon that catered primarily to Vietnamese tourists visiting the city for its fine seafood. The descending sun hovered well behind them as they watched a fleet of one-man basket boats make its way through the surf toward the anchored fishing boats in Quy Nhon Bay. In each of the circular boats, a man J-stroked an oar to propel his little vessel through the frothy surf. Each stroke moved the craft three feet forward before the surf pushed it two feet back. The collective motion of all the men in all their little boats resembled an assortment of tiny microorganisms wiggling about on a microscope slide.

"That went well, all things considered," Trutch said, in reference to their visit with Ngoc. He lifted a chilled bottle of Bier Saigon to his lips and drank from it. "It's clear to me that he's my son. And I want to help find Lien, but realistically, what are the chances of finding Vu?"

"Slim," Andrew said. "Going to the police, even armed with his full name and photograph, would be fruitless. Unless we take them evidence of criminal behavior, they won't invest resources to find one man in a city of eight million people. Even if they did, it would take a huge bribe to get any action. Worse, if Lien's been sold, there's a good chance she's no longer in Vietnam. I can only suggest that we meet with the STOK people and ask if they can help in any way."

Trutch noted Andrew's use of "we" with satisfaction, as it signaled their shared, if unspoken, understanding that they would be partners in this endeavor. But the suggestion itself was anything but encouraging. "What can STOK do?" he asked.

"In the child prostitution game it's easier to move girls out of Vietnam and market them in neighboring countries like Cambodia, Thailand and Malaysia, even China. Enforcement of anti-prostitution laws is spotty when it comes to mature prostitutes, but the government takes a dim view of the sexual exploitation of children. Pedophilia and child pornography are serious offenses in Vietnam, and the penalties for those caught are severe. The Ministry of Public Security has established a unit that investigates child sex tourism. They're aggressive and enforcement-minded. Because STOK uses a network of informants, they're sometimes able to supply the enforcement unit with information that leads to arrests."

Sometimes. Trutch felt that same sense of foreboding that had haunted him earlier. This was going to be an ugly experience with slim chance of success. He and Andrew had embarked on a fishing expedition, and this was not the way he liked to do things. He was conditioned to act pragmatically in solving problems and seizing objectives, to evaluate the facts bearing on any problem, and then to select the option that had the best chance of success with the lowest possible cost in casualties. In this case, the paucity of concrete facts made evaluation difficult. He was left with assumptions — Vu had sold Lien into bondage; Vu had a woman in Saigon. What they needed was good solid intelligence — information about the enemy, his location, his strengths and weaknesses, his capabilities and limitations. Solid facts. "Okay, then," he said. "Let's talk to the people at STOK."

CHAPTER NINE

On Sunday afternoon, the square in front of the People's Committee headquarters in Ho Chi Minh City was crowded with families enjoying themselves amid the carefully tended flower beds and manicured topiary, snapping photos of their children by a statue of a benevolent Uncle Ho, posed seated and reading to a little girl.

Trutch strode past the statue and crossed Nguyen Hue Street, his pace brisk as the mass of motorbike drivers anticipated his path and wove their way around him. After climbing an ostentatious marble stairway, he approached the doors of the Rex Hotel, where a uniformed doorman bowed slightly and held the door open for him, allowing him to enter the spacious, high-ceilinged lobby. He turned left and walked past a row of brightly lit shops to the elevator that would take him to the famous rooftop veranda bar.

Bill Anderson, his business partner in Seattle, had mentioned that during the war the Rex had been leased by the US military and used as an officer's billet. The rooftop bar had been a popular watering hole, where military brass stationed in Saigon could sip martinis and watch artillery flashes and the slow descent of parachute flares. After the fall of Saigon, the hotel fell into disrepair, but with a series of renovations, the most recent in 2007–2008, a luxurious five-star property and adjoining casino was born.

With about 80 percent of the tables occupied, mostly by Westerners, Trutch found an empty table near the low wall at the roof's edge and ordered a Bier Saigon. While he waited for Andrew, he leaned back and took in the expansive view of downtown Saigon and its many neon-lit skyscrapers. A short city block up Le Loi Street, bathed in floodlights, The Ho Chi Minh City Opera House sat regally, a classical example of French Colonial architecture.

He had never had the opportunity to come into the city during his combat tours, but to hear Bill Anderson describe it, the city was a seething fleshpot of a place, hemorrhaging raw sex from every doorway. He tried to imagine it now, and couldn't. Even the most notorious red light district, Tu Do Street, renamed

Dong Khoi Street and barely a block away from the Rex, now boasted glitzy retail shops instead of sleazy bars and hotels.

"Good afternoon, Pete." Andrew drew up a chair opposite Trutch and ordered a bottle of Perrier from the hovering waiter. "Okay, we have an appointment with a Ms. Judith Grinder and two other people, tomorrow morning at ten o'clock. She's the in-country director for STOK."

"Who are the others?"

"Duc is one of Judith's investigators. The other is Captain Minh, a policeman of questionable character."

"Questionable how?"

"He's thought to be cunning, maybe working both sides of the street. Like many policemen, he augments his salary in nefarious ways. Some also suspect he's in on the trafficking business himself."

Trutch's eyebrows shot upward. "Why the hell will he be there?"

"Because Judith thinks it's good politics to invite him. The investigators she uses sometimes go to him when they uncover evidence of trafficking, in hopes the police will intervene. Sometimes he's helpful. Other times he's not."

"Apart from asking if anyone has any ideas we can pursue, what's the agenda?"

"That's pretty much it. Hopefully, Judith or Duc can provide some insight into the whole trafficking culture in Ho Chi Minh City. They may know of some rocks we can turn over."

"If nothing else it should be interesting," Trutch said, and then silently chided himself. *Interesting*, what a useless noncommittal word. Uncertainty wasn't interesting.

***

In the second-floor office of STOK in Saigon's District 4, Trutch sat opposite a man in a forest green uniform, three gold stars adorning each of his epaulettes. Recognizing the insignia as that of a *dai uy*, he regarded Captain Minh with wariness, conscious of Andrew's warning of his possible duplicity.

Minh was of medium height and pot-bellied, with buzz-cut hair that bristled over a no-nonsense face. He occupied a straight chair, his left leg crossed over his right, his hand resting on his knee with a lit cigarette gripped between his fingers.

When Judith Grinder made the introductions, he didn't offer his hand.

"I'm just here to take the full name of your granddaughter," he said to Trutch, displaying teeth rimmed with gold. "A photo may also help."

When Trutch produced the photo, Judith copied it and gave the copy to Captain Minh.

"We'll circulate this information. But just one more thing." He looked first at Trutch then at Andrew and finally at Duc, Judith's investigator, dressed in a Hawaiian shirt. "Leave investigations and law enforcement to us. People who interfere get hurt sometimes."

Trutch noted that Duc suddenly found something interesting to examine on the floor.

When Captain Minh had gone, Judith, in her Aussie accent, explained. "Duc here walks a narrow tightrope, trying to obtain police cooperation and action without stepping on their toes, and we try to liaise with the police whenever we uncover evidence of child trafficking. I asked Captain Minh here today in a spirit of cooperation. There's probably little the police can do to find your granddaughter without good leads and evidence of criminality, but at least he knows we're consulting with him."

She moved to the window and looked out for a moment, and then she motioned for Trutch and Andrew to join her. "Step over here, I want to show you something."

With the men beside her, she pointed to a block-long triangle of green on the other side of the street. "That's Hoa Binh Park. Whenever the police aren't heavy into enforcement mode, it's a meat market. What you see going on between that young man and that girl is a price negotiation for a toss in the hay."

Below, a slender young man sat astride his motorbike, smoking a cigarette. The girl was overly made up and wore a leather miniskirt and stiletto heels. In response to his lascivious grin, she was speaking rapidly and gesturing suggestively.

"The hookers in this area are known as 'butterflies of the night,'" Judith said, "although they clearly don't limit their activities to nighttime. She's probably no more than 15, and likely from a poor village, duped into becoming a prostitute."

Trutch looked away and stepped back from the window, frowning. "Then the police aren't doing as much as they could."

"Trafficking takes several forms," Judith said. "Some young women in their late teens are willingly recruited and sent to Kuala Lumpur or Singapore for arranged marriages to businessmen, who pay well for doctor-certified Vietnamese virgins. The girls, usually from poor villages, see it as an opportunity for upward mobility. They're treated to the adventure of a flight at the buyer's expense, and often met by a uniformed chauffeur, so they're somewhat bowled over by that and the big modern cities. Unfortunately, they're often discarded by their husbands after several months and left stranded without airfare or means of support or friends in the big city.

"Some young women are lured to Saigon with the promise of a job as a waitress or nanny only to discover that they're now 'owned' by a *mama san* or a pimp who puts them to work immediately on the streets or in the bars of Saigon. But the saddest cases are the underage girls, and to a lesser extent boys, who are kidnapped or sold for the purpose of transportation to another Asian nation, where they feed the insatiable appetites of traveling sexual predators and suffer unspeakable abuse and privation. These children are in particular demand in Cambodia."

"Why Cambodia?"

"For two reasons. The Khmers have no great love for the Vietnamese and regard them as inferior, so abuse of the ethnic Viets is seen as okay. Secondly, the Vietnamese typically have lighter skin than Khmers and are more physically desirable for Khmer men, and many tourists, who see white skin as a mark of beauty."

Trutch had already read much of this information during his research in the States, but having it corroborated from a source much closer to the problem, while overlooking a live negotiation for sex in the park below, left his stomach knotted.

When Andrew's cellular phone jangled, and he politely stepped into the corridor to take the call, Trutch moved the conversation with Judith off the general issue of trafficking and back to the question of finding Lien.

"Duc can circulate copies of her picture and description to his resources and ask them to be on the lookout for her," Judith suggested. "We just have to hope someone spots her. That is, of course, if she's still in Ho Chi Minh City."

"Resources?"

Duc spoke for the first time. "Many people in Saigon are concerned and want to help — students, clergy, social workers and many Westerners working for NGOs as well. Some do undercover work by visiting bars and karaoke parlors. They keep their eyes open."

"Isn't that dangerous?"

"Could be, if the pimps and bouncers suspect something. But they pose as young people out to have a good time. They observe passively."

Duc himself, with his broad shoulders and muscular physique, looked like a bouncer from the neck down. His face, though, Trutch thought, reflected the wholesome countenance of a choirboy.

Andrew reentered the room looking pleased. "We may have a break. That call was from Le, the director of the care home at An Nhon." He remained standing by the door, as though poised to take off on an urgent errand. "He says that Vu has wired a small sum of money to the home for the support of his mother. He gave me the transaction number and said it originated from a branch of the Phuong Dong Bank at 246 Khanh Hoi Street, here in Saigon."

"That's just two blocks from here," Duc said. "Let's go." Then to Trutch, "Do you have a photo of this Vu?"

"Right here." He pulled out the grainy black and white snapshot.

CHAPTER TEN

Two hours after Lotus and Diamond underwent their pelvic exam, Boupha returned, looking gloomy. "Follow me. You'll see what you have to do with customers."

She led them past several curtained doorways and then pushed one beaded curtain aside. With her index finger over her lips in a warning sign, she gestured for them to enter with her. Inside, pushed against a wall, was a pallet bed and bamboo mat. A two-drawer nightstand held a pink lamp, its fringed shade glowing with soft light. Opposite that hung a wall sink with rusty taps and no outlet pipes. Dark stains below suggested that the sink emptied its contents onto the concrete floor, where they snaked to an open drain.

Boupha extinguished the lamp, but through a connecting doorway, also curtained, a few rays of light leaked in from the adjoining room. Again she signaled for silence, and then parted the curtain just a crack and motioned for Diamond and Lotus to peek into the other room, a carbon copy of the one they occupied. A girl Lotus recognized from their dinner earlier sat on the bed staring down at her hands, which rested palms up on her knees. About 12, she was heavily made up with rouged cheeks, lipstick and mascara. She wore a red miniskirt that barely reached her thighs and a pink and white floral top, the entire look incongruent with her slender hips and flat chest.

She rose when Nakry appeared in the hall doorway and showed a middle-aged Caucasian man into the room. "This here girl name Moon," Nakry said.

The man, florid and balding, had wet stains under his arms. He clutched an opened bottle of beer in one hand and a burning cigarette in the other. He grinned at Moon, showing tobacco-stained teeth.

Moon smiled demurely and then lowered her eyes.

After Nakry left, the man lifted Moon's chin. "Hey there, little Moon."

"You want boom boom?"

"You bet." He pantomimed that he wanted Moon to remove her blouse and then his voice grew raspy. "You're well trained, Moon."

Moon removed her blouse and then glanced up, an apprehensive furrow between her brows, as though seeking approval.

The man set his beer and cigarette on the nightstand without benefit of an ashtray. He reached around behind her with both hands to unclip and remove her bra. He brought it to his nose to give it a sniff and then tossed it beside her blouse. He stepped back and looked approvingly at the little knobs on her chest. His upper lip shone with flecks of perspiration and a drop of saliva appeared at the corner of his mouth.

Paralyzed by the scene, Lotus was unable to avert her eyes. Diamond gasped and covered her mouth with her hand.

Next, the man gestured for Moon to remove her miniskirt, which she did. Naked, she stepped forward, and without command, unbuttoned and removed the man's shirt. He kicked off his shoes. Now barefoot, his feet grimy, he stepped around behind Moon and roughly pinched at her chest while kissing the nape of her neck. She flinched and let out a subdued squeal.

Ignoring her discomfort, he was now wheezing and breathing rapidly.

Lotus sucked back a sob. At her side, Diamond's breath caught in her throat as she grabbed Lotus's hand.

The man stepped back around to Moon's front and pointed at his crotch. "Okay Moon, yum yum."

With a bland, resigned expression, Moon unbuckled his belt and lowered his zipper. She tugged his pants down to his ankles.

Now panting heavily, he pointed at the bulging erection barely concealed by his shorts.

Lotus flinched. She had seen penises before when small children in her village ran around naked during the warm months, but she had never seen one as large or menacing as this.

As though an automaton on remote control, Moon got down onto her knees.

"That pig," whispered Diamond, a little too loudly.

The man turned to look over his shoulder toward the curtain and shouted, "What're you little bitches gawking at? In training, are you?"

Diamond and Lotus lurched back from their vantage point, and Lotus jerked the curtain shut.

"Well you watch real good. This is how it's done," he roared.

Lotus cowered in a corner of the room with Diamond at her side, next to an indifferent Boupha. As the man grunted and groaned, she squeezed her eyes closed tight. The sounds didn't last long. Then she heard Moon gag and spit into the sink. Water ran, then splashed on the floor, as if someone were urinating there.

Then the customer slapped the side of the wall next to where the girls huddled and lumbered out of the room.

"You don't have to do that the first time," Boupha said. "Just take his thing into your secret, dark place. It will hurt the first time, but you should pretend like you're having a good time. Wiggle around a little and groan. But you won't have to do it for at least a week. Nakry will put the word out that she has virgins and will wait until someone pays a high price."

Lotus trembled, her chin jutting out, her arms crossed. "I don't want to do that. I won't do that."

"Then Nakry and Mau will beat you," Boupha said.

CHAPTER ELEVEN

Captain Minh departed the STOK office. As he exited the narrow building, he checked the sidewalk in both directions and walked a few steps before his eyes met those of a beefy man with the wide, flat nose of a kickboxer. The two nodded at each other. Five minutes later they met in a booth at a Highlands Coffee outlet a block away. Luong had arrived first and was already drinking *ca phe sua* — coffee with sweetened condensed milk. Captain Minh ordered nothing.

He handed Luong a photograph. "You might have a problem. Do you recognize the girl in the picture?"

Luong sipped his coffee and fingered the photo, his shifty eyes darting between the picture and Captain Minh.

Minh considered the ash at the end of his cigarette. "Well?"

"It's one of the girls we took to Svay Pak about two months ago. We've moved a lot of meat to Cambodia in the past six months. But I remember this girl's eyes. They look different than most Vietnamese."

"An older American, who seems to have some money, is asking STOK if they can help find her. He claims to be her grandfather."

"So what? What does that have to do with me?"

"If this old American man learns anything while he's sniffing around here, he could end up in Svay Pak. Maybe with Mr. Duc, an experienced investigator, and a nosy *Viet Kieu* from Australia named Quang. I don't have to tell you Svay Pak is a much smaller pond in which to go fishing than Saigon. You wouldn't want them to find anything there that could interrupt your tidy little cash flow. You won't have me or my men looking the other way in Cambodia."

"True, but we do have some cooperative Khmer officials there."

"The American and this Quang think the child was brought to Saigon by her uncle, a man named Tran Duc Vu. Do you know him?"

"No. We get all our meat from middle people. Not directly from family or kidnappers."

"Of course. I know some of your suppliers — the middle people. It's good that you don't know the sources."

"My friends and I will keep our eyes open. We'll let you know if anyone is getting too close."

"It will be in all of our interests for you to do so. If this Trutch learns too much, he could be a threat to our operation."

***

Across the street from Highlands Coffee, Trutch, Andrew and Duc walked briskly on the uneven sidewalk, toward the Khanh Hoi Street branch of the Phuong Dong Bank.

"I didn't appreciate his not-so-veiled threat," Trutch observed of Captain Minh. "How often do you work with him, Duc?"

"When we find evidence of underage children being held, we go to him. Sometimes he takes action. Sometimes he makes trouble for us."

"How?"

"About a month ago we stopped a truck going to Cambodia at Go Dau. We freed three children, and brought them back to a safe house here in Saigon."

"How did you stop the truck?"

"I paid another truck driver to put his truck across the road and lay a motorbike on its side in front of the truck. We had one man lie in the road by his motorbike. When the truck stopped, I had four other men open the back and take the children. The driver and the other man in the cab tried to fight us but we were too many — six of us."

They stepped off the sidewalk and into the street to go around a cluster of motorbikes parked in front of a sundry shop. When they regained the walkway Duc said, "Later in Saigon, Captain Minh arrested me for 'interference.' The police kept me for one day then made me pay a big 'fine' — three million dong, 150 dollars. That's what Captain Minh meant when he said 'people get hurt sometimes,' but he may have meant physical harm too."

They arrived at the bank, a small storefront in a four-story building, and entered. Three young women in ao dais sat behind desks at the rear of the room. Trutch felt his usual twinge of admiration at their delicate beauty. The country had more than its fair share of beautiful women, and yet to what advantage when so many were exploited? One in twenty were sold by their parents, Andrew had told him.

He pressed the machine by the door and took his number, and then sat with Andrew and Duc and several other customers waiting for service in two rows of folding chairs.

When it was their turn to see one of the clerks, Trutch showed the picture of Vu while Duc spoke to her in Vietnamese.

She shook her head.

Duc showed her the transaction number of the transfer and she tapped a few computer keys. "Yes," she said. "The wire transfer was sent from this office but the customer paid in cash. I don't remember the man in the picture."

She rose from her chair and showed the picture to each of the other two clerks. The one in the green ao dai hoisted her eyebrows for a fraction of a second but then shook her head. The other one paused and studied the photo. Then she said *khong*. No.

Trutch and Andrew shared glances of commiseration as they left. Discouraged, they followed Duc down the sidewalk. They hadn't gone 15 meters when the young woman in green ran after them. She raised her voice and shouted to be heard above the steady stream of buzzing motorbikes and the blaring horns of high-end SUVs surging in both directions. "I know the man," she said in English. "He stay with my sister. She bring him to my bank for wire the money."

"Would you tell us where your sister lives?" asked Andrew.

"I don't want to get her in trouble."

"She won't be in any trouble. We just want to talk to the man in the picture."

"She live in Cholon District. I write address for you. Her name is Mai."

Trutch handed her a business card and a ballpoint pen. She glanced at the business card then turned it over and scrawled an address on the reverse. "You can give me some money?"

Trutch gave her 200,000 dong, and thanked her.

As she turned away she yelled, "You not go there until tomorrow morning. Best time. I don't think anyone there now."

The three men resumed walking. "Screw that," Trutch said, his voice elevated to be heard over the traffic. "We'd better go now in case she tips off her sister that we're interested in seeing Vu."

"Probably best to wait until morning, as she says," Duc said. "Cholon is a tightly packed warren of walk-up apartments. If we go today and no one's home, the neighbors are likely to tell them later that three men were nosing around."

"And if they know that one of the men is a tall Caucasian that's sure to arouse suspicion," added Andrew.

Reluctantly, Trutch accepted their logic. "Okay. First thing tomorrow then."

***

On the bank of the Saigon River, as the sun rapidly descended, Trutch sat on a stone bench among lengthening shadows. With the darkening sky, dinner cruise boats, outlined with tiny strings of lights, became dragons and castles. Chattering tourists filed up the gangways in excited anticipation of the cruise down the busy waterway and the spectacle of the twinkling city floating by. Ferries gobbled up hundreds of motorbikes, their taillights bobbing and blinking as they squeezed together on the decks.

Thoughts flickered and shifted in and out of Trutch's mind, much like the motorbike lights. This city, the events of the last few days, his confusion about Ngoc, his desperate longing to be with Catherine, all collided, interrupting each other, none complete.

Two elegant women passed in front of him, their graceful ao dais and long silken hair fluttering in the evening breeze. He admired them as they glided past, and watched their swaying bottoms. He had only succumbed to temptation once in his 43-year marriage, but when he was young, those derrières would have stirred something more than the appreciation of graceful beauty which he felt now. God, he was getting old.

He forced his mind to shift gears. This could be a dangerous undertaking, this search for Lien. He recalled Bill Anderson's warning — "If you start poking around in Saigon for this supposed granddaughter, you're biting off way more than you can chew, my friend."

But the soldier in him knew this was a problem to be attacked aggressively. He had known fear and apprehension in this part of the world before and had always found that the best way to deal with it was to get on with the mission, to gather as much information as he could, develop a meticulous plan and execute it vigorously. But be flexible, he reminded himself, because the situation can, and will, inevitably change.

The city used mercury vapor streetlights, and he sat in the humid night by the Saigon River and watched them cast their marmalade corona onto the water and roadways. The courage of his son Ngoc lanced its way into his reflections. How had he, as a little boy, withstood the taunts of the other children without becoming ruined by anger? How had he survived the loss of his mother and his wife? How did he go on despite the pain, both physical and emotional?

His son's bravery in the face of overwhelming adversity cemented his resolve. He would get on with the job. And he would start in the morning by finding this man, Uncle Vu.

CHAPTER TWELVE

Catherine met Bill Anderson in the Alaska Air Lines lounge at Sea-Tac airport. She helped herself to coffee and added soymilk, while Bill ordered an extra-spicy Bloody Mary. They carried their drinks into the high-ceilinged seating area and found two comfortable leather chairs near the windows. Outside, baggage was being loaded or unloaded and a variety of ground service vehicles, tugs and tractors shuttled back and forth among the six or seven jetliners parked at gates along the C concourse. It was a fabulous Indian summer day with clear skies, puffy cumulous clouds here and there, and the crenellated peaks of the Olympic Range visible in the distance to the west. "A good day for flying," Bill said, using a celery stick to swizzle ice cubes in his tall glass.

A week earlier, Bill, who still spoke a little Vietnamese and understood much of the culture, had consulted with the Viet community in Seattle and obtained their help in constructing the ads that Catherine wanted to run in several *Viet Kieu* newspapers. Two days ago they got a hit when Catherine received an e-mail from a man who said his grandmother had seen the ad and thought she remembered Nguyen Thi Tuyet from the Xuan Loc re-education camp.

As soon as he heard, Anderson volunteered to accompany Catherine to California. "Two sets of ears are better than one," he said. "Besides, I'm curious. I've read about, but never seen, the Vietnamese enclave in Orange County."

They couldn't hear flight announcements within the fancy lounge, but wall-mounted video displays of departure and arrival information would remind them when to head down to their gate.

They each sipped in silence until Bill said, "God damn, but you're a loyal wife, Catherine. I can't imagine many women who would put up with the expectations of an army wife — the teas, the charity bake sales and all that crap — for over 20 years and then travel a thousand miles to try and locate her husband's former lover."

"You know why? I endured over two decades of Pete's army career, as

70

contemptuous as I was of the norms and mores defining my role, because he is a good man, doing something he truly believed in. Yes, my own career as a teacher was on hold as I followed him around the world, doing my best to decorate and make homey the sometimes dingy housing we occupied. But the devotion and loyalty was reciprocal, at least that's what I believed until I heard about his dalliance in Nha Trang."

"Yeah, but any woman who can put up with the institutional strictures of the army has my respect *and* bewilders me at the same time. We used to say, if the army wanted you to have a wife, they'd issue you one."

"I never once felt that I played second fiddle to the army. Pete has a strong sense of duty, but during those military years, he never allowed his oath of office and his responsibilities as a husband to come into conflict. I always felt like it was 'Catherine first, the army second.' Now I'm hurt that, at least at one point, it may have been Catherine and Dream tied for first."

"Then why are you doing this for him?"

"Because, even as angry as I am right now, one of the things I love most about Pete — and probably the driving force behind him right now — is his strong belief in human dignity and human rights. He's doing the right thing. He's owning his probable paternity and he's trying to help his alleged son."

"Right." He took a long drink. "On a different subject, how much do you know about this woman we're meeting?"

"According to her grandson, she speaks no English. He'll be there to help with the translations. Her name is Ha Thi Loan. She is 74 years old. She spent just over three years in the re-education camp at Xuan Loc. Her crime? She worked as a dining facility manager for the US Air Force at Tan Son Nhat Air Base." She shook her head, causing the discreet platinum hoops in her ears to quiver. "Let's head down to the gate, Bill."

***

A stooped Asian woman in slacks and a yellow blouse opened the door to a single-story bungalow near the Asian Garden Mall in the city of Westminster, south of Los Angeles. Her gray hair pulled tightly into a bun at the back of her head, she peered over the top of a small pair of spectacles, which rested precariously on the end of her nose. "*Vo di, vo di,*" she said while gesturing that they were welcome to come in. Her grandson then appeared and introduced himself as Chau.

The living room, sparsely furnished with Ikea products, had a distinct musty smell like old library books, possibly emanating from the carpets and draperies, as the three-shelf bookcase opposite the sofa contained no literature, only framed family photographs of several generations. A shelf over the bookcase constituted a shrine. Featured dominantly amid a cluster of offerings that included several pieces of fruit, a package of Marlboro cigarettes and a vase containing unlit joss sticks, was a faded photo of a middle-aged Asian man in a suit. A bronze image of Jesus hung from a cross on another wall, his hands and feet bleeding, a tear clinging to his left cheek.

Catherine and Bill sat on the sofa.

"My grandmother welcomes you to her house," said Chau. "She was in Camp Z-30 at Xuan Loc from June of 1975 to October of 1978. She knew this woman, Nguyen Thi Tuyet."

Catherine said, "Please tell Mrs. Loan it's very kind of her to see us. We realize it must be painful for her to dredge up old memories of the re-education camp."

Chau and Mrs. Loan conversed for a full five minutes in their tonal sing-song Vietnamese, the old woman fingering the hem of her loose-fitting blouse as she spoke. Her voice cracked from time to time and she paused to collect herself several times.

"My grandmother tells of the hardships the women in the camp faced. They worked 12 or 13 hours a day in the fields, to produce the meager food they ate, and then listened to lectures at night. They were kept separate from the men prisoners but were often…um…sexually harassed, sometimes molested, by the male guards."

Catherine placed her hand over her mouth and Bill looked sadly at Mrs. Loan.

"They slept on bamboo mats on the dirt floor of their building, which had no walls, only a roof, and during the rainy season it was cold. Most of the women had merely two changes of clothing and no soap for washing them. After a year or so in the camp, their clothes were in tatters."

"Oh, those poor women," Catherine said.

Chau nodded solemnly. "Some of the women were pregnant when they came to the camp. In spite of their growing stomachs they had to dig ditches, service latrines, plant corn and tend to crops while the brutal sun beat on them."

Loan interrupted her grandson with a 45-second flurry of Vietnamese, gesturing demonstratively as she spoke.

"My grandmother says that most of the pregnant women wondered where they would get clothing for their babies, and how they could nurse when they worked in the fields all day. They already knew they would get no extra food. Every person in the camp was sick and always hungry."

Mrs. Loan spoke again for a couple of minutes. Bill Anderson nodded in recognition of several words, and Catherine discerned the name *Tuyet* several times.

"When the women had their babies, Tuyet was like an angel, offering the new mothers some of her own food. She held babies and rocked them to sleep. She showed the mothers how to change the thin cloth diapers made from their own clothing and how to clean the babies' bottoms to avoid rashes. She invented a way to augment the babies' inadequate clothing and diapers with banana leaves and showed the mothers how to do that."

By this time Catherine had tears in her eyes. She said, "Mrs. Loan. Thank you for telling us these things. Do you know what ultimately became of Tuyet? Was she released?"

When Chau translated this, Loan squeezed her eyes closed and steepled her hands as though in prayer. She spoke again in Vietnamese, her voice subdued.

Chau spoke directly to Catherine. "She says that Ms. Tuyet was raped by a particularly mean guard who took pleasure in hurting them. He raped several of the other women inmates as well. Tuyet became pregnant, but my grandmother was released before Tuyet gave birth. The last time she saw her, Tuyet was about seven months pregnant and sick, but even so, the guards cut her no slack."

"Does your grandmother know what happened after that?"

"No, Ma'am."

"Would she have had anybody to help her when she gave birth in the camp?"

"Let me ask." Chau spoke again with Loan, whose response lasted for a full minute.

Chau smiled apologetically at Catherine. "Sometimes the Vietnamese language must seem cumbersome to Westerners. It often takes about three times longer to get an idea across than it would in English. My grandmother said that when the women in the camp went into labor, they were taken into the town of Xuan Loc, accompanied by a guard or two, and a midwife would assist with the delivery."

"Were there many midwives in Xuan Loc? Does Loan know their names?"

Chao consulted with his grandmother, and then said, "Only one worked with the women from the camp. Her name was Ngo and she was about 35 years old, herself the mother of three or four children."

Catherine and Bill stood to leave, and Catherine said, "Thank you Chau, and please thank your grandmother for us."

"Well," Bill said, when they were back in the rental car. "What will you do with that information?"

"When we get back to Seattle, the first thing I'll do is send that dear woman a bathtub full of flowers. Beyond that, I'm not sure. But I have an inkling."

Bill started the engine. "I don't suppose it involves a visit to the town of Xuan Loc?"

CHAPTER THIRTEEN

Saigon awakens early. Trutch, accompanied by Andrew Quang, strode out for his morning run. They picked their way through the clutches of sidewalk food vendors and small crowds of patrons lining both sides of Nguyen Hue Street, the city already abuzz with motorbike traffic, exhaust fumes mingling with the smells of richly seasoned *pho* and fresh baked goods.

At the river, they turned away from the city center and ran at a steady pace in a northerly direction for about a mile, and then slowed. A young woman in orange coveralls and a hard hat blocked their way with a handheld stop sign. Behind her a backhoe loader and a bulldozer clanked on the roadway adjacent to the riverfront sidewalk. Rather than wait, they turned around and jogged back a half block to Dong Khoi Street. Although much less congested, the infamously uneven sidewalks, with their jutting stones and tiles, forced them to walk in order to watch their footing and avoid tripping.

"How did your family end up in Australia?" Trutch asked, somewhat breathless from the run.

"We are *Viet Kieu*. That's what residents of Vietnam call their countrymen who've left and live abroad. My father was an ARVN officer during the war. He spent four years in a re-education camp in the Mekong Delta after the Communists took over. When he was released in 1979, after a year of plotting and scheming, he and my mother and my older sister made it down the Mekong one dark night, on a former French yacht with 30 other people. Somewhere off Vung Tau, they rendezvoused with a larger boat that took them to a refugee camp in the Philippines. It took another year, but finally they were approved for immigration to Australia. My father found work as a janitor and my mother worked in a laundry."

"They were lucky," Trutch said. "I've read estimates that half the boat people perished at sea, or at the hands of pirates."

"My parents never speak of the voyage. I was born in Melbourne in 1986, and I had a confusing childhood. Once I started school, I never quite knew if I was Australian or Vietnamese. I wanted to fit in, so I participated in sports and joined Boy Scouts. I lived as an Australian boy when I was outside the home, but my parents worked hard to ensure that I understood and honored my heritage. Sometimes I felt like I had one foot in each of two worlds, and I struggled to find a balance."

"You obviously found that balance somewhere, Andrew."

"Yes, I'm a proud Australian, mate. But I also identify with my Vietnamese heritage. Now that I've lived here in Vietnam, I can honestly say I love this country as much as I do Australia. But I'm not wild about the one-party system. Or the government, or any of its repressive policies here."

They reached the steps of the Continental Hotel and Trutch glanced at his watch. "Jesus," he said. "We have 45 minutes before we meet Duc to go to Cholon. I'll grab a quick shower and a breakfast of spring rolls. Then let's meet in the lobby. I'm ready to nab that prick. Let's hope he hasn't already run off."

***

They met up with Duc outside the four-story walk-up where they hoped to find Lien's Uncle Vu. Each window in the concrete apartment block looked out on a narrow iron balcony filled with laundry or bicycles.

The three men sprinted up several flights of stairs. On the third floor, down a dark and narrow hallway, Duc pounded on the door to room 34 until a young woman dressed in shorts and a tank top opened the door partway.

"*Gi day?*" she yelped, registering surprise.

"Are you Mai?" Duc asked, and then, at the sound of an immediate commotion behind her, Duc pushed the door open the rest of the way.

Wearing only a singlet and a pair of khaki shorts, a man, clearly Uncle Vu, dashed toward the window.

Duc pushed past Mai and lunged toward the fleeing Vu. He shouted in Vietnamese, "Wait. We want to talk to you."

Vu went through the window and over the balcony rail just as Duc grabbed for him, missing by inches.

Andrew swiveled on his heels and headed back for the stairwell, shouting at Trutch, "The side alley!" He and Trutch bolted down the stairway and swung into the alley.

A female vendor, standing by her collapsed canvas-covered stall, pointed down the alley and screamed curses in Vietnamese at the fleeing Vu.

Duc stood on the third-floor balcony, also pointing, and shouted, "Left! There at the small lane by the garbage cans."

Around the corner Trutch and Andrew pivoted into the smaller lane, where Trutch sideswiped a man pushing a bicycle loaded with caged ducks. The bike, the man and the ducks crashed over and sprawled across the pavement. Trutch stumbled but managed to right himself and continued to run, now several paces behind Andrew.

Fifty yards ahead, he could see Vu running frantically, rudely pushing vendors and pedestrians out of his way. One woman fell to her knees. An alley-side display of stacked pots and pans clattered down and rattled onto the paving stones as he brushed it with his hip. Andrew and Trutch ran through the clutter, further scattering the cookware.

A large open-walled, single-story building loomed up in front of the lane and Vu dashed in under a sign reading *Cho* — the public market.

Andrew and Trutch followed him into the dimly lit building, a warren of small crowded stalls, narrow aisles, aggressive vendors and pushy shoppers.

Vu, slowed by the crowded aisles to a fast walk, pushed and shoved his way through the chattering clutches of buyers and sellers, with Andrew and Trutch now closer behind him. He made an abrupt turn into an even smaller aisle, and knocked over a stacked display of fabric bolts.

Trutch leaped over the rolls of fabric. White cotton and patterned silks unrolled over the dirty sidewalk in wide, colorful ribbons. "Sorry, sorry," he said to the furious vendor as he rushed past, Andrew close behind.

At the end of the passage, Vu turned again into a wider aisle through the center of the meat section. He picked up some speed and trotted between stainless steel tables showcasing pigs' heads, animal entrails and other bloody cuts of raw meat, all of them under investigation by swarms of shiny black flies.

As he approached the street on the opposite side of the market, he slid in a puddle of water on the concrete floor, where a vendor was hosing animal blood off a table. He went down onto one knee and then fell sideways onto his butt.

Andrew and Trutch, both panting and sweating profusely, were on him in seconds. Leaning over to offer his hand and assist him, Trutch gasped, "We merely want to talk to you."

Andrew started to translate, but before he could get the sentence out Vu grabbed the edge of a table laden with fish and yanked hard, pulling the table onto its side so that the slimy and stinking fish spread like a viscous oil slick across the concrete floor. Instantly, he was on his feet and scrambling off in the direction of the street.

Andrew and Trutch stepped carefully through the slippery piscine clutter before they resumed the chase.

On the street, they spotted Vu a half block away, just as he ducked into a sundry store.

They entered the store but once inside, saw no sign of Vu.

"Where'd he go?" Andrew asked the proprietress.

She pointed toward the rear of the building.

Andrew and Trutch pushed aside a curtain and entered a small, sparsely furnished living room. Although a color TV was on, broadcasting a speech by a somber official in uniform, no one occupied the room. Behind the living room, they walked through a tiny kitchen, also empty, and then passed through the back door and into another alley. Trutch looked left and saw no one, but when he looked to the right, Vu lay flat on his back on the cobblestones.

Trutch and Andrew approached cautiously. They squatted down and Andrew spoke to Vu, who remained unresponsive. Andrew checked for a radial pulse but found none. He wore an expression of incredulity. "I think he's dead. All that exertion probably triggered a heart attack. Bloody Hell."

Trutch nodded in disbelief. Dead. What a fuck up.

"I'll call the police," Andrew said, and pulled his cell phone from his pocket. "But I think we should get out of here before they arrive."

"A good plan," Trutch said, still panting. "Let's go back to that apartment and see if Mai knows anything."

***

They found Duc talking to Mai in the third-floor flat. He looked up as Andrew and Trutch entered. "She doesn't know much. She thinks Vu drunkenly muttered something about dropping his niece off at a backpacker's hotel. Where is he? Did he get away from you?"

"Dead," said Trutch. "Lying in the street near the market. Probably a heart attack. Unfortunately, we didn't have a chance to talk to him."

"Oh no." Duc said something in Vietnamese to Mai that caused her to move a few feet away, as if he had dismissed her. "He was our best lead. Our only lead. Must have been scared shitless to try to run like that. "

Mai was watching them, as if hoping to learn something. She had turned sharply toward Trutch at the word "dead." But she looked curious, not distraught, as she might if she understood what had happened to Vu.

"So, how do we find this backpacker's hotel?" Trutch asked, now eager to leave.

"Not so easy. There are many small hotels in the backpacker district."

"Could the police help?"

"I doubt it. They wouldn't tie up the manpower needed to ask questions at every hotel in that part of town. Besides, I'd be reluctant to tell Captain Minh that we obtained this information partly by chasing a man until he died. He warned us not to investigate or try to enforce the law. He'd be ... how you say ... pissed off."

"So," Andrew said, "we're back at square one."

"I'll ask our network to keep their eyes open in the bars and karaoke parlors and to watch for anything suspicious at the backpacker hotels," Duc suggested. "But their surveillance must be strictly passive. No questioning of clerks or doormen. I think the chances of success are slim, but it's something."

Duc's voice trailed off as two uniformed policemen entered the flat, their expressions alert and stern.

CHAPTER FOURTEEN

Three terrifying weeks had passed since Lotus had arrived in Svay Pak. She had learned to answer to her new name, and spent all day, every day, in the sultry upstairs living space. There she talked with the other girls or played repetitive and predictable rounds of *tien len,* a Vietnamese card game in which the aim is to get rid of your cards as soon as possible by beating combinations of cards laid down by the other players. Even preoccupied by fear and anxiety, Lien frequently won.

With each story heard from the other captives, her sadness grew deeper. Hong Hanh's brother had tricked her into going with him on an errand to the next village. Her mother had packed her a lunch of quail eggs and rice cakes on the morning of her abduction. She fed Hong Hanh a breakfast of porridge and kissed her goodbye. Then her brother took her off — not to the next village as he had said, but to the highway, where they caught a bus to the city of Da Nang. There he introduced her to a strange older man and, without looking back, walked away. The stranger took her to Saigon, where she was put in the back of a truck and smuggled into Cambodia and the village of Svay Pak. All of the stories were similar. Someone they trusted had promised a better life and a way to help the family.

None of the girls were permitted to leave the premises of the brothel. For Lotus, days were tedious and boring, but nights were filled with terrifying anticipation of the inevitable. The horrors of her situation magnified with each passing night as the other girls, all of them under 15, were repeatedly dressed, made up and delivered to the "working rooms" downstairs.

***

Nakry and Mau came for Diamond early one night. When she resisted being taken to one of what Lotus now thought of as the rape chambers downstairs,

80

Nakry beat her with a stick across the back of her legs.

Lotus stood by, terrified, unable to help, while Diamond continued to resist by throwing herself on the bed and curling into the fetal position.

Then Mau climbed the stairs, carrying a dangerous-looking metal rod.

Lotus shrieked, "Diamond, stop. The man comes, he has a metal stick."

Diamond curled tighter.

Nakry bent down and held her motionless, bearing down on Diamond's hip and shoulder with her forearms.

Mau then applied the metal rod to the soles of Diamond's feet and pressed a switch on its handle.

Witnessing her friend's pain, Lotus screamed almost as loudly as Diamond did when the electric current coursed into her body through her feet.

Mau had used a *picana,* Lotus would be told later, an adaptation of an electric cattle prod, which uses high voltage to maximize pain but low current to minimize marking the skin. In less than a minute, Diamond was compliant. When Mau lifted the prod and Nakry asked if she was ready to go, Diamond nodded her head amid her sobs. She continued to sob, her thin shoulders wobbling, while Nakry skillfully applied light makeup to her face and dressed her in a white ao dai.

When would they come for her, Lotus wondered, shuddering as Diamond was led downstairs. Would it be tonight? When it was her time, she wouldn't go. Her father and grandmother would be shamed. No one could make her do those disgusting acts with such beastly men. She would fight them.

Diamond returned to the stuffy upstairs space 90 minutes later. Her tear-streaked face wore a catatonic expression, her eyes staring fixedly into the near distance, unseeing, as though they were merely marbles. She walked with tiny, mincing steps to the pallet, where she sat trembling, her face and eyes blank.

Lotus sat next to her and draped her arm around her shoulders.

Diamond failed to respond, as though all her senses had been numbed.

Lotus held her tighter and stroked her hair. She cooed and whispered, trying to give her friend some small comfort, all the while feeling sick to her stomach, terrified that she would soon experience the same unspeakable horror.

One by one, between midnight and 1 a.m., having serviced several clients each, the other girls returned to their quarters. Moon and Boupha helped Lotus get Diamond undressed, and pointed to blood spots on her silk pantaloons.

Deep furrows of concern etched Lotus's face as she covered her friend, who coiled again into the fetal position. The room filled with sobs — Diamond's anguished, Lotus's fearful, the others' tired, broken, helpless.

***

Diamond remained rigid and unresponsive for much of the next day. The other girls attempted to comfort her with touch and gentle conversation, and encouraged her to sip herbal teas, a kettle being the one small luxury they were allowed to possess. By five o'clock in the afternoon, when their supper arrived, rice with bits of chicken, her eyes had focused and she was speaking in short, subdued sentences. "I won't do that again. I would rather die."

"You must live," Boupha said. "We all must survive and hope that one day this nightmare will end. In the basement of this house, there's a room where they torture girls who refuse to go with customers or girls who customers say did not please them enough. Two months ago they took one girl to the basement and we never saw her again. Diamond, you must learn to shut off your heart and your feelings when they make you go with a man. That way you can survive.'"

"How do I shut off my heart?" asked Diamond, her voice tremulous. "I can't quit feeling."

Moon said, "You're stronger than us, Boupha. There is nothing to hope. We just go to the working rooms every day until we get sick. I've been here longer than you. I saw that when Pham got so sick she looked ugly to the customers and couldn't work, Mau just put her out and told her to go away. She had no place to go. Every day she came back and begged to come in to sleep and eat. But Mau called the police and they took her somewhere. We don't know where."

Boupha said, "Sometime Nakry gives us the little white pill, *yama*. It makes you feel good before you go to the working room. Maybe you can ask Nakry for one tonight, Diamond."

Lotus held Diamond's hand and listened without contributing to the conversation. Why was this happening to them? And what about Papa? He must be frantic with worry that she hadn't called. She needed to get a message to him or to Grandma Quy. But she couldn't get a message downstairs, much less to Tuy Phuoc. Soon they would come for her. It could be a matter of days, or hours. And then what? With her free hand she fingered the small polished-stone image of Buddha, which she wore on a thin chain around her neck.

***

Diamond had been led downstairs on two more evenings before they came upstairs for Lotus on a Sunday afternoon, Nakry accompanied by Mau. Nakry had her hair down for the evening and wore a sleek black ao dai with simple gold jewelry. A cloying scent wafted into the room with her. She stood over Lotus with a no-nonsense expression and said, "Come and get ready, it's your turn."

Lotus cringed and slid back on the bed until her spine touched the wall and she felt the prickle of woven bamboo through her thin t-shirt. She would never go and return as empty-eyed as Diamond. They'd have to carry her downstairs as stiff as a broom handle, and even then she would not do what the other girls had done. If she did, how would she ever face her father when she saw him again? She pressed her back more firmly into the wall and shook her head. "I don't want to," she whispered.

Nakry stepped back and crossed her arms in front of her small chest. She made an impatient sound and turned to Mau, "You know what to do."

Mau stepped onto the bed and squatted over Lotus. With a quick yank, he pulled her away from the wall and pinioned her shoulders to the bed with his knees and lowered himself until he sat on her chest. Then he grabbed her cheeks between his thumb and forefinger and squeezed cruelly until her mouth opened.

Lotus gagged and tried futilely to turn her head.

Nakry leaned over and dropped a white pill onto Lotus's tongue. She pushed the rim of a tin cup against her lower lip and tipped the cup up. Warm water filled Lotus's mouth and washed the pill into her throat, where it caught. "Now swallow," Nakry said.

Lotus tried to cough but gagged instead.

Nakry poured more water into her throat.

Her attempts to twist and wriggle free of Mau were futile. She succeeded in forcing a cough but the pill had already washed down her throat. "Someone help me," she croaked. She coughed again.

The other girls watched with concern, but no one dared move.

Lotus struggled until struggling no longer seemed important. Drowsiness replaced her need to move, and she lay quietly, strangely calm, until Mau released her. She sat up and moved to the edge of the bed. What was happening?

Nakry and Mau left the room.

The room swirled, and Lotus pressed her hand against the wall nearest her to steady herself. With blurred vision, she turned toward Boupha, who sat on the floor in a corner, applying lipstick with the help of a tiny mirror. "Was that yama?" Her speech was slightly slurred.

Boupha put the tube of lipstick down onto the upturned wooden box that served as their make-up station. "You'll be okay," she said, her expression kind as she gently touched Lotus on the shoulder. "The yama will make it easy."

Nakry returned, her impatient expression gone. Now she looked almost motherly and concerned. "Come Lotus. Someone wants to meet you." She handed Lotus a white ao dai. "Here. Put this on."

Wrapped in the numbing cocoon of the methamphetamine, Lotus dressed in the pretty ao dai. She no longer cared as much that she would have to go with a man. As she followed Nakry down the narrow stairwell, the walls passed by in slow motion. She floated unfeelingly toward whatever awaited.

Her sense of well being diminished and her heart ticked rapidly when she entered the living room and saw her client, a handsome Khmer with dark hair, receding at the temples. He was dressed in a short-sleeve khaki uniform, with four rows of colorful ribbons adorning his left chest. His wrist was wrapped in an expensive gold wristwatch, and a large gold signet ring, with a black gem on its flat, top facet, decorated his third finger. He sat on a red vinyl settee next to the half refrigerator. With one finger hooked over his upper lip and his thumb beneath his chin, he partly concealed his lascivious smile.

Ice formed in Lotus's stomach. In her home district, the men who wore uniforms were seldom kind. She took a step backward, only to bump into Nakry who gripped her shoulders and propelled her forward again.

"This one is lovely," the man said to Nakry. "She is a virgin?"

"Of course. I guarantee it, Colonel Khlot." Nakry continued to grip Lotus by the shoulders.

Lotus thought he looked important. She now knew enough Khmer to recognize the words "colonel" and "virgin," but she did not know that the five broad gold stripes on his epaulettes identified him as a senior officer in the

Cambodian National Police. In her clouded state, she thought he looked fatherly, despite what he wanted of her. She trembled as Nakry introduced her as Lotus.

The colonel appraised her up and down, maintaining his smile. "She will do," he said.

Lotus lifted her hand and caressed her Buddha.

Nakry led the way to the first working room down the corridor. She whispered to Lotus, "He's a very important man. Give him everything he wants." She remained in the room for a brief time to make sure everything was satisfactory.

Colonel Khlot laid a hand on Lotus's shoulder, said something softly in Khmer, then bent slightly and kissed her on the nape of the neck. He said something else in Khmer, and gestured for her to undress.

Not understanding the Khmer, Lotus waited awkwardly in front of him, unmoving.

Nakry translated into Vietnamese.

Lotus slowly and methodically complied. She undid the buttons of her white bodice, removed the long, two-paneled dress and lowered the baggy silk pantaloons.

Meanwhile, Colonel Khlot removed his uniform and carefully hung both the trousers and the shirt on a wooden clothes hanger. He handed the hanger to Nakry with a polite nod.

Nakry left the room, leaving the two of them naked. Lotus fell onto the pallet bed as her client stood ogling her. The room swam into motion and the colonel's image wavered before her.

He moved to her, pressed her shoulders until she lay flat on the bed and forced her crossed legs apart.

In her drugged state, Lotus lay passively, even as he climbed on top of her. He fumbled for a few moments between her legs and then a sudden burst of pain caused her to call out.

"Shh," he said.

She held her breath and lay rigid beneath him as he thrust in and out. The man's heavy weight felt as if it would crush her, and yet it didn't. She felt the hot scraping of her insides, the terrible sting between her legs, and yet she did not feel it. She had wondered how the other girls had survived and now she knew. The white pill was magic. She would not refuse it again.

Later, when Colonel Khlot dressed, he checked to ensure that Nakry had pressed his trousers, and had kept the creases sharp. He leaned over, kissed Lotus fully on the lips and whispered, "Good bye, precious one. I will see you again."

Lotus remained supine on the bed, still somewhat anesthetized by the yama, although its effects had begun to wear off. A growing understanding of what had just happened to her now registered, and her limbs trembled.

"Very good, Lotus. The colonel liked you" Nakry said, after he had gone. "He wants to see more of you, and he is a very big man, important to our business."

Dazed and unmoved, Lotus said, "I want to go to bed now." She walked insensate past the other working rooms, now alive with sounds and lurid with the odor of men taking their pleasure from young girls.

Nakry accompanied her up the stairs and unlocked the door to the dorm. It was unusual for the girls to service only one client a night, but this was a special occasion. Lotus had been deflowered and Colonel Khlot had left satisfied.

Lotus lay down and wept.

CHAPTER FIFTEEN

In Saigon, Trutch slipped the uniformed doorman at the Continental Hotel an American dollar for hailing their cab and then slid into the vehicle after Andrew. He showed the driver the card a policeman in Mai's flat had handed him yesterday. "It has the street address on it," he said. "We need to be there by 10."

When the driver acknowledged the address, Trutch sat back. "Okay, let's see what the cops want. I don't suppose they plan to give us hints on how to find Lien."

"No," Andrew said. "But they're likely to have plenty of questions about Vu's death."

Duc was waiting on Tran Hung Dao Street in front of the imposing four-story police headquarters when they arrived. The three of them entered the low-ceilinged lobby, which was small and tired looking, with chipped and soiled cinder block walls and a floor of filthy flesh-colored tiles, many of them broken. An unsmiling officer behind a gray metal desk lifted his eyes from his newspaper and glowered at them.

Trutch presented the card, "*Xin Chao, Em.*"

Without a word or change in facial expression, the cop held up three fingers and pointed toward a set of wooden stairs.

"Thank you. You've been very helpful," said Trutch. Then, under his breath, "Asshole."

Duc led the way up the creaky stairs. "I've been in this building before. It gives me the creeps, as if I'm walking among unhappy spirits."

"It wouldn't win any interior design awards," said Trutch.

Andrew agreed. "Nor would the guy at the front win one for good manners."

On the third floor, they found the office two-thirds of the way down a dingy corridor. Another dour-looking young cop sat just inside the door. Trutch wondered if they were encouraged to look so unapproachable, or only learned to look that way by emulating their superiors.

Andrew went through the door first. "We have an appointment with someone in this office."

The cop pointed to a bench just beyond an inner doorway. "Wait there."

The windowless room was tiny, no larger then three by three meters, austerely furnished with just the bench and a vacant metal desk across from it. A pair of weakly blinking fluorescent tubes on the dirty ceiling barely illuminated the room with their melancholy light. Behind the desk, a whitewashed wall featured an obligatory picture of Ho Chi Minh, who managed to look both imperious and benevolent at the same time.

Dressed in an open-collared white shirt and blue polyester slacks that had not seen an iron in some time, Captain Minh entered the room, his head encased in a turban of swirling cigarette smoke. Without bothering to greet them, he plopped into the desk chair and scowled at the memo or report he clutched, his expression suggesting that he was either having a bad day or was desperately constipated.

Both Andrew and Duc glanced at Trutch, as though they expected him to start the dialogue.

Trutch stared at the cop.

Captain Minh looked Trutch in the eyes. "I thought I told you to leave the investigating to us. But you decided to find this man Tran Duc Vu and now he's dead. What do you have to say about that?" He took a drag off the cigarette held between his nicotine-stained fingers.

"Look Captain, this is bullshit. We stumbled upon a piece of gratuitous information that we thought was time sensitive and would lead us to Vu if we acted fast. We wanted to ask him some questions. And we sure as hell didn't trespass on your turf. Not deliberately anyway." Trutch felt as charged with adrenaline as if he were commanding troops. A good feeling.

Minh slammed his fist on the desk. "You can't talk to me that way. I'm a police Captain."

"I don't give a damn if you're a drag queen drum majorette. We're not here to step on your toes. I'm here to find my granddaughter and I'll pursue any *legal* means to do so. It's obvious we can't count on help from you or your stalwart legions of men in green."

Andrew and Duc both winced.

Minh grew red in the face. His cheeks puffed out and his ears glowed crimson. "Mr. Trutch, you ..."

The scar on Trutch's cheek turned rosy. "*Colonel* Trutch, to *you* if you please."

This time Andrew struggled to suppress a smirk.

Minh took a deep breath, sucking in smoke. "Okay *Colonel* Trutch, I suggest we both calm down. But you need to know, I have a great deal of authority and the latitude to interpret our laws and police policies. I'm warning you not to meddle in our business another time."

"You're right Captain. We should both calm down, and I'll stay out of your backyard. But I'm aware that prostitution is illegal in this country, although typically winked at by the police. I'm further aware that you're hard on the practices of child trafficking and pedophilia, and I'm grateful for that. So here's my pledge to you. If we come across information of any kind, while we also avoid 'meddling' as you say, we'll make that information available to you, in hopes that it will help your investigation and enforcement mandate. In turn, I'm asking you to provide any assistance you can to help us find my granddaughter."

Minh glanced at both Duc and Andrew as though to acknowledge them for the first time in the meeting.

Both nodded, signifying their agreement with Trutch that they would avoid meddling.

"That's a reasonable give and take arrangement for both of us, Mr. ... uh, *Colonel* Trutch. I agree. But I'm obligated to collect a fine of ... shall we say ... oh, 100 dollars? For your ... how you would call it ... per-pe-tra-shun."

Trutch snorted but nonetheless opened his wallet and waved two 20-dollar bills. "I think this is as large a *fine* as I can pay today." He dropped the banknotes on the desk.

"Fine," Captain Minh offered his hand.

Trutch shook to cement their deal, then asked, "Okay, now what can I expect in the way of help from you, Captain?"

"Normally, in this office, I'm the one to ask the questions. But since we now have an agreement, I'll think about it and contact you. Now, I have other business."

"This feels like a brush off, Captain. In my country that's rude."

"We're not in your country, Colonel Trutch. Now go."

Trutch glared at him for a moment while Duc and Andrew hastily stood. Finally he rose. Andrew and Duc followed him out.

As they left the station, Andrew shook his head, "Jeez, Pete you really let him have it. Good thing that 'drag queen' insult went over his head."

"I think he was in a good mood today," Duc said. "He could have sent us to the basement. That would not have been pleasant."

"What now?" Andrew asked.

"All we can do is bide our time and hope that either Duc's network of observers discovers something useful or that Captain Minh comes through."

***

After lunch, Trutch heard a knock on his door. He opened it to Andrew, who was holding up his cell phone. "Captain Minh wants to speak with you. He said to meet him on the sidewalk in front of the hotel."

When Trutch stepped onto the street, Minh, still in civilian clothes, said, "The breeze off the river is refreshing this afternoon. Let's go for a walk."

They crossed the square in front of the opera house and started down Dong Khoi Street toward the river. Minh lit a cigarette and took a deep drag. He exhaled. "I have a reason for inviting you to meet with me in front of the hotel."

"I want to hear what you have to say, but just for the record, it didn't feel like an *invitation*. It sounded like I was *directed* to meet you."

"Oh, I must have been misquoted. These young people. They haven't learned how to be ... how you say? ... *subtle.*"

They walked in silence until the river came into view, slow moving and murky.

Captain Minh spoke first. "I had the opportunity to attend a course on procedure with the San Francisco Police Department three years ago."

"That's a beautiful city. I hope you had some free time."

"Yes, North Beach and the Broadway areas are exciting. But I also visited Alcatraz. It seemed like a luxury resort compared to our Vietnamese prisons."

"I'll bet. I've heard about your prisons. During the war all Americans feared being captured and sent to your Hoa Lo prison in Hanoi. We called it the Hanoi Hilton. You have to appreciate the American penchant for dark humor to understand that nickname."

"Colonel Trutch, as an Army officer serving in the South, you would not have been sent to Hoa Lo if captured. We had even less hospitable facilities hidden in the jungles of War Zone C and over the border in Cambodia for your soldiers who became our guests. Our prisons are still ugly. But we have become much more civilized. They are not in the jungle anymore. Still, you would not want to see one from the inside."

Trutch only nodded, biding his time, waiting to learn more about the purpose of this little walk.

They wandered past high-end retail shops and boutique four-star hotels that now lined the street. Elegant window displays and tasteful signage trumpeted designer brands like Bally, Burberry and Gucci. Known as Tu Do Street during the war, this had been the red light district of Saigon, teeming with hookers and pimps eager to separate American and Australian soldiers from their money.

Now Minh said, "Some police departments in the US sponsor charity events. Some raise money for internal, departmental funds to support the morale and welfare of their own members when they have family hardship or illnesses to cope with."

"That's true. They're like the military in that respect. We take care of our own when the chips are down."

"I would like to start something like that for our members here in Ho Chi Minh City."

"That's big of you." If this was to be a solicitation, Trutch had no illusions about who would be the first beneficiary.

"Our resources are spread thin. But I was thinking that if I could raise funds to compensate them for extra hours, perhaps I could have some men canvass the hotels in the backpackers' area. The extra wages would be helpful to those men who are struggling with hungry kids or sick parents."

They stopped at the river and Trutch watched the waterborne traffic. A Japanese freighter made its way slowly upriver and a tugboat towed a string of three barges downstream through the sluggish, brown water.

"I'm afraid I'm on a budget. I couldn't afford to help defray overtime costs," he said. He had yet to see a policeman in Saigon who appeared hungry or destitute. Every one of them looked well nourished and contented, especially Captain Minh, who packed a conspicuous bulge above his belt.

Minh's brow furrowed as he listened and his facial features hardened.

"But if your men developed some information about the location of my granddaughter," Trutch added, "out of gratitude, I would contribute to the charity of your choice, including your police welfare fund."

***

For the next four afternoons Trutch and Andrew walked the streets of the backpacker district. In the evenings they popped into karaoke parlors and bars, staying only a few minutes in each one to not draw attention, alert always for anything or anyone who might provide a lead into Lien's whereabouts. Learning anything was a long shot, but at least they were doing *something* while they waited and hoped that either Duc's network or Captain Minh's "resources" would produce something they could act on.

Late Thursday evening, Trutch phoned Catherine, eager to hear what she had learned on her whirlwind trip to Los Angeles. As so often happened, Skype was not up and running, possibly something to do with atmospheric conditions, he had been told, so he resorted to the more expensive alternative, his smartphone.

As Catherine filled him in on the details of her conversation with Mrs. Loan, his grip on the telephone tightened. When she finished, it took him a moment to speak. "My God. Raped. Pregnant. I need to make a side trip to Xuan Loc to try and find this midwife." Again, he lapsed into silence.

"Pete, are you still on the line?"

"Yes."

"What if I came to Vietnam and tried to find this Ngo woman."

Trutch said nothing, considering.

"Pete?"

"I'm not sure that's a good idea, this is a long way to come to search for the proverbial needle in a haystack."

"Isn't that what you're doing? And as long we're into idioms, I could submit that 'what's good for the goose is good for the gander.' Besides, I've already applied for my Vietnamese visa."

"You what? Shouldn't we have talked about this first?"

"Don't shut me out of this. Let's not have another chapter in your life where I'm not involved."

"I appreciate the sentiment, Catherine. But this can be dicey. I'm already into some scary stuff. This isn't like learning to be brave when the sailboat heels over."

"Pete. This is Catherine. Remember?"

Trutch went quiet again, then, "When are you coming? I have to admit I'm really missing you."

"I'll wait for the visa to arrive, then book myself out on the first available."

"Have I told you lately that I love you?"

"Not nearly enough."

***

Trutch sat in the pleasant courtyard of the Continental Hotel eating a "Western" breakfast of unbuttered toast, pink sausages and watery scrambled eggs. In four days of pub-crawling he had learned nothing. He poked at one of the sausages and weighed the pros and cons of eating it. A bellman approached him. Trutch tipped him 20,000 dong in exchange for the envelope he offered and then pried open the flap.

Cercle Sportif. 13:00.

Minh

Trutch alighted from a cab on a boulevard lined with huge mahogany trees. The Cercle Sportif was no longer what it had been in its heyday. Situated in a park-like setting behind the Reunification Palace, the once opulent country club now looked tired.

The signage had been changed from French to Vietnamese, and much of the paint had faded and was peeling. The grounds looked unkempt against the pictures he recalled seeing 40 years ago.

Captain Minh invited Trutch to join him at a glass-topped table beside the pool where he was sipping a beer. "Ah, Colonel, have you been keeping well?"

"Yes, thanks. And I see you have too." He nodded at the two empty beer bottles sitting at Minh's elbow. "Why did you want to see me?"

Minh sighed. "You Westerners. So impatient. Wouldn't you like to join me with a beer and enjoy the pleasures of this club? During the war years, it was the focal point for social life among the Westerners living in Saigon. In the afternoons, ladies in white tennis skirts would bat balls back and forth on these red clay courts. Gentlemen sat around this pool sipping cognac, served by white-coated Vietnamese waiters, and smoked Cuban cigars."

A waiter approached Trutch. He waved him off. "I'd rather you just got to the point, Captain."

Minh leaned back in his chair, grinned, and lit a cigarette. He took a long luxurious drag and then slowly expelled the smoke, turning his head to the side and consciously blowing it away from the neighboring table, occupied by two well-dressed, middle-aged Vietnamese women. "My grandfather worked as a waiter in this club. He resented being a servant to the decadent Westerners who occupied our country, but he kowtowed to them anyway, to make a few piasters each month."

Trutch leaned on his elbow and rested his chin in his palm, unconsciously fingering the scar on his cheek. "I understand how he must have felt. Colonialism has never been fair to indigenous people. But why am I here, Captain?"

"Then in 1955, the French left and the Americans replaced them. My grandfather was still a servant to white men. But the Americans smoked less offensive cigarettes than the French. Compared to Gauloises, Marlboros and Winstons are almost mild. Do you notice my brand, Colonel Trutch?" He tapped the red and white package of Marlboros lying on the table.

"Tolerance for petty chit chat is not one of my virtues."

"Very well. Your granddaughter, who is now called Lotus, is in Phnom Penh."

Trutch tried to read Minh's inscrutable expression. He stared intensely into his eyes as if through windows onto the gears and cogs that turned in the policeman's mind.

"Can you tell me how you developed this fact? In my former career, we would have called it intelligence, and the reliability of the source would be extremely important."

"My men used good old-fashioned police work. They interviewed the proprietors and clerks of every hotel in the backpacker district. Naturally, I personally supervised and followed up on every lead they developed."

"How can you be sure Lien is in Cambodia?"

"When we exerted a little ... persuasion on the proprietor of one particular hotel, she gave us the name of the thug who picked Lotus up at the hotel and drove her to Cambodia. He is called Luong. He is a slippery little people smuggler, easy to recognize, stout, dark skin, ears that poke out like handles. He and his partner, a petty criminal from Cambodia, have been known to us for a long time. We're familiar with their MO — they deliver their 'goods' to various brothels in the village of Svay Pak, an ethnic Vietnamese hamlet, I'm sorry to say. Regrettably, we've never been able to nab Luong or his partner."

Trutch tried to read on Minh's face the veracity of what he had just said. Finally he spoke. "Okay, I will contribute to your police "welfare fund." I certainly hope your men who did such fine police work are able to feed their kids and provide medicine for their sickly parents." With that he peeled two one-hundred dollar bills off of a wad and handed them to Minh.

***

Two hours later, Minh met with Luong in the same Highlands Coffee shop as before. "My friend. Somehow the old American I told you about during our last meeting has found out that his granddaughter is in Svay Pak. He will travel there, probably with the Australian-Viet Kieu and maybe with the STOK investigator, Duc. They are smart men. You need to be certain there is no way they can go to the Khmer Authorities with evidence that would disrupt your business, or worse, put you in jeopardy of going to prison in Cambodia."

CHAPTER SIXTEEN

Lotus sat next to Diamond on the edge of the pallet, her head hanging. "I can't go on. That was the worst time ever." Though still early afternoon, she had just come from one of the working rooms, where Mau had taken her.

He had ripped off her pants and thrown her on the bed. "Let's see how well broken in you are," he said, and then he mounted her. He pumped and slammed against her until she thought he would split her body in half. To distract herself, she imagined the coconut palms that grew alongside the rice field back home, and tried to remember how it felt to sit in the shade of their fronds among the cool grasses. Then as the scraping and pounding grew worse, she attempted to empty her head of any thoughts at all. When that didn't help, she imagined sitting in a tub of hot, hot water. But the water scalded and she could no longer stop herself. She opened her throat and screamed until Mau climbed off and pressed his fingers around her neck.

"Shut up, bitch. Even after 80 times with other men you still don't know how to get wet enough. If I'm sore later, you'll be sorry."

Most of the men she had been with, Westerners as well as Cambodians and other Asians, were coarse, rough men who treated her as their temporary property, something to buy or sell. Some had shown interest only in straight boom boom. Others wanted more specialized favors. A white man, older than her father, had insisted that she lie on her back and masturbate, while he watched and recorded her with a video camera. But none had been as rough with her as Mau.

"I hate him," she said to Diamond. "I hate them all. Before, when I was with my Papa, I thought all men must be like him. But they're animals. Worse than animals."

"You said the one called Colonel is kind."

"He is. He's not like the others." He had sought her company every week since their first encounter and remained gentle, polite, almost like a father, and

96

never demanded any special service. He had kind words for her on each call and after the third visit tipped her a few riels. She had no place to spend the money but folded it away in an inside pocket of her cardboard suitcase, which stood in a corner of the upstairs dormitory along with the other girls' meager possessions. She welcomed his visits as a reprieve from abuse at the hands of the other customers.

"I hated them at first, too," Diamond said. "Now, I can't feel anything. I can't feel anything about them. I can't feel anything about myself. My soul is dead. Only my body is alive." She turned and faced the wall.

With the conversation ended, Lotus flopped onto her back and stared at the ceiling, her eyes fixed and unfocused. In the afternoons she looked forward to the white pill, which would mask the pain she otherwise felt in the working rooms. When she did not have the numbness of the yama, or the diversion of Colonel Khlot's visits, she lay on her back in a deep inner place. She no longer spent time wondering about what might become of her. Instead, she clutched the stone Buddha and willed herself into light trances that helped her escape the windowless confines of the dormitory room.

She suspended the horrifying reality by bringing to mind ethereal images of her father and grandmother, even her friend Ha. Papa's kind visage shone with love and adoration, and grandmother always moved about in the kitchen or tended her vegetable plot. Ha pedaled her bicycle through the rice paddies, and wearing a white, flowing ao dai, she looked like a beautiful swan taking flight.

She ran her finger over the tiny scratches she had made on the wall. With no night or day to identify days of the week, she separated days by the meals offered and with the late afternoon and evening trips downstairs to work. According to her scratches, August had given way to September.

Nakry jolted her back to reality when she entered the room and beckoned for Lotus to follow.

Lotus wondered why she hadn't been given the white pill first. After Mau's treatment, she didn't think she could be with a man without its warming comfort. She held back as long as she could, until Nakry looked back impatiently over her shoulder.

"Come," she said. "Before I change my mind."

Nakry led her past all of the working rooms, into the front room and then up the spiral staircase to the part of the upstairs Lotus had never seen before. "This is my house," Nakry told her.

The linear kitchen — counter, sink, half refrigerator and two-burner gas cooker — stood along one wall. A large flat-screened television sat atop a wooden chest and a table and five chairs comprised the rest of the furnishings. An open doorway revealed a bedroom with an attached bathroom.

The glare of natural daylight stunned Lotus for a moment. The room looked so ordinary and homey it could belong to her grandmother or to one of the neighbors at home. She squinted into the daylight flooding in from the one large window on the street side of the building. The light gave her spirit a lift, almost euphoric.

"Why are we here?"

"You're my best girl," Nakry said. "I give you special privilege. You will work up here one hour each day. Clean my house, do laundry in sink."

Lotus nodded.

"You will get extra food — more rice, some meat. Sometime mangoes and bananas. In time, if you earn my trust, you can go to the village market and obtain the supplies we need every day."

"Thank you," Lotus said flatly.

***

Early the next morning, after the effects of her nighttime yama had worn off, Lotus lay awake listening to the light snoring of the other girls. Her life in the brothel had been so consumed with surviving, at least when she wasn't anesthetized by yama, that she had lost the ability to think straight.

But now something hovered at the back of her mind, the germ of an idea that lacked clarity and definition. She kept her eyes closed and grasped at the smoky thought and tried shaping it into a meaningful image. Still it teased her, and she fought mentally and spiritually to crystallize it, until gradually the idea began to form, like small pieces of a jigsaw puzzle coming together, first at the corners and then along the straight edges. Awareness crept over her. If she worked in Nakry's apartment ... what? ... What? ...

Pop! Her eyelids sprung open as the rest of the thought broke through. Maybe there would be a chance to escape.

Then, like monsoon winds, new thoughts swept in ... and questions. What about Diamond? They had become sisters. Could she help Diamond to escape too? And where would she, or they, go? She knew that they were near a big city in Cambodia. In which direction was Vietnam? How would they get there? How many days would it take? She had about 8,000 riel, from Colonel Khlot's tips, put away in her suitcase. Was that enough to buy bus tickets to Vietnam?

Then a new, terrifying question: would her family accept her — damaged, broken and dirty as she was?

Charged and full of purpose for the first time in weeks, she dared to hope.

***

Two days later, a new girl arrived, Thanh. Mau delivered her to the dorm room, where she stood scowling defiantly at the other girls.

Lotus tried to speak with her. "I'm Lien, but here I'm called Lotus. Do you come from Vietnam?" Lotus took her hand. "Come. Sit with me. We have a kettle and some tea."

Thanh's expression softened as she allowed Lotus to lead her to a seat on the edge of a bed. "Yes. From Ho Chi Minh City. A man brought me here on his motorbike."

"Then do you know the way to Ho Chi Minh city from here?" Lotus's mind had been in high gear for 48 hours.

Thanh opened her mouth to respond but before she could speak, Nakry burst into the room with the smarmy little doctor.

Lotus warned Thanh as they approached. "He's going to examine you in your secret place, Thanh. It will hurt a little bit, but if you just close your eyes and clench your teeth it'll be over in a hurry."

"No," Thanh leaned up against Lotus, clinging to her.

Lotus knew it would do no good to struggle, so she sat passively as Nakry and the doctor pried Thanh away and held her down on the bed.

While Nakry pinned her upper body to the bed, Thanh screamed and kicked violently. When the doctor fumbled with her pants, Thanh called upon God and her mother to help her, then hurled profane Vietnamese insults at Nakry and the medic, "*Du ma may, du ma may,*" and "*cho de, do cho de.*" When Nakry flailed her legs with a bamboo switch, Thanh only screamed louder.

As the struggle continued, Nakry backhanded Thanh across the face so viciously that she collapsed, stunned into semi-consciousness. Her legs ceased kicking long enough for the doctor to remove her pants and go to work with his hand. At his touch, Thanh exploded into violence again.

Even so, the doctor completed the procedure and made his pronouncement: "Yes. Still a virgin, Nakry."

Mau burst into the room and smacked Thanh on the side of her head with his fist. When she crumpled, he threw her over his shoulder and carried her out of the room.

Lotus stood to the side rubbing her Buddha pendant. Thanh would be handcuffed to a U-bolt anchored in the cinder block wall in the basement and tortured until she was compliant or injured and unconscious. Lotus squeezed her eyes tightly to blot out the scene, then covered her ears and cowered, trembling in the corner.

In the very early morning, after the front door had been closed to customers, Lotus and the other girls upstairs heard a piercing shriek from below.

Towards 3 p.m., Mau carried Thanh back upstairs and tossed her on one of the pallet beds. Her right eye was swollen shut and the surrounding flesh the color of an overripe plum. The fingernail had been ripped from her left index finger, the sensitive flesh of the nail bed pulpy and bloody.

When Mau left, the girls bathed Thanh's injured fingertip with hot water from their kettle and dressed it with strips of cloth torn from a towel.

Thanh's shoulders quivered.

"They won't come for you until the swelling is gone from your face," Lotus assured her. "It would be better, Sister, if you swallow the white pill when they come."

CHAPTER SEVENTEEN

The morning after his meeting with Captain Minh at the Cercle Sportif, Trutch surfed the Internet for information on prostitution in Cambodia, aiming to equip himself with as much knowledge as possible before he traveled there. Within minutes, he spotted a provocative headline:

Make your Sexual Fantasies a reality in Phnom Penh! Get the most out of your sex vacation in Asia's best city for getting laid.

The advertisement offered a $20 downloadable PDF, purporting to provide essential information for sex tourists in Cambodia.

This book has been created for one reason, to transform your dull and lifeless holiday into the most exciting sex vacation of your life. Learn how to get the best piece of ass for the best price in a city loaded with some of the finest nookie on the planet.

Trutch's stomach turned sour as he read. Unbelievable, he thought, that he could find such debauchery so easily. Especially in Vietnam, where the Ministry of Information and Communication is known to have armies of techies scanning web pages for inappropriate content.

He spent another hour perusing sites. They ranged from religious condemnations of rampant sinfulness, to journalistic reports on the cultural reasons for promiscuity in Cambodia. One account profiled a 12-year-old from a poor village in western Cambodia. Her parents had sold her to a trafficker for the equivalent of $800. Her earnings would help her older brother live while he served as a monk for two years. In this way, the girl would secure karmic credits for the family, she had been told. She ended up in a cheap brothel in China, where she died of AIDS.

According to what he had been reading, most Cambodian men had their first sexual experience by age 15, usually in a brothel. For a Cambodian man, the articles suggested, a wife's purpose was to bear children. A 13-year-old on the side was needed for sport.

Next, he Googled the village of Svay Pak.

Up popped the image of a girl Trutch gauged to be about 12. Forlorn looking, clad in a faded red dress, she stood in the doorway of a crumbling wooden building, her hair askew, her smile forced. The caption read:

The cheap brothels of Svay Pak, largely an ethnic Vietnamese hamlet, eleven kilometers from the center of Phnom Penh, specialize in child sex. Young girls, such as the one depicted, are lured or sold into whorehouses. Virgins are particularly valuable and can produce a lofty sum for the person, often a parent or uncle, who sells them into slavery.

Trutch closed the lid on his computer. He felt as if he was moments away from being sick.

***

At 2 p.m. he joined Andrew and Duc in the Saigon office of STOK, to meet with Judith Grinder. Within minutes, they had all agreed that a trip to Cambodia offered the best hope of finding Lien. But Duc would stay behind, Judith said.

"He'd be a big help to Andrew and me if he came with us," Trutch told Judith. "His investigative skills would be invaluable."

"I'll accompany you to Phnom Penh," she said. "I've been to Cambodia half a dozen times on STOK business. I know my way around the network."

It seemed to Trutch that muscle and fact-finding savvy would be more important than knowing people, and Duc had already proven his worth. A woman would only get in the way if the going got tough. But he knew better than to express that concern aloud. So he said, "Even so, couldn't Duc still come along? I've enjoyed working with him."

"I understand, but I need him to look after things here while I'm gone. One of us needs to stay, and in Svay Pak, I'll keep you out of trouble. Any single man roaming the streets of Phnom Penh is assumed to be up to no good. Even older ones," she said, looking pointedly at Trutch. "You can't hang around a place like Svay Pak drinking coffee and asking questions. You'll arouse suspicion. The thugs and pimps will be watching, so you put yourself at risk. Several concerned networks and organizations work with tuk-tuk and moto drivers. Also with hotel clerks, travel agents and Internet café operators. They're all on the lookout for sexual predators who may be in town to exploit children. If you're mistaken for a pedophile, they'll circulate your photo and you won't even know it's been taken."

"Perhaps," Trutch said. He looked to Andrew and Duc for support, but both men had become unusually preoccupied with their cell phones. "Can't you call ahead and let them know that's not why I'm there?"

"From here it would be impossible to cover all the bases. Your photograph could make the rounds — the volunteer child protection agencies; the Ministry of Education, Youth and Sports; possibly even Western embassies. Several Western embassies, including yours, take a dim view of their citizens exploiting underage children. You want to avoid being put in a position where you have to defend yourself."

Trutch sat back in his chair and studied her. She worked for an overburdened and underbudgeted charity with a shabby office in downtown Saigon. No doubt she was underpaid. He guessed her age at about 50, and a plain gold band on her left ring finger suggested a partner somewhere. Taking a different tack, he said, "What will your husband think of your going?"

"My husband is the Australian Consul General here in Saigon. He's fully supportive of my work at STOK. He'll entirely understand and support my travel to Cambodia to help you find your granddaughter."

That explained a lot, Trutch thought. If she was comfortable financially she'd be working in child welfare out of deeply held convictions. She was also a strong and confident woman. He needed to ease off. "I didn't mean to probe into your personal life," he said. "I just wanted to know more about who you are, and how we might work together. *Safely*," he emphasized.

Judith held his gaze for a moment and then nodded and tapped her pen on the table as if she had just made a decision about him. "I appreciate that. If we're to work together, we need to know we can count on each other. Let's talk more on the plane tomorrow."

"There's a good chance we could get our hands dirty during this little expedition, and if that happens, I'd still prefer to have the benefit of Duc's experience."

"Look. Duc hasn't been to Cambodia and I have. I think you'll find it useful if I take you around to one or two other NGOs. They're involved in the rescue and rehabilitation of trafficked children. You'll get a better sense of the local situation. And with my husband's connections, I can arrange for you to meet someone in the US embassy in PP. They may provide some insight and assistance."

He made one last attempt. "I'm still thinking Duc would be an asset."

Her jaw took on a determined set and she picked up the phone. "It doesn't matter. If you want STOK's help that's the way it'll be."

While Trutch waited, she made reservations on Vietnam Airlines for the three of them. She booked a flight for the next afternoon and reserved rooms for an indefinite period in the Blue Lime Hotel, near the National Museum, in downtown Phnom Penh.

Just before she concluded the telephone conversation. Trutch scraped his chair back and left the office.

***

In the morning, they arrived at the airport in time to greet Catherine's 11:15 flight. Still angry that she hadn't caved concerning Duc, Trutch offered Judith only a slight nod, and then turned to Duc and Andrew. He'd meet the three of them in one of the coffee shops on the departures level after he met Catherine.

Now he stood amid the sea of greeters, tour guides and taxi drivers just outside the customs hall at Tan Son Nhat. The overhead monitor indicated that Catherine's flight had been delayed 30 minutes, meaning that he'd have less than an hour with her before his own flight left for Phnom Penh. He wished he could delay his departure another day and make everything right with her, but the old soldier in him knew that the sooner they got on the ground and into action in PP, the better. He and Catherine would have to settle for a quick hug and a kiss.

Trutch stepped outside the arrivals area and walked to a small patch of lawn between the two terminals, where it was a bit quieter. If he had to wait, he could at least put the time to use. He made the connection with the An Nhon care center and asked to speak with Ngoc.

During a long delay, Trutch heard several women speaking in their singsong dialect in the background. He imagined someone walking down the long hallway toward Ngoc's room or to the rec room where he might be watching TV.

Finally, Ngoc's voice came through the handset, "Hello, Ba. I'm glad to talk to you. Is everything good in Saigon? You find something about my daughter?"

Trutch brought him up to date — Uncle Vu's demise, Captain Minh's announcement that Lien was in Cambodia, his plan to go there today with Andrew and Judith Grinder, Catherine's discovery about Dream, and her plan to go to Xuan Loc and find the midwife.

Ngoc's voice caught as he said, "Ba, I thank you too much. I don't know how to say that enough. I am happy and proud to say that I am your son. You're a good father and grandfather. I think you will find Lien — bring her back for us."

Trutch gulped back a sudden flood of emotion as his son's sweetness touched him in a tender spot, long hidden from anyone but Catherine. "I will," he said. Then he stepped back into the arrivals area and checked the airport monitors. Catherine's flight was now on the ground.

People in the waiting crowd outside the doors jostled for position. Many waved cardboard signs and placards on which they had scrawled in felt tip handwriting the names of those they had come to meet. Groups of passengers made their way into the rabble of chattering and shouting greeters, most pushing and pulling luggage trolleys overloaded with suitcases and cardboard boxes.

Trutch stood apart from the melee and scanned the shoving mass for Catherine. He had left Seattle on September 11th and hadn't seen her for 22 days. As a result, and despite his outwardly cool demeanor, his heart raced. Taller than most, he looked over the heads of the crowd and watched the electronic sliding doors leading from the customs hall.

When the double doors slid open on an Asian family of four, and they surged through with their mountain of luggage, Catherine appeared in the line behind them, her lithesome physique and auburn hair distinct from the shorter, dark-haired Orientals surrounding her. Trutch's breath caught in his throat as he watched her move gracefully through the crowd. He waved, caught her eye, and then elbowed his way toward her. *Xin loi*, he said as he bumped into a woman. Then again as he bumped into others. *Xin loi, Xin loi,* he said repeatedly. He turned sideways and squeezed past a man and a woman. Then he reached out and encircled Catherine.

She wrapped her arms around his neck and pressed her body against his. She kissed him fully on the mouth and drew back far enough to coo, "You taste *so* good." She kissed him again and added, "I've missed you, Colonel Trutch. I'm over my hurt, I just want to be with you."

"Me too," he said. "God, it feels good to hold you."

They clung to each other for several seconds and then, with her hand clutched in his, Trutch led Catherine through the crush of people to the small coffee shop on the departures level, where Andrew, Judith and Duc waited.

When he had made the introductions, they sat and he said, "Duc will drive you downtown to the Continental. He's also made himself available to serve as a guide and translator when you make the trip up to Xuan Loc."

Catherine's smile radiated outward as she turned from Trutch to Duc. "That's very kind of you, Duc."

Trutch couldn't look anywhere but at her. Even after 20 hours flying across the Pacific, she looked alert and ebullient. "Duc's an experienced investigator," he added, "so he can help you with your enquiries as well."

"Have you been to Vietnam before, Mrs. Trutch?" Judith asked.

Catherine flashed her the same warm smile. "Please call me Catherine. And no, this is my first time. And not exactly the circumstances I would have chosen. I barely had time to get shots and close the house, much less prepare for the tropics and a lost grandchild. But I hope I can help Pete solve the puzzle of Dream and connect with Lien. The bonus will be learning as much as I can about the culture of this fascinating place. How long have you been here, Judith?"

"Going on three years."

"Have you traveled widely in-country?"

"The foundation work centers on Ho Chi Minh City, but I've been to Vung Tau, Nha Trang and Hoi An. And I've accompanied my husband on official visits to Hanoi several times." She set her tea down. "I've gone by car up Highway 1 from here to Nha Trang, and I've passed through Xuan Loc. The traffic on the segment between HCMC and Xuan Loc is ferocious … and deadly. Don't let Duc talk you into going by motorbike. Hire a substantial car, like an SUV, and a driver to take you there."

Trutch relaxed. Judith's answer to Catherine's question affirmed that she knew her way around and had her priorities straight. And Catherine, with her easy social skills, had just paved over his slight rift with Judith. Between Judith and Andrew, he thought, he would have ample backing in Phnom Penh.

***

On the mezzanine level above the cavernous departure lounge, Captain Minh and Luong sat unseen in the airport security office staring at the Trutch party through one-way glass. "There is your threat," Minh said. "Study the faces of Trutch and Quang closely."

CHAPTER EIGHTEEN

Shortly after the bellman delivered his luggage to his comfortable room in the Blue Lime Hotel, Trutch set off for the US Embassy. He waved off several tuk tuk drivers who approached him, preferring to walk the two kilometers, where he would meet with the senior FBI agent at the embassy. His hope was that the agent would offer advice and/or assistance in finding Lien.

The roadway was clotted with motorbikes, tuk tuks, commercial and military vehicles, horns blaring, unabashedly spewing tons of pollution into the humid air. He walked briskly alongside them on the cluttered sidewalks, wishing he had remembered to don one of the medical facemasks he had in his luggage.

It took 20 minutes to reach the embassy, an imposing complex of gleaming white concrete buildings surrounded by a high iron picket fence, topped with razor wire. Although designed for functionality and security, the array of three-story buildings and the surrounding fence had charm, its grassy and expansive grounds landscaped with palm trees, manicured shrubs and flowers, making the overall effect stately and attractive. The gatehouse, a single-story, rectangular structure about the size of a Western three-bedroom bungalow, was set into the fence, a smaller replica of the main building. Behind the gate, four blue-uniformed and well-armed Cambodians stood guard.

Trutch found the pedestrian entrance, a single door with a sign that read: Visitors and Employee Entrance, Consular Entrance on Street 51.

Beyond that entrance two more security guards directed him through a metal detector and then up to a heavily glassed window, where a clerk beamed at him and asked through an amplified speaking grate, "May I help you, sir?"

Trutch returned her smile and presented his passport and military ID, explaining that he had an appointment with the Legat, meaning Legal Attaché, a thin euphemism for the FBI's presence in US embassies around the world.

Still smiling, she picked up a phone and spoke a few words. Moments later a door behind her opened and a Marine Corps Gunnery Sergeant in dress blues stepped out and approached the window. "Yes sir, Colonel Trutch, they're expecting you. Just follow the walkway up to the chancery building and in the lobby you'll be further directed to the Legat section. You're to see Mr. Brad Cassidy." He pressed a button and a buzzer sounded as the back door of the gatehouse opened onto a sidewalk.

Cassidy acknowledged Trutch in his office with a warm handshake and a broad smile. "Nice to see you, Colonel. We received your e-mail yesterday and we stand ready to help you in any way we can."

"That's good to know, Mr. Cassidy."

"Call me Brad, please. Understand, though, that we have no police jurisdiction here. We're basically present to help keep foreign crime as far from American shores as possible. We serve as liaison to the Cambodian National Police and other law enforcement and security agencies. Our mandate is to coordinate investigations of interest to both countries. That's the official party line."

"I understand. It's comforting just to know you have a presence here. I'm hopeful I can use you as a sounding board if I uncover any leads or have any bright ideas."

"And we'll keep our antennae tuned for anything that may be helpful to you. Beyond that, we can't do much without the cooperation of the locals."

"Understood."

"Now to take that a step further, we're vitally interested in combating child trafficking. In fact, we have a mandate to do so. Under the provisions of the TVPA — that's the Trafficking Victims Protection Act — part of our mission is to capture and prosecute US citizens who travel to Cambodia to engage in sex acts with children. We also lend what assistance we can, including limited forensic aid, to the NGOs involved. I can't say any more about that."

"How big is the problem of US citizens coming here for that purpose?"

"It's big enough to be shameful and disgusting. There are Americans — I won't even call them men — they're predatory *animals*, who come to Cambodia, and several other Asian countries, for the purpose of having sex with children. It makes me sick."

***

As Trutch passed through the embassy gate on his way out, one of the Marine guards said to him, "Be careful if you're walking, sir. There's some kind of protest going on about two blocks south of here. Thousands of angry Cambodes and several hundred armed policemen near Freedom Park. A guy named Rainsy has them all stirred up."

Trutch had read about Rainsy, leader of the Cambodian National Rescue Party — the primary opposition party in Cambodia — and an articulate critic of the government's corrupt economic policies. Born in 1949, and educated in Paris, he returned to Cambodia in 1992 to embark on a checkered career as an activist and politician. He was elected to parliament and appointed to a ministerial position but then removed and ejected, first from his party and then from the National Assembly. Since, he had founded a succession of political parties. Seen as a thorn in the side of the long-ruling Cambodian People's Party, he regularly faced government intimidation and criminal charges. At one point, accused of various transgressions, including defamation and allegedly accepting bribes, he fled the country rather than be imprisoned for 18 months. Finally granted a royal pardon, he returned to Cambodia only to resume his agitation. In recent weeks, he'd organized a number of protests and public rallies against the CPP and its leader, Hun Sen. Apparently this was another.

Although curious, Trutch nevertheless heeded the guard's advice and walked a block farther east before turning south on Preah Norodom Blvd. to head back to the hotel. But as he approached the intersection with Street 106, wisps of fog drifted above the street. Irritation in his eyes and nostrils told him instantly that the fog was Agent CS — a tear gas used by military and police forces worldwide to help control unruly crowds. Aware that the odorless riot control gas would soon cause a rowdy, thundering panic, he quickened his pace.

Already, down Street 106 toward Freedom Park, an enormous crowd of people surged forward like ocean breakers and then fell back. The roar of the protesting crowd and the harsh blare of loudspeakers increased as he reached the middle of the block. A rolling, ghostlike fog of tear gas engulfed the crowd and they backed away screaming as one, but then individually, and frantically, sought to escape the swirling chemicals. For Trutch, everything seemed to be happening in slow motion, and he'd be caught in the stampede if he didn't move quickly. He bolted across the street and broke into a run, heading south.

Too late. The surging crowd overtook him, elbowing and jostling until he fell to his knees. Someone bumped heavily into his back and he fell forward. Instinctively, he shielded his head and neck with his arms, and rolled onto his side to minimize his exposure to the trampling feet until he managed to get onto his knees again. Several others around him had also fallen, and a woman near him was bleeding from her forehead. With one hand on a curb, he attempted to haul himself to his feet, but he was knocked over again.

Then a strong pair of hands seized him under his arms and jerked him off the sidewalk and into the lower half of a doorway. "This is crazy, but you should stay here for now," said a strong male voice in English.

Trutch looked up into the face of a young man, likely a student and one of the protestors. "Thanks."

He heard several sharp cracks. Through years of conditioning he recognized them as shots fired from an AK-47 Kalashnikov assault rifle. More cracks. Then sirens and European-style police klaxons sounded from several directions, converging on the turbulent scene.

He got to his feet and braced himself in the rear of the doorway until the running feet and shouting wave of humanity thinned. The tumult continued farther up the street as he dashed down a side lane and turned the corner onto an avenue that appeared calm.

In a last glance over his shoulder before a building eclipsed the grim scene, he saw high-pressure jet streams from truck-mounted water cannons being directed into the crowd. The force of the water knocked many off their feet and several scudded along the pavement, tumbling and rolling in the torrents.

A block or two away from the chaotic scene the roars of the crowd and wailing sirens could still be heard, but with a noticeable absence of the normally heavy currents of traffic, the streets were eerily calm.

Minutes later he entered the tidy lobby of the Blue Lime Hotel, where the reception clerk looked up, her eyes widening at his disheveled, sweaty appearance. "Better to stay inside the hotel for a while, sir."

"I believe you're right," he said.

He flopped into a seat and joined a clutch of guests and hotel staff watching a wall-mounted flat screen TV with BBC coverage of the disturbance happening a few blocks away. The camera appeared to be positioned within the front ranks of the protesters and panned back and forth to show upraised fists and the backs of many heads, while a few meters beyond, phalanxes of helmeted policemen stood backed by fire trucks with their mounted water cannons. Just in front of the front rank of cops a high-ranking policeman stabbed an index finger at the crowd and spoke through a handheld bullhorn. The camera zoomed in closely enough for viewers to see the distended and pulsating arteries of his temples, his eyebrows knit together and lowered to form a hedge of bramble. But contrary to his fierce appearance, he spoke calmly and rationally, apparently trying to appeal to the crowd to disperse and go home. The plastic nametag on his breast pocket flap read *Khlot*.

The screen changed and a male commentator with a British accent spoke into the camera. "At least two people are dead in Phnom Penh today, as Sam Rainsy, leader of the opposition party, the Cambodian National Rescue Party, or CNRP, has been leading a series of protest rallies. He alleges voter fraud in July's national election and calls for an independent probe. We understand that in today's action, several policemen opened fire. Although recent political gatherings in Cambodia have been largely non-violent, today's events demonstrate the potential for spontaneous escalation into deadly confrontation without warning. Mr. Rainsy has told reporters that the protests will continue on at least a weekly basis until the government either addresses their grievances or the Prime Minister, Mr. Hun Sen, steps down. Hun Sen has said that he would neither resign nor call for a re-vote. The Asian edition of BBC World News will continue to monitor the situation. Meanwhile, in Hong Kong today…"

***

"We're entering Svay Pak," Judith said, as their vehicle turned off the main highway and into a village. "I'd like you to get a feel for the place before we devise a plan to look for Lien. I think *you'd* call this a reconnaissance."

They drove slowly through the muddy streets of the impoverished suburb in an SUV with a hired driver. To Trutch it looked pretty much like any other poor village in Southeast Asia, with run-down stucco buildings, dilapidated shanties, haphazardly constructed of wood, canvas and sheets of corrugated metal — a ghetto of despair. Most shopfronts had wide wall-to-wall openings for customer access, with folding iron grates for non-business hours. Half-naked children stopped playing in the streets to smile and wave as the vehicle rocked through the potholes. Scrawny chickens scratched and pecked in the mud and between paving stones. On one corner, men on tiny stools played cards under a plastic tarp around a rusted metal table. A mix of Western and Cambodian men hung about the coffee shops and the shoddy carts of street vendors.

"A lot of these men are just waiting for pimps to come by and set up liaisons for them," Judith said. "It's a little early in the day for the pimps to be out. This place is a magnet for traveling pedophiles and for local men as well."

"How many of these buildings are brothels?" Trutch asked.

"Hard to say. Many of them. The village is popular because they advertise virgins."

"How's that different from any other whorehouse in Cambodia? I've read that virgins are much in demand."

"I've heard that too," Andrew said.

"That's true, virgins are a valuable commodity anywhere in Cambodia. A man who can afford to will pay a premium for raping a teen-ager, or an even younger girl, though he wouldn't see it as rape."

"What's the attraction in that?" Trutch asked. "Is it an ego thing? Does it give these losers special bragging rights to say that they've robbed a young girl of her chastity?"

"I suppose so. This is definitely a culture of male supremacy. Many Cambodian men believe that raping a virgin will make the man stronger, more virile. Others subscribe to the ridiculous myth that sex with a virgin can cure AIDS."

Trutch shook his head in disbelief, and then focused on the road, where a small gray delivery truck partially blocked the narrow street in front of a mold-covered concrete building.

The driver inched the SUV forward, his head swiveling from side to side to check his clearance, little more than several inches on each side. Through the open driver's side window of the delivery van, Trutch locked eyes with the driver, a stout, dark-skinned man with prominent jutting ears. He recoiled from the malevolence he saw in the man's expression. Definitely a pimp, he thought.

***

The SUV turned and thumped up from the mire of the Svay Pak side road onto the hardtop of National Highway 5, accelerating southward back to Phnom Penh. The brief reconnaissance over, Trutch fought a feeling of sadness and repugnance.

"Next stop," Judith announced, "PPWS, the Phnom Penh Women's Shelter. You'll have a chance to understand the work of a rehab center and possibly meet one or two girls who've been victims in the brothels. Their stories may provide you with insight into what we're up against, along with some hope."

"Good. I've read a little about it, an isle of humanity in this sea of depravity," Trutch said.

"And it's one of the few charitable organizations run by local people rather than expats. The girls and women in this shelter have been raped or trafficked. Usually both."

"Who runs it?" Andrew asked.

"The founding director is a dynamite woman by the name of Chakra Dith, and she lives up to her first name — she is a center of energy, a former victim of trafficking herself, who has since earned a law degree and now devotes her life to combating abuse against women."

Trutch felt a flash of admiration. "How does someone with that background manage to pull herself up and get a law degree?"

"The short version of her story is that both parents were killed during the Pol Pot reign of terror in about 1977, when she was seven. She essentially lived hand to mouth on the street from the time of Pol Pot's defeat in 1978 until she was kidnapped and sold to a brothel in 1984 at the age of 14. A New Zealander serving with the United Nations Transitional Authority, UNTAC, rescued her in 1992. He sponsored her immigration to New Zealand, where she eventually completed law school at the University of Auckland. She returned to Cambodia in 2000 and initially went to work for the government in the area of child protection law, but she soon became disillusioned with the rampant corruption. With financial backing from friends in New Zealand, she started this center on her own."

"How did she survive as an eight-year-old alone on the streets after her parents died?"

"She never talks about that."

Trutch lost all sense of direction as the SUV, oversized for the narrow lanes and alleyways through which it attempted to crawl, navigated the complicated labyrinth of back streets in Phnom Penh. Several times the driver needed to back up and try another passage. Once or twice he laid on the horn until someone emerged from a shop to move a parked motorbike out of the way.

At last they arrived at a compound surrounded by seven-foot concrete walls topped with razor wire. A security guard opened the gate and when they stopped Ms. Dith and two younger women met them, all three dressed in slacks and white blouses.

Judith made the introductions and then, as they entered the building, she said to Trutch, "This will crack your heart wide open."

Chakra was tall and statuesque for an Asian. She turned on her high heels, worn with fashionable slacks, and led the group to her office, where she gestured toward a modest conference table. "Please join me for tea. I suppose Judith has told you that I'm a ball of fire, or something like that. Although I like that metaphor, I think it's more apt to say that I can be a dragon at times."

"I'm hoping that we can see you breathe fire, then," Trutch said.

"I would have to be very angry with you, Mr. Trutch," she said, her smile a wide slice of delight. "Perhaps next time." The smile faded as the scraping of chairs also subsided. "And now," she said, "time to be serious.

"At the moment we have 14 girls here in various stages of rehabilitation and counseling. They usually spend three to five years here before they have the necessary self-esteem and life skills to reintegrate into society, but sometimes that's insufficient. We've had cases where, after months of intensive counseling, basic education and skills training, girls have left here feeling good about themselves only to be demeaned again. Imagine how you would feel as a 17-year-old who had been subjected to unspeakable abuse. You spent three years in rehab and reached the point where you had the confidence to apply for work as a seamstress, only to be told by prospective employers, 'You're just a whore. You're damaged and worthless.'"

Chakra reached into a credenza drawer at the side of the room and withdrew a cloth-bound scrapbook while one of the other women filled their demitasse-sized teacups with hot herbal tea from a plastic thermos.

Trutch noted out of the corner of his eye that Andrew was furiously taking notes. He reached for his own pen, but then checked the movement. Andrew could be the scribe for both of them.

"These are two of our successes," Chakra said. She turned to a page containing two portraits of young women with wide eyes and showcase smiles. "This one, on the left — we managed to place her into an apprenticeship of sorts as a hotel receptionist at a boutique hotel run by an empathetic woman here in P.P. She's now the front desk manager, responsible for supervising three other receptionists on shift work."

Trutch wondered how damaged they would find Lien, and what kind of work she might succeed at after a period of rehabilitation.

"Her story is miraculous because she spent five years as a sex slave, having been sold by her own parents — not so uncommon among ignorant, impoverished families in my country. At the time of her rescue from the brothel she was nearly spent — thin, gaunt, jaundiced, undernourished *and* HIV-positive. As you can tell by this photo, she now carries herself well, has a healthy countenance and is well nourished. Of course, she is still HIV-positive. That won't go away. But we pray that with good nutrition and competent medical attention she can stave off the inevitable for many years."

"That's quite a story," Trutch said. He stared pensively at the picture, unable to find words for further comment.

"And the other girl?" asked Andrew.

"She is Vietnamese. Sold, or perhaps kidnapped, I'm not sure which, into the hands of the criminal trafficking network at 12, smuggled across the border by foot, as one of a gaggle of about seven girls herded by thugs and consigned to a brothel in Svay Pak. She managed to escape, found her way to our shelter, and then spent three years with us. Once we thought she was ready for reintegration, we repatriated her to Vietnam through STOK, with Judith's help, of course. Judith and her people found her on-the-job training in Hoi An, at a restaurant called Streets. The restaurant caters to Western tourists, but exists primarily for the purpose of providing skills training to street kids or children from abusive backgrounds. It's operated by an American couple with hearts the size of bathtubs. They've invested their retirement in helping unfortunate and marginalized kids in Vietnam. She — our former victim — now runs her own restaurant in Hoi An, a successful enterprise. And she is married, about to give birth to her first child."

"We're very proud of her," added Judith.

Now Chakra frowned. "I'm sorry, gentlemen, that I cannot give you a tour of our facility. Some of our girls are still so tender that if they see an older white man and a robust young Asian, they'll think you're just here to exploit them."

"God. They're that damaged, are they?" Trutch asked.

"I'm afraid so, Mr. Trutch. But I would like you to meet one of our girls who has been here for four years and is pretty well recovered. The trauma of her years as a sex slave will always be with her just below the surface, but she has succeeded in subduing her fear and now looks forward to a future."

Chakra left the room for two or three minutes, and returned with a tall, slender girl of indeterminate age — she could have been anywhere between 13 and 18. "This is her name." She wrote "Ai Huynh" on a scratch pad and held it up. "It is pronounced like 'I Won' in English. We hope that is a prophecy. She is ethnic Vietnamese but was born here in Cambodia. She has learned to speak

English reasonably well since being here with us."

Trutch, Andrew and Judith all stood and smiled politely. Ai Huynh smiled demurely and said softly, "I am pleased to meet you." She made eye contact with Trutch and said, "I hope your granddaughter can come here."

Chakra invited her to be seated at the conference table and poured her a cup of tea from the thermos. "Ai Huynh, will you tell these people a little about your life?"

Ai Huynh's gaze moved from one person to another as she spoke. "My parents are very poor. I am number five child, the only girl. Only number one brother went to school, no money for other people. My father took me to a house in Svay Pak for him to get money when I was nine. Then my life turned black. Every day I had to work many hours — sometimes 15 or 20 men in one day. If I got sick, I still had to work. One time I was so sick I couldn't get up off the floor, so the owner beat me with a bamboo stick. He said if I didn't go to work, he would poke out my eye with the stick." She paused and wiped away a tear that had spilled to her cheek.

"One time the owner's wife caught me sleeping in the working room, between times with men. She poked me in my breast with a pair of scissors and made me go back to work with blood dripping down my front. They never gave us enough to eat. We were hungry and sick all the time. Two girls died and were carried out in rice sacks. We knew no day or night, no sun or stars. I lived in the shell of my body. My spirit was dead. No hope. The future is black I thought. Then I came here for three years. Now a flower blooms from the black mud and like a lotus I think my life can be beautiful."

Trutch swallowed hard. Instinctively he moved to pat Ai Huynh's arm but caught himself and pulled back, afraid he might startle her or cause her to cringe.

Andrew's watery eyes fell on his teacup. Neither found words to speak.

Judith reached across the table and placed her hand on top of Ai Huynh's. "Thank you for telling us your story," she said kindly. "Understanding will help us work together to prevent other young girls from suffering."

After Ai Huynh had left the room, Trutch turned to Chakra with an expression of pain and disgust. "This is all so inhumane. I don't understand how human beings can make a business of exploiting and ruining the lives of babies. What is the profile of a typical brothel owner in Svay Pak?"

"First you must understand that, even though it sits on the edge of PP, Svay Pak is a poor village, with many like it throughout Cambodia. Most of the residents are ethnic Vietnamese who immigrated, or whose parents immigrated, right after the war. They're largely despised by the Khmers. They have little or no education, no skills and no understanding of ethics. They're often involved in, or on the fringes of, criminal activity. The brothel owners, usually Mom and Pop operations, typically fell into the business through circumstances, as a way out of poverty or debt. Sometimes a relative or friend brings them on board as a business partner to earn money themselves, and it's all they know. Usually Mom is the mama san and Pop either traffics or pimps. Frequently other villagers, not directly involved in the business, deliver their kids to the brothels on a 'rental' basis. As you already know, they can get, by their standards, a large amount of cash for a virgin daughter."

"This is what I don't understand," Trutch said. "How does a *parent* justify selling a child into sexual slavery?"

"Many parents, mothers in particular, have been asked that question. Typically it's about some debt the parents have accrued with loan sharks. They've already reached the end of their financial options. Maybe they're sick or starving, or loan sharks have threatened them. The parents have heard of virginity selling, or someone raises it as a possibility. Sometimes a woman in the community approaches them, offering money. Now the potential sale exists for the parents as an option, as something others do — it's normalized to some extent — and they see a daughter as their only hope. By selling her virginity, they can reduce or eliminate the debt altogether."

"So they see it as a one-time thing?"

"At first, perhaps. And when the daughter comes home from that transaction, changed but still alive, withdrawn, maybe bruised, but otherwise not visibly damaged, some parents will justify renting her out again. Maybe they need money for food, or maybe they get greedy. In their minds, the daughter is already 'spoiled goods,' and she has the opportunity to earn, so now it becomes her duty. We've seen girls as young as 4 in safe houses."

"Jesus," Trutch said.

"Are the brothel owners linked in some way to organized crime?" Andrew asked.

"We have a loosely connected network of criminals known as the

Cambodian Mafia. They extort a cut from the mama sans. The village chief and informal leaders will also take more. This has become a way of life in Svay Pak and many other villages. To the gangsters, girls are lucrative business. To the poor villagers, including brothel operators in Svay Pak, it's all about survival."

"But the charities and NGOs must be making some dent in the problem," Trutch said.

"Yes. But every success is like a few grains of sand on a vast beach. Many of us believe that the ultimate solution must go beyond the three R's — raid, rescue, rehabilitate — and work toward changing the subculture of these communities by helping the villagers learn trades like plumbing, carpentry and so forth. The idea is to build honor and dignity into their lives — to build community, to build pride. It's a slow process."

***

"Unless either of you has a better idea, I think we're on our own," Trutch said, as the vehicle threaded its way back to the Blue Lime. "At least until we develop some information that might persuade the police to look for Lien in Svay Pak. We know that they're not particularly trustworthy. Some of them are involved in the game."

When Andrew glanced back at Trutch from his seat beside the driver, Trutch directed his next comment to him. "The local FBI agent, Brad Cassidy, was supportive when I spoke to him, but we can't expect any help from the US Embassy either. We need to go into Svay Pak on foot and nose around. It's a long shot, but I'm thinking Judith and I might pose as a tourist couple and walk around with our cameras. If we ask dumb tourist-type questions of other tourists or even of the locals, we may hit upon something to generate police interest." He turned to Judith, "Are you game?"

"I'm willing to give it a try, but the cover's not very credible. The only foreigners on the streets of Svay Pak are male predators. And maybe a few do-gooders trying to win hearts and minds. We can have a go at it tomorrow afternoon, but if we don't find anything useful we'd better think of something else. We can't do it for more than one day."

"Here's another thought," Andrew said. "While you two play tourist in Svay Pak, how about I noodle around the bar and disco scene downtown? I'll see if I can recruit a few college students or backpacker types to join me in some window-shopping in Svay Pak. I'm sure I can find some young people out for a good time, but firmly opposed to pedophilia. We'll pose as prospective johns on the prowl."

Trutch shook his head. "I couldn't ask that of you. It could be risky."

"No more risky than what you and Judith are doing, and I'll have a couple of other guys with me. There's strength in numbers."

"All right. But only if you have a car and driver standing by. And don't stray more than a couple hundred meters from the car."

"I can arrange that through our local volunteers," Judith suggested. "We have several reliable drivers here. You should also keep an open cell phone connection with the driver while you're on the prowl."

"Done," Andrew said.

CHAPTER NINETEEN

Catherine slid into the Toyota SUV alongside Duc, keen to find the midwife in Xuan Loc. Ngo could be the key to learning what had become of Dream.

Smudgy morning air blanketed the vehicle as they drove through the shabby suburbs of Ho Chi Minh City. Their driver bullied his way along the clotted four-lane highway with loud and liberal use of the vehicle's horn. It took an hour and a half to traverse the 33 kilometers between Saigon and the city of Bien Hoa, but once beyond that, the pace of traffic on Highway AH-1 improved and they averaged about 60 kilometers an hour.

The chaotic conglomeration of roadside shacks, hovels and small family-owned shops gradually receded and was replaced by vast stands of mature trees, planted in neatly aligned rows and columns. Mesmerized by their symmetry, Catherine thought they resembled soldiers in formation. "How long ago were these trees planted?" she asked Duc.

"These are relatively recent," he said. "You'll see a lot of rubber plantations in Vietnam, mostly planted during the French occupation."

"This one looks huge. Is it part of the Michelin plantation?"

"That's farther along to the north and west, and much larger. It was important to the South Vietnamese Government."

Catherine glanced out the windows at the orderly plantations rolling past on each side of the highway. Well groomed and free of entangling underbrush, the trees formed a matrix of tidy ranks. A few pickup trucks and farm-type vehicles could be seen in the lanes between rows, as workers collected latex from bowls attached to the sides of the trees. "I remember reading something about that," she said, "that Michelin was one of the mainstays of the French Indo-China economy."

Duc gestured toward the plantations on each side of the road. "During the American war, this area was mostly jungle and forest. It was wild and raw, until heavy fighting and Agent Orange destroyed most of the forest. The South

Vietnamese Army made its last stand here in April of 1975, probably their most bold and courageous engagement. They held off the North Vietnamese in the Xuan Loc area for many days before they finally caved in to the onslaught. There was nothing left here."

"You'd never know it to look at the area now," Catherine said.

"After the Communists took over in 1975, they declared this the New Economic Zone. They forced many former merchants and small business owners in Saigon to relocate here and become peasant rice farmers. It was an "economic zone" in name only, though. They had no economy here at all — just bomb craters, scorched earth and a few trees left struggling for survival. I grew up here in the '70s and '80s. As a boy, my friends and I would foolishly hunt for souvenirs in the woods."

"You mean shells?"

"Unexploded artillery rounds and bombs. Foolish, dangerous stuff, but we were hungry and could sell scrap metal. One of my friends was killed and two ten-year-old friends seriously injured when they attempted to handle a mortar round we found."

Catherine shuddered at the thought. Looking out the window, she attempted to picture this area at a time when ragamuffins scavenged for unexploded ordnance. "Was your family one of the ones moved here from Saigon after the war ended?"

"My parents owned a small business in Saigon, so they were deemed evil capitalists by the new Communist government. We were moved to a commune here. Along with other families, we had to clear the land, install irrigation ditches and make it suitable for rice cultivation. I was four when we moved here in 1976, and like everyone else, I had to labor in the fields all day every day. My parents knew nothing of rice farming. Neither did many of the other families, so we didn't do well. I was constantly hungry. Often we ate roots from the forest. A few bites of meat, if someone managed to kill a rat or a snake, was a treat."

Catherine listened attentively, and hoped Duc would continue.

Around them, a steady stream of large trucks rolled by in each direction, horns blaring, headlights flashing to assert their dominance. But the drivers of smaller vehicles and motorbikes neither swerved away nor flinched, forcing trucks to cross the roadway in order to pass.

"Eventually the Communist Party concluded that the economic model they had installed wasn't working, and they made reforms and eased their policies. My family was allowed to move back to Saigon and start a small business again in 1985."

"Did anyone have money to do that after the years here?"

"Fortunately, my mother had managed to keep some gold hidden, so we had the capital to start another shop. I went to school for the first time at age 13. When the Communists recognized that collective rice farming wasn't working, they allowed farmers to again control their land and do with it as they wished. That's when this area was cultivated for rubber trees. Many of these former peasants control small rubber plantations and have become very comfortable."

"I noticed you said *control* not *own* with respect to their land ..." She cringed and trailed off as a truck ahead of them veered over the centerline and squeezed past a bus moving in the opposite direction. For a second, the drivers could have kissed through their windows.

Duc followed her gaze and laughed. "We won't worry until our driver tries to squeeze between them," he said. Then, "The state ultimately owns all land in Vietnam. Farmers lease land cheaply for 20 or 30 years. At the end of the term the leases may be renewable. If I buy a house in Saigon or Nha Trang or anywhere else, I'm just buying the previous owner's lease."

Minutes later, they approached the outskirts of Xuan Loc. The roadside rubber plantations gave way to ramshackle buildings that lined the highway. Brake lights blinked in front of them as traffic slowed to a near standstill. Some of the motorbike drivers, thinking they could maneuver around the problem, whatever it was, began pulling off the roadway and onto the verge to pass larger vehicles on the right. At the same time a number of cars and trucks pulled into the oncoming lanes on the left and accelerated. Horns blared. Trucks, cars and motorbikes swerved this way and that, like wriggling snakes, each driver attempting to gain as much advantage as he could.

"*Troi oi*," shouted the driver and pointed to a cluster of flashing blue lights up ahead.

"What is it?" asked Catherine.

"It looks like a police roadblock," Duc said.

Their driver contributed to the cacophony by leaning on his horn and maintained his position in the lineup as they crept forward. Nine or ten helmeted policemen blew whistles and made threatening hand and arm signals as they screamed instructions at motorists in an attempt to control the river of vehicles. Despite these attempts, traffic surged madly onward with vehicles dodging and swerving as they competed for the limited space to pass the blockage.

Their vehicle inched forward, toward the wreckage of a demolished SUV that blocked the left lanes. It had smacked head-on into a tour bus, its front end flattened as though it had hit a brick wall. A body, covered by a plastic sheet, lay near the passenger side of the vehicle, and a rivulet of blood leaked out from under the tarp and ran across the road. The front portion of the bus was also heavily damaged. The bus driver sat dead at his station, still embracing the steering wheel. The steering column had penetrated his bloody chest.

As they came abreast of the wreckage, Catherine cracked her window a little and heard those trapped inside the SUV still screaming. She closed the window.

Bloodied, panicked passengers slithered out of the emergency exits on the roof and sides of the bus. Horns continued to blast and vehicles twisted and turned in their attempt to wriggle through the logjam. Incredibly, the other drivers seemed oblivious to the carnage, intent only on passing this obstruction.

Once, when Pete had returned from his second tour of duty in Vietnam, he'd said, "Life is cheap in Southeast Asia," a frustrated comment on what he saw as a devaluing of human life. His words came back to Catherine now.

In flagrant disregard of the signals given by one of the policemen, a motorbike gunned its way across two lanes of creeping northbound traffic and plowed onto the shoulder, partially blocked by a police vehicle. When the driver attempted to swerve around the police car, one of the cops jammed his truncheon into the spokes of the bike's front wheel causing its rear wheel to buck momentarily before the vehicle fell over on its side, the operator still saddled. Another policeman, who wore the chevrons of a more senior cop ran up and commenced to beat the driver about the head and shoulders with his truncheon.

"My God, how can they be so brutal?" she asked.

Duc nodded. "They're drunk with power, Mrs. Trutch."

The cop dealt about five hard blows which rendered the bike operator bloodied and crumpled in the mud, and then he swaggered away with his chin jutted out, much impressed with his own importance.

***

Thirty minutes later they were within the gritty city of Xuan Loc, where Duc intended to make inquiries as to the existence and possible whereabouts of the midwife, Ngo. As they cruised down the main street, lined on both sides with shanties and dilapidated storefronts, he kept a sharp lookout for locals over 60 years of age.

Up ahead, an old woman came out of a store. She wore the cotton black pajamas and straw conical hat of a peasant and was carrying a large basket of mangoes.

Duc asked the driver to stop, and then stepped out of the vehicle and approached the woman with the deference required of a middle-aged man addressing an older woman. "Excuse me, Grandmother," he said in Vietnamese, "Do you know of a woman named Ngo, who delivered babies here in the 1970s?"

The old crone smiled, her lips and sparse array of irregular teeth stained red with betel nut. She shook her head but then said, also in Vietnamese, "Go to pagoda. Most women who pull babies in this town are nuns."

"Where is the pagoda, Grandmother?"

She pointed down a lane to the right and said "Two kilometer. Now in rubber trees."

***

The pavement ended and the built-up area gave way to raw countryside within 500 meters of their last turn. The SUV bounced and jerked down the muddy, rutted road as they encountered ancient trucks and motorbikes, carts pulled by water buffalo, pedestrians and bicycles, all moving slowly in both directions.

Soon the tires became mired in the claylike laterite. The driver blurted out what Catherine assumed was a Vietnamese expletive and pressed hard on the accelerator. The wheels spun and the vehicle sunk further into the goo.

"I think we'd better push," Duc said.

He and Catherine stepped into the red mud and pushed from the rear while the driver spun all four wheels in at attempt to gain some traction. Catherine and Duc grunted and groaned and leaned into the vehicle with all their strength. The driver shifted back and forth between reverse and drive until the SUV rocked with good momentum, and still the wheels dug deeper into the goo.

After ten minutes of futile effort and numerous spontaneous curses, a passing peasant hitched his water buffalo to the front bumper. With much caterwauling on the farmer's part and a good deal of switching across the beast's rump with a piece of bamboo cane, the animal was persuaded to lunge ahead, pulling the SUV free of the quagmire.

Another kilometer along, a well-manicured plantation of young rubber trees appeared along the north side of the dirt road. Well off the road, and down a dirt path suitable only for foot traffic or motorbikes, Catherine spotted the yellow stucco pagoda, its red-tiled roof perforated with gaping holes.

***

They left the vehicle and driver at the edge of the road and walked down the path toward the temple. The sultry air felt laden with water, but the countryside had an earthy, appealing aroma, like freshly dug potatoes. Somewhere a rooster crowed.

About halfway down the path, Duc grabbed Catherine by the upper arm and jerked her violently to the side.

"What?" she shrieked.

"Snake! You were about to step on it." He pointed to the right of the path. The creature was bluish-black with faint white crossbars. Over a meter in length, it was semi-coiled into a rough S-shape, the top of its long body curled into a loop, the head resting on the body, tongue darting in and out.

Catherine looked at it and shuddered. "Is it venomous?"

"It's a krait, Catherine. One of many poisonous species we're favored with in Vietnam. They're not aggressive during the daytime, but if you had stepped on it, it would probably have bitten."

"Is it known as Mr. Two Step?"

"I have never heard that. What does it mean?"

"Pete told me that during the war soldiers referred to a certain snake as Mr. Two Step because if it bit you, you would only take two steps before dropping dead."

Duc laughed. "It *is* deadly but the toxin doesn't act quite that fast."

The single pagoda they had seen turned out to be a cluster of buildings occupying about half an acre, built around several paved courtyards. The surrounding rubber trees afforded some cooling shade and the courtyards themselves were landscaped with many large outdoor pots holding plants, flowering shrubs and small trees.

They walked through an opening in a low wall into the first courtyard, where a few motorbikes were parked. Catherine stopped and attempted, without success, to brush off the muddy red spots on her slacks and top. ""I'm a mess," she said. "I certainly hope this pays off."

A young nun in gray robes looked up from where she worked pruning shrubs. As she approached Duc and Catherine, she put her palms together and bowed slightly. She said in English, "You are welcome." Then to Catherine, "We do get some Australian visitors here. Are you Australian?"

Catherine smiled and offered her hand. "I am an American. My name is Catherine."

"I am Le. We invite you to come in and have tea."

Duc and Catherine followed her into a large room, cooled by two overhead fans and furnished with heavy, highly lustrous wooden furniture. Le seated them at a long conference table of polished mahogany, embellished with mother-of-pearl floral inlays. "I will find our head nun, her name is Sister Minh Tu." While they waited for Le to return with Minh Tu, another young nun appeared through a side door carrying a tray with a ceramic teapot and small porcelain cups. She silently poured the tea and set two plastic bottles of cold water on the table.

"*Cam on,*" said Duc, bowing a little.

Seconds later, a heavyset woman in her 60s joined them, with Le following close at her heels. Sister Minh Tu wore a pair of tiny wire-rimmed glasses perched on her nose and also wore simple gray unadorned robes. Her shaved head glistened with light perspiration, noticeable when she steepled her hands and bowed several times, the smile on her face as bright as a full moon. She shook hands with both Catherine and Duc, then spoke several sentences in Vietnamese. Le translated:

"Sister Minh Tu says you are welcome to our temple. She is pleased to see you and hopes that your health and that of your family is good. If you would like to meditate, we will show you to a quiet place. And she hopes you would like to have a simple vegetarian lunch with us."

Uncertain of what protocol demanded, Catherine glanced at Duc.

In Vietnamese, Duc told the two nuns that their offer was very kind, but that Catherine actually had another reason for visiting. Then in English, "You should tell them why we're here, Catherine."

Catherine explained in detail, pausing every two or three sentences to allow for translation.

Sister Minh Tu listened attentively and, when Catherine had finished, sat silently for a few moments. At last she spoke. To Catherine she seemed almost to be thinking aloud, as her monologue rambled on for fully two minutes.

Finally she smiled to signify that she had finished, and Le reported in English.

"Sister Minh Tu says the nuns here have a long history of doing midwife when Xuan Loc was a village and there was no *bac si* — excuse me, *doctor* — here. For many years when the sisters start to get old they trained other younger nuns to be midwife. Until a few years ago, there was always one sister who was a midwife. She say to tell you there *is* an older nun here named Ngo. She helped the women of the work camp when they have babies. When she was younger she did not live in the pagoda, just come during the day to meditate. But now she is 83 and ... I think *feeble* is the word ... and her husband is dead. Her children all have important jobs in cities, so she lives here now."

"May we see her?" Catherine asked.

This question produced another lengthy exchange between Le and Minh Tu. Even Duc jumped in from time to time. At last Le spoke in English again. "Minh Tu says I can take you to see her, but you must wait here for a while so we can check on her and make sure she is okay first. But please do not expect too much. She is not always in her mind. She has good days and bad days."

CHAPTER TWENTY

"And there's the pile of laundry," said Nakry from the top of the stairs, on Lotus's first afternoon in Nakry's second-floor quarters. "You can use the sink to wash and rinse. After you've wrung them out, hang them in the bathroom to dry. I've put a cord in there for that. Now get busy." She descended the spiral staircase, leaving Lotus alone.

Light flooded through the raised window and bathed the room in a glow the color of rice straw. Lotus drank in the soothing natural light and soaked up its warmth. Before the horrors of the past few weeks, she had taken daylight for granted and hadn't appreciated its soul-feeding qualities. Reunited with its restorative presence, she felt an overwhelming urge to escape. In a bid for freedom, she needed to get Diamond and Thanh, who knew the direction to Ho Chi Minh City, out from the dorm room and onto the street.

So far, Thanh had remained uncooperative and belligerent, in spite of two torture sessions in the basement. But if Lotus were to count on Thanh's help, and help Thanh escape in return, she would need to act fast.

While she stood at the window, a large SUV came into view on the rutted street below, an unusual sight alongside the tuk tuks, motorbikes and bicycles. It squeezed through the narrow gap created by a parked delivery truck.

Lotus's veins turned to ice. No doubt the vehicle contained more Westerners or rich Japanese or Chinese who had come to buy sex, she thought, her moment of comforting warmth in the sunshine eclipsed by renewed desperation. She could no longer endure this captivity and the servitude to coarse, animalistic men. She needed to make her move soon. But maybe they *weren't* sexual predators. Could this vehicle be an opportunity in disguise? With a flash of optimism, she pressed closer to the window to see if she might shout to them for help with any chance of being heard.

Before she could weigh the situation, Nakry squawked from behind her. "Lotus. I bring you up here to clean my room and do laundry, not to stand in window light like a plant."

Lotus turned.

Nakry stood at the top of the stairs, her face now flushed. "You get to work." She pointed at the soiled sheets and towels stacked by the kitchen sink.

It was all so unfair, Lotus thought. She should be home with her Papa who needed her. She raised her fist to Nakry. "I don't want to be treated like an animal anymore, you old cow. Leave me alone."

"Shut up. You don't talk to me like that. You're nothing but a whore."

"*You're* the whore," she screamed, tears streaming down both cheeks. "I'm a prisoner here and I hate it. I hate you. I hate Mau. I hate this house. I hate all of it."

"Yes, you're a slave. I own you and don't forget it. If you don't please me, I can have you beaten. I can have you killed." Nakry did not raise her voice so much as spew venom across the room, each word drenched in toxicity and spat with wrath. "We got rid of your friend Thanh this morning. The same can happen to you."

"I don't care what you do to me. I hate it here. I want to die. You and Mau aren't even human. You're worse than animals." Then, as Nakry's last words registered, "What do you mean you got rid of her? What have you done to Thanh, you bitch?"

In two strides Nakry crossed from the top of the spiral staircase to the window and with a furious swipe of her open hand slapped Lotus hard across the cheek. "You will obey me or you're dead. Do you hear me? You're nothing but a whore and a slave and I own you. You do as I say."

The force of the blow knocked Lotus sideways. She sidestepped to regain her balance.

Mau came limping up the stairs. He crossed the room and without a word grabbed Lotus by the wrist and twisted her arm around into the hammerlock position in the small of her back. "You little piglet, you're coming to the basement with me."

***

Thirty-one kilometers north of Phnom Penh, Luong turned the truck off National Highway 5 and headed west into the countryside, on an unimproved gravel road. Thumping noises from the back told him that his unwilling passenger was still feisty. He frowned. He hated this aspect of his job. He just wanted to get it done, make his way back to Svay Pak and collect the money due him when he completed the grisly chore.

He had been working at the bottom rung of the ladder for too many years and saw no chance of advancement in this loose network of petty gangsters. Even Mau and Nakry enjoyed a higher standard of living than he. Certainly the big bosses who gave him his assignments were doing better. And that corrupt *thang khon nan,* Captain Minh, ordered him around as though he was a peasant and then extorted him for protection. That snake definitely enjoyed a better life. And yet who had to take most of the risk?

Kidnapping and smuggling children through Vietnam was dangerous work. Police from the Ministry of Public Security were constantly on the lookout for traffickers. And the Cambodian border guards — he could never be sure whether they would take a bribe, arrest him on the spot or confiscate his cargo for their own sport. Once inside Cambodia, he had to kowtow to the police, the Cambodian Mafia and even the low-life brothel operators.

This morning one of the thugs who controlled some of the child sex market in PP had given him orders — pick up an uncooperative girl from the brothel of Nakry and Mau and take her out into the countryside.

He slammed his palm on the steering wheel and shouted over his shoulder, "Shut up back there. Lie still and don't struggle. It won't do any good."

The thumping and banging got louder.

In response he sped up, the increased speed on the uneven and rutty surface causing the vehicle to bounce and sway vigorously. Pebbles and clods of earth pecked against the windshield like little missiles and larger rocks smacked into the undercarriage. In the cargo compartment he heard the girl, gagged and securely bound, a rice sack tied around her head, roll from side to side on the dirty metal floor.

When he came to a paved crossroad, he slowed slightly. He swiveled his head in both directions to scan the highway but ignored the rusty stop sign that leaned at a 15-degree angle into his muddy path. With a protesting groan from its ancient leaf springs, the vehicle bounced up onto the hardtop and rolled to the other side. As it dropped back onto gravel, he accelerated sharply, causing the rear wheels to spin and kick up a spray of gravel before they found traction.

A few meters more and a blue flash refracted off his side mirror and caught his attention. The image of a helmeted policeman on a motorcycle filled the glass.

Di Tieu, he thought. Where had he come from? He considered gunning the engine in an attempt to outrun the cop, but his rattling old vehicle could not outperform the motorcycle. He applied the brakes and pulled to the edge of the road. As he did, he reached around to the small of his back and felt for the plastic handle of his pistol.

The cop approached. "You went through the stop sign," he said, and scowled through the open window. "You're from Vietnam? Let's see your driving license and your National Identity Card."

Luong produced the tattered documents from his wallet and handed them to the cop, just as the thumping from the rear began again. He clenched his teeth and sucked in a deep breath.

"What's in the back?'

"Pigs."

"Did you bring the pigs in from Vietnam?"

"No, no. I picked them up in Phnom Penh."

"Why do you speak Khmer so well?" The thumping grew louder and the cop cast his eyes toward the back of truck.

"I have relatives living here in Cambodia, so I come often. I've learned your language." His sphincter tightened as he spoke.

The policemen took a step toward the rear of the vehicle. Over his shoulder, he asked, "Where are you taking these pigs?"

Luong reached again for the gun. "To my cousin's. He asked me to buy them in Phnom Penh and bring them to his house. He doesn't have a truck."

Alongside the rear wheel, the cop stopped and turned to look at him. "Where does your cousin live?"

Luong spat out the first village name that came to mind. "In Svay Pak."

"You're almost 20 kilometers north of Svay Pak. If you're coming from Phnom Penh, you missed the turn." He walked back to the window, laughing, his eyebrows raised with incredulity. "How could you be so stupid as to go 20 kilometers past your destination and turn on the wrong road?"

Luong heard his own heart beating. "I don't know. My mind must have been elsewhere." The noises from the rear continued at a steady tempo, like percussion instruments. "I was thinking of getting home to my wife tomorrow."

The cop lowered his eyebrows and pointed back to the crossroad. "OK. You can back up to the paved road and turn around there. I'll stop any traffic for you." He turned and strode back to the motorcycle.

Luong slumped backwards in his seat and expelled a long breath. He turned around as ordered and drove south on Highway 5, glancing repeatedly in his side mirror.

When he saw the cop turn, satisfied that he no longer followed him, he drove five minutes farther and turned onto a dirt road, little more than a tractor path. A kilometer down the trail, near a small copse of coconut palms growing on a slight rise, he stopped the vehicle and took his time inspecting the grove, no longer distracted by the thrashing in the rear of his vehicle. That would soon be over.

The girl's agitation intensified when he pulled back the curtain and opened the tailgate. She banged both bound feet up and down against the metal bed of the truck. Blood seeped through her clothes from the beatings at the brothel, and the ends of several fingers were pulpy where fingernails had been ripped off. Guttural, inarticulate protests and distorted whines emerged from beneath her gag.

He reached in to grab one ankle and with a furious tug yanked her from the vehicle and let her drop onto the ground. "It'll be over in a minute, bitch."

Panting in the heat, he dragged her by the ankles through the dirt and stones and deeper into the undergrowth that grew thick below the tall, slender boles of the coconut grove. When he released her legs, the girl rolled and jackknifed until he put a foot on her back and pressed hard. Even then, she struggled, right up to the second he put the gun to the back of her head and squeezed the trigger.

He watched the red stain blossom and grow against the whiteness of the rice bag. Then he turned away. Time to get paid. He strode back to the truck with determination in every step.

An hour later, he sat as instructed in the cab of his van on the side of a muddy street in Svay Pak. He didn't know who would show up to pay him, Mau or one of the thugs. Briefly, he opened the driver's door and leaned out over the muddy street. What a shithole this village is, he thought, wishing he could avoid ever coming back to its garbage, its stench, its horrible ugliness. He flattened one nostril with his index finger alongside it and cleared the other one by blowing vigorously, then repeated the procedure with the opposite side of his nose.

He had just closed the door when a four-wheel-drive SUV approached from the opposite direction, the driver extra cautious, rolling over bumps and potholes with the brakes on, as if to protect his lily-white Western passengers.

As the vehicle came abreast of his truck, Luong peered into the passenger compartment. A surge of adrenaline hit him as he recognized the three foreigners Captain Minh had pointed out in the Saigon Airport. So they had made it to Svay Pak. This was not good news. If they found what they were looking for, they would disrupt his business. He knew what he had to do.

CHAPTER TWENTY-ONE

Catherine ducked her head to enter the small, dimly lit room, furnished with a pallet bed, a metal trunk and a wooden table, on which a single joss stick burned in a sand-filled bowl, its rising stream of smoke a light irritant to her eyes. The room's occupant sat at the table in a narrow, armless wheelchair, like those used to assist disabled passengers on and off aircraft. Now we'll know, Catherine thought, and her heart sped up.

With a yellow-handled paring knife the woman frenched long green beans into thin slivers and dropped them into a battered tin pan. Le introduced her, "Miss Catherine, Mr. Duc, this is Sister Ngo. She is preparing vegetables for our lunch. Again, you're welcome to eat with us." She touched Ngo on the shoulder and spoke louder in Vietnamese, introducing the two visitors.

Wispy silver hair framed Ngo's wrinkled features like a pale cloud. Her smile, when she turned to them, revealed a partial set of teeth, several of them gold. She spoke briefly.

Le chuckled before she translated, "She say your hair is like the color of a bright flower that grows in the jungle. She has never seen hair that color before."

"She's being kind. If the light were better she'd see that it's streaked with gray. It may more closely resemble a *fading* flower in the jungle. Would you tell her that we apologize for intruding like this?"

"That's not a problem. Sister Ngo is pleased to have company and she'd also like you to join us for lunch."

"Well, I guess we should then. What about our driver?"

"Of course. He is included too."

Catherine looked at Duc, who looked a little uncomfortable, his shoulders awkwardly broad in the tiny room, then back at Le. "I'm afraid we've been remiss. I didn't think to bring a gift for the pagoda."

"It's not expected, Miss."

But Duc chimed in. "We can leave something in the offertory box at the main shrine, Catherine. That's where people leave money for the pagoda."

"Wonderful." She turned back to Le. "Would you please tell Ngo that we're here to enquire about a young woman who was in Camp Z-30 in the late 70s? She would have given birth to a baby in late 1978 or early 1979. Her name was Nguyen Thi Tuyet. She also had a reputation for helping the other women care for their babies in the camp."

"Of course. This may take a few minutes."

Le and Ngo conversed for several minutes in an exchange that, to Catherine, felt repetitive and ceaseless, with much gesturing, nodding and shrugging on the part of both nuns as they chattered, often both speaking at the same time. Catherine looked anxiously at Duc who only shrugged and smiled. She listened to the words, meaningless to her, and carefully watched Ngo's face for a hint, any slight nuance, that signaled a sparked memory.

She caught a quick, anticipatory breath, when Le turned toward her and began,

"Sister Ngo remembers many of the women from the camp. She says the pregnancies were hard and the women miserable. Never enough good food. She remembers that outside the re-education camp there were graves of women and their babies who did not survive because of the bad conditions. She asks if you remember what this Tuyet looked like, the shape of her lips, her nose, her ears. Was her skin darker like a Montagnard or a Khmer? Did she speak with a northern or a central dialect? Could she have been of Chinese descent?"

"Oh my." Catherine blushed. What a fool she'd been. Prancing in here expecting this poor old soul to remember one woman from those days so long ago. "I'm afraid I know none of these things. I've never even seen a picture of her. I don't know anything about her except her name ... Oh ... and that she is from Nha Trang and worked for the American Army as a medical assistant. So she probably had some training in medical procedures. She had one other baby. A son born in 1971." Catherine hoped that would trigger something.

"Ah, good. Let me tell her that."

This resulted in another dialogue, with gestures and nonverbal signals, none of which Catherine could understand. She felt crestfallen when she detected a slight shake of the head on Ngo's part, but heartened a moment later when her eyebrows rose in apparent recognition of something.

At last, Le turned again toward Catherine with the corners of her mouth turned downward and said, "I am sorry, Miss Catherine. Sister Ngo says she never knew the names of the mothers from the camp. She doesn't know of anyone who had any medical training. I'm truly sorry."

Catherine took a moment to absorb the disappointing words and shake off a feeling of despair. She hadn't traveled halfway around the world to hit a dead end. There had to be other stones to overturn, and she wouldn't give up. Not now.

"*Cam on* to both of you. You both worked hard to help me."

***

They left the cloistered room and walked through the courtyard back toward the main part of the pagoda.

"Lunch will be served in about 30 minutes," said Le. "You'll hear a gong. Please enjoy the garden while I attend to some duties. The toilets are down this hall and the dining room just beyond them."

Duc went to the vehicle to let the driver know about lunch. No doubt he'd also have a quick cigarette with him, Catherine thought. She welcomed a few minutes alone to breathe the fresh air and wander in the garden at the rear of the pagoda where she admired the neat rows of deep greens. Her deep disappointment at the lack of information surprised her, but at the same time she chastised herself for having been so naively optimistic, and for foolishly fantasizing about delivering news to Pete. This wasn't some childish story wherein the good fairy would make sure she got her wishes. This was real life, in a country far from home, where she understood neither the language nor the culture, a place where history was harsh and where suffering made up the everyday fabric of so many lives.

When the gong sounded, the thought of lunch held no appeal, but she moved into the dining room anyway, wondering if there might still be something to learn before she left this pagoda.

The plentiful food filling the long table looked more beautiful than many a painting in the art gallery on whose board Catherine served at home in Seattle. The greens, both cooked and fresh, and including Ngo's beans, were vibrant in color. Bright orange carrots, carved into tiny animal sculptures, with pieces of red pepper for eyes, adorned platters of grilled eggplant. Some food she recognized — the spring rolls, rice and noodles — but many dishes remained a mystery. One dish looked somewhat like chicken wings in a tantalizingly aromatic sauce.

"They're tofu wings," whispered Duc, who had come up beside her, "and the other round-shaped ones, which look like your meat balls, are made of bean paste."

The nun on her other side placed a small portion of delicate-looking salad on her plate and demonstrated how to eat it on a small piece of crispy rice cracker. "Lotus root salad," she said.

The nuns engaged in little conversation, but Minh Tu spoke quietly with Duc while Sister Le occasionally chimed in. Le turned to Catherine in an aside as the other two continued to speak, "Duc has been telling Sister Minh Tu about the meeting with Sister Ngo. Minh Tu said you should go to the prison, to see if they can help. She say Camp Z-30 is now a permanent prison southeast of the city. I didn't know that."

Hearing, Duc said to Catherine, "I know about the prison. It's 25 kilometers southeast of here along Highway AH-1. It's where the government keeps the highest profile political prisoners. I'm sure we'll be turned away, but we do have time to drive by and see if we can talk to someone in authority."

***

An hour later, they rounded a curve into the village of Thu Duc and Catherine pushed herself forward on the edge of her seat.

"Just a few hundred meters to go," Duc said. "I hope we learn something here."

"If we're turned away, is there still a way to speak with someone?"

"I'm hoping we can persuade the gate guards to ask someone to consult with us, preferably someone with access to prisoner records."

"Oh, let's wish for that. This feels like my last hope."

"We'll know in a minute or two."

The prison appeared on their left, where a broad, paved driveway led from the highway up to the main gate, set back even farther into a recess in the yellow stucco prison wall. Beyond the wall, six two-story buildings with red-tiled roofs looked like they could be cellblocks or dormitories, but the densely treed grounds made it difficult to see much of the buildings.

Twenty meters into the drive, two heavily armed guards stepped off the sidewalk in front of the car and officiously signaled the driver to turn around. Clearly, they meant business.

The driver stopped and said to Duc, "What shall I do?"

"Just roll up enough that I can talk to the one on the left."

The driver complied, but barely. He eased the car forward about three meters at an extremely slow speed and stopped again.

Duc rolled his window down and opened his mouth to speak with the nearer of the two sentries.

In an almost imperceptible flash of movement the soldier whipped his AK-47 assault rifle from its slung position over his shoulder and presented it in front of his body at an angle, butt at his hip and barrel at his opposite shoulder. In another blindingly quick motion he pulled back and released the charging handle allowing the bolt carrier to slide forward, chambering the first of thirty rounds with an audible metallic click. This was no idle threat. "*Khong*," he commanded, red faced. "*Di di. Di di mau.*"

The driver required no further persuasion. He slammed the vehicle into reverse, and with tires squealing, sped backwards ten meters. Then he executed a three-point turn and pulled back onto Highway 1.

"Oh my God, would he have shot us?"

"Not likely," Duc said. "But it would have been foolish to provoke him further."

"I'm thinking of the cop who bludgeoned the motorcycle driver. Is everyone who wears a uniform in this country that charming?"

Duc flashed her a grim smile but didn't answer.

Two hundred meters beyond the gate, the wall made a 90 degree turn, away from the highway. The vehicle was now abreast of a run-down cemetery.

Duc motioned the driver to pull onto the right shoulder. "Catherine, I hesitate to suggest this, but this was the prison cemetery. I think we should spend some time looking at graves."

They spent an hour wandering through the random pattern of unkempt graves and corroding concrete markers. Catherine remembered reading that Vietnamese traditions of fealty demand that ancestors be revered, with their graves well tended in perpetuity. Those who can afford to will ensure that their forbears are memorialized with ornate monuments of marble and granite, often engraved with likenesses of the deceased. But this was the Vietnamese equivalent of a pauper's field, next door to a prison and doubtless holding the remains of many forgotten tenants.

Catherine was investigating a crude marker where someone had recently burned joss sticks — not all the remains here were totally forgotten, she thought — when Duc shouted, "Catherine! Over here!"

He pointed to a chipped, mold-covered concrete headstone. Catherine strained to make out the engraving which, along with the marker itself, had decayed considerably with age. The barely discernible lettering read:

Nguyễn Thị Tuyết 29 tuổi
Con Trai 1 ngày tuổi

"I recognize her name, and I can guess that the bit following means age 29. But what's the second line?"

"Baby boy. One day old."

CHAPTER TWENTY-TWO

Lotus had no idea if it was night or day. She only knew that it had been many hours since Mau had tortured her with the picana, touching the electric cattle prod first to the soles of her feet and then to the insides of her thighs. The unbearable pain burned like fire through her flesh and into the bone. Her entire body had quaked with each jolt, as spasms swept like waves up and down her legs. She had fallen into a fitful slumber a couple of times during the long hours since, but her sleep had been perforated with nightmarish images and sounds. Her own screaming jolted her awake and frightened her even more. Now she sat handcuffed to the U-bolt in the basement wall, nauseous, irritable and anxious. How long had it been since she had been given the relief of a white pill? A day? Two days?

The door moved and then opened violently to bang into the wall behind as Nakry burst into the room.

Lotus screamed and jerked her arms in an attempt to pull free of the handcuffs anchoring her to the wall.

"If you ever again speak to me the way you did yesterday, I will kill you," Nakry said, her tone still seething. "You need to remember that you are alive only at our pleasure. We feed you and house you because you produce money for us. No other reason. If you no longer please us, we can do away with you."

A wave of nausea caused Lotus to gag, but her empty stomach could produce only a thin stream of vomit, which dribbled down her chin. Her head pounded with pain and her skin tingled. "I … need to pee," she mumbled.

Nakry unlocked the handcuffs and marched her upstairs to the girls' quarters. "Be ready to work in an hour. I'll give you yama then."

Lotus squatted over the porcelain toilet recessed into the floor and voided her nearly empty bowels.

Then three unmistakable pops sounded from the front of the building.

Lotus sprang to her feet and flung herself into the arms of the girl nearest her, something wet dribbling down her legs. "Now they're shooting at us," she said.

CHAPTER TWENTY-THREE

In the Pussy Cat Bar on Street 136, Andrew waited for his eyes to adjust to the dim lighting. He found a table and gradually took in the action swirling around him while he waited for his beer. The tables were occupied mostly by men under 40, who sat in semi-circles facing a huge pane of glass. Behind it a clutch of young, scantily clad women danced to modern pop music. Each wore a printed number emblazoned across the clingy fabric of her tight dress. Others sat at tables with men of various ages, who had chosen them by their numbers. Andrew allowed himself a minute or two to observe the timeless ritual of men, women and alcohol concentrated in a smoke-filled room.

The waiter, a tall baby-faced Cambodian, set the foamy mug of beer before him. "You want meet girl, sir?"

"No thanks. For now I'm just looking."

"Ha ha. You crazy, man. Plenty girl here. Lots of boom boom."

"No worries, I'll just coast for now."

The waiter screwed up his face. "What this mean, *coast?*"

"It means I'm happy just to sip my beer and watch what's happening, mate."

"You crazy, man. One girl — all night — only 50 dollah. You tell me number when you ready."

"You'll be the first to know."

"My name Hank. Just call me when you know what number you want."

"Okay, Hank. It's a deal."

Andrew settled into the serious business of looking for prospective candidates to help with the undercover gig in Svay Pak, which he, Pete and Judith had ginned up. One table held three intelligent looking Caucasian chaps but they also appeared to have imbibed a bit too much. Off in a corner, he spotted two other possibilities. The men, uninterested in the mini-dramas playing out in the rest of the room, were instead engaged in a conversation that

Andrew assumed, by its intensity and the nature of their gestures, had some intellectual depth. He picked up his beer and approached their table.

"Gentlemen," he said, smiling modestly. "Sorry for the interruption. It looks like you're into a heavy conversation. But I wonder if I can join you. Just for a couple of minutes."

They both glanced up at him, clearly annoyed.

"I'm not a pimp, mates. My name is Andrew. I'm a social worker and an Australian graduate student, here on what I'd call moral business. I'm looking for a couple of adventuresome guys who could help me with some field research tonight. Maybe tomorrow night as well."

The taller of the two indicated a chair. "I'm Roger, and you have my curiosity piqued. Let's just hear what he has to say, Sherm."

"OK. Have a seat, Andrew. I'm Sherman. Roger and I are grad students at UCLA. But *field research?* Is that an up-ticked euphemism for whorehouse hopping?"

Sherman had an impish grin and brilliant white teeth, showcased against a tanned face. Probably a surfer, Andrew thought. Aloud, he said, "Well, sort of. But, if I have you two pegged right, the kind of whorehouse we'll be looking for will make you sick."

He reached into his hip pocket and pulled out a set of photocopies of Lien's picture and handed one to each of the Californians. "Her name is Lien and she's 13. She was kidnapped from Vietnam. Her grandfather is a retired American Army officer. I'm trying to help him find her."

The two Americans shared a glance, and then Roger said, "Let's hear more."

Andrew spent half an hour filling them in on background, describing the plan and answering their questions, their beers untouched. Finally he said, "Are you in?"

"Let's go," said Sherman.

"Right," Roger added. "Let's do some brothel prospecting."

When they got up to leave, Hank looked crestfallen and hastened up to them. "You not want girls? What's the matter? Not like these girls? I get other ones. You sit back down. Beer free. I get more girls for you to look at."

Andrew handed him a five-dollar bill. "Don't take it so hard, Hank. When we finish what we have to do, we'll all come back here and have a big party. Spend lots of money."

Hank pocketed the fiver and grinned.

***

Forty-five minutes later the Lexus, hired by STOK, dropped Andrew and the two Americans off on the side of National Highway 5 at the edge of Svay Pak. The driver agreed to hover and move slightly into the village as he saw the threesome progressing down the dirt street. He'd also keep his phone open with a connection to Andrew's phone.

As they trolled the street, they acted inebriated and full of testosterone. Their first hit came within minutes, when a young man of about 14 rose from a metal table in a roadside refreshment stand and approached them on the muddy road with a self-assured swagger. "You want boom boom? Yum yum? I can get for you. Boom boom, yum yum very good."

"How much?" Roger asked.

"Just 20 dollah. Very clean pussy. No get sick."

"Show us the place," Sherman demanded.

"You give me money first. 20 dollah each."

"We need to see the girls first."

"No can do. This no shit. Fine young girls. But I need money first."

"Okay. Show us." Andrew produced three 20-dollar bills and handed them to the young pimp. He wished he could push the young punk's face into a pile of shit. On the other hand, he realized that Cambodia's social system had failed him so badly that he was only doing what he could to survive.

The youthful pimp led the trio down two narrow back lanes and through a tight doorway into a nondescript cinder block building, where they were met by a middle-aged woman with chipped teeth. The rest of her face was camouflaged with badly applied makeup, her eyebrows simply slashes of black pencil lines. "This Miss Nga. She show you girls. Fix you up nice." With that the punk disappeared.

"You sit down. Drink beer," said Miss Nga. She pulled three bottles of warm Chinese beer from a drawer and popped the tops. "I bring some boom boom girls." She left the room but reappeared moments later with five bedraggled prepubescent girls, no more than eleven or twelve, dressed shabbily but provocatively, their short cotton pajamas so tight their clefts showed through the skimpy material. Fear and apprehension showed on each child's face.

Sherman's face went ashen, "This is fuckin' sick. My God. I've got a kid sister about their age."

"Are these all of the girls you have?" Andrew asked.

"Yes. You each pick one. Take to room I show you. Already paid for. Very good boom boom."

"Let's get out of here," Andrew said to the other two. "None of these is Lien."

"This is seriously fucked up," Roger said. He pointed his index finger at the mama san's face and managed to locate a sturdier voice, "This is criminal. You're despicable."

They found their way back to the street on which they had been dropped and paused to catch their breath. "I'm not sure I can do this," Sherman said. "This scene is beyond evil. It's not human."

Roger swiped at a bead of sweat on his forehead. "We've come this far, Sherm. I don't like it either. But if we do find this Lien, maybe we can help save one little life. Jeez, did you see the big brown eyes on those little girls? That cracks my heart. I don't think I can ever forget those pleading looks."

"All right, let's get on with it. I'll be okay."

About every third doorway opened into a brothel. They entered the first two cautiously and were shown the available girls, none of whom was Lien.

By the time they reached the third one, they had taken control of their revulsion and settled into their little charade.

They passed through a metal gate and crossed a small brick courtyard. They had almost reached the door to the building when it opened and a stout man with jug-handle ears appeared and aimed a pistol at them. The man was shouting something in Vietnamese.

The three men whirled around as though a single entity and sprang back through the gate. They ran down the muddy street.

"*Dung lai! Dung lai!*" the fat man shouted.

Andrew shouted into his cell phone, "Driver. Driver. Straight down the street where you dropped us. One block."

He heard a zing and then a loud crack, which caused his companions to bolt like racehorses, mud flying from their feet with every long stride. He felt the wind of a second bullet pass by his ear just before he heard the shot. The third shot entered him before he heard it, and he pitched forward, face down into the muck.

CHAPTER TWENTY-FOUR

Catherine was almost oblivious to the swirl of activity surrounding her in the big, airy breakfast room of the Continental Hotel. Groups of tourists and businessmen noisily made their way around the various islands of assorted Eastern and Western breakfast offerings, filling their plates, then sitting in clusters to chat their way through the meal, doubtless discussing the adventures or business meetings awaiting them on this day. Sitting pensively, struggling to understand her feelings, Catherine nursed a cup of tea and brooded on yesterday's events in Xuan Loc. On the one hand, while no longer hemorrhaging, her heart still felt bruised by Pete's revelation of infidelity, and she had not yet mended entirely. Paradoxically, it saddened her to learn of Dream's death at age 29. Had she died in childbirth? And the baby, who apparently died on the same day it was born, must have been a stillbirth. Part of her wanted to be angry with, and jealous of, her husband's former mistress, but intuition told her that Dream was gentle and loving and had truly cared for the man they had shared.

She took another sip of tea and nibbled around the edges of a rice cake. Now that the quest for Dream had concluded, how would she occupy herself today, tomorrow, the next day? Should she head back to the States or wait for Pete to return from Cambodia?

"Mrs. Trutch?" A paunchy Vietnamese man in a forest green uniform interrupted her reflection. He wore three gold stars on each of his epaulettes. "I'm sorry to intrude. I am Captain Minh with the Ho Chi Minh police. May I sit with you for a moment?"

An icy grip squeezed her heart. "Has something happened to my husband?"

"No no no. I merely wish to chat with you." He sat, still uninvited by Catherine, and lit the inevitable cigarette. He drew deeply and tipped his head back to expel the stream of smoke upwardly. "I believe you witnessed one of our policemen abuse a motorbike driver near Xuan Loc yesterday. I only wish to get a statement from you."

Already Catherine, whose momentary terror had been replaced with revulsion, had formed an unfavorable impression of this man. How on earth would he know that she had witnessed the highway accident? Unless ... would Duc have told him? What reason would he have had to do so?

As if reading her thoughts, Minh said, "We followed you to Xuan Loc. I know your husband, and I know about his purpose here in Vietnam, and that he is now in Cambodia. I want to ensure your safety while you are alone in our country. At times it can be perilous here."

Catherine stared at his inscrutable face and tried to discern the real message behind his words. She knew enough about Southeast Asia, where "OK" seldom means "yes" and prevarication is a way of life, to recognize the beginning of some kind of tea dance. "I don't really think I need police protection ..." she glanced at his nametag, "Captain Minh."

"One cannot be too careful, Madame. What do you hear from your husband in Phnom Penh?"

"That question is personal. But I can tell you I last heard from him yesterday morning before we left for Xuan Loc. He will be calling me again, this evening."

"What was the purpose of your trip to Xuan Loc yesterday?" He pulled a note card from his breast pocket and glanced briefly at it. "I understand you spent over an hour in a pagoda evidently visiting with the nuns. You attempted to enter our Prison Z-30, but were turned away by the guards, and you spent over an hour in a cemetery next to the prison."

Others in the room had turned to stare, so Catherine spoke quietly. "Captain Minh, would you do me the courtesy of explaining your agenda with me?"

"I don't know this word, *agenda*."

"It means, what is the purpose of this conversation?"

"I told you. It's my duty to ensure your safety while you're in Vietnam. In order to do this, I need to know why you went to Xuan Loc."

"I don't believe I need police protection." Unless she needed protection *against* this glib cop. "I wanted to determine what eventually became of someone my husband knew in Nha Trang during the war. At war's end she was incarcerated in Camp Z-30. As near as I can tell, that's the last place she was known to be."

"Ah. Now I am putting two and two together, as you Americans say, and understanding that perhaps this person who went to Xuan Loc re-education camp is the reason he has a Vietnamese granddaughter. Would this woman who went to Xuan Loc be the mother of the son who produced Colonel Trutch's granddaughter who is now in Phnom Penh?"

Catherine bristled inwardly. She had the impression that he already knew the answers to his questions and wanted only to rub salt in Catherine's still festering wound. What an arrogant prick. "Yes, but I fail to see how any of this is relevant."

"In police work, Madame, we must assume everything is relevant. Now, please tell me, what did you learn about this woman who was your husband's concubine in Nha Trang? Is she a resident of the cemetery next to the prison?"

The pompous ass. Who the hell did he think he was to crow this way? "Actually, yes. We found her grave."

"What was her name?"

Catherine sighed, reluctant to give him any more grist for whatever mill he was operating. But she felt trapped. "Her name was Nguyen Thi Tuyet."

"How did Colonel Trutch meet her?"

"He was *Captain* Trutch at the time. She worked for an American medical facility in Nha Trang. They met when he was at the hospital having shrapnel from an old wound removed from his jaw."

"Ah. That explains the scar on his cheek. So at some point he was in combat in this country. And that explains why this Miss Tuyet was sent to the re-education camp. She sold her country out to work for the American puppet masters. Many Vietnamese paid for that same mistake after the reunification. When your husband was in combat did he kill any Vietnamese people?"

"He never speaks of his combat experience. I just know that on his first tour of duty in this country, he was an infantry platoon leader. He saw plenty of battle."

"What was his unit on that first tour?"

"Captain Minh, I fail to see the reason behind this. I thought you were here to get a statement about an incident I witnessed yesterday."

"That's true. But in order to ensure that you remain safe while you visit my country, I need as much background about you and your husband as possible."

"I have a busy day. I'd appreciate it if you would leave me."

"As a general rule in my country, people don't tell the police when their business is concluded, Mrs. Trutch."

"Well, I certainly don't want to step on any cultural norms here. So I'll just ask if I might be excused … *sir*."

"OK. Thank you, Mrs. Trutch. Please give my regards to your husband when he calls tonight."

"And my statement about the policeman beating the motorbike operator?"

"Write it up and e-mail it to me. Here's my card."

***

Later that afternoon, Catherine took a long, shower, hoping to expunge the distasteful conversation with Captain Minh. As she toweled off, her skin creped slightly and she straightened to examine her nude body in the mirror over the dresser, turning first one way and then the other. A small wave of grief hit her. Her body wasn't bad for 63, but its preservation had come at a cost. She had almost drowned in grief at 30, when she learned that she could never bear a child. How odd to be childless all these years and then become in an instant a stepmother and a step-grandmother. A Nanny? A Grammy? She could be either, or something different altogether. If Lien were found, she hoped they would have a relationship. For the moment, she would wait it out in Saigon to see what developed with Pete in Cambodia.

CHAPTER TWENTY-FIVE

Trutch was jarred from a fitful sleep by the jangling phone in his room in the Blue Lime Hotel.

"Mr. Trutch, my name is Khlot. I'm a senior officer in the Cambodian National Police. We'd like you to come to the mortuary in the Khmer-Soviet Friendship Hospital to identify the remains of Andrew Quang. I will be waiting for you at the hospital's admissions and disposition desk."

"Oh God," Trutch whispered. "Which hospital was that again?"

"The Khmer-Soviet Friendship Hospital. Any taxi driver will know it."

Unable to respond, Trutch listened to Khlot end the conversation and replaced the receiver. He swung his bare feet to the floor and sat on the edge of his bed without moving. Icy disbelief coursed through him until he felt numb and dazed. His gut had been talking to him all night about the undercover mission that Andrew had so bravely or naively ventured upon the previous evening, and now here it was, the news that he had dreaded. Throughout the night his uneasiness had mounted. His sleepless pacing had increased when he talked with Catherine on the phone and she described the sinister meeting she had had with Captain Minh in Saigon. Now, Colonel Khlot's abrupt, matter-of-fact announcement of Andrew's death confirmed his worst fears.

He gave his head a shake and dressed hurriedly, stumbling into his trousers and nearly tripping when he scuffed too quickly into his shoes. As he did, he wondered if Andrew had been whacked by the police, if this call could be a ruse to set him up for an ambush as he left the hotel with the sun barely rising. This thought gained momentum in his imagination as he entered the lobby, where the desk clerk dozed lightly in his chair behind the reception counter.

To guard against the possibility of a trap, he exited the hotel through a back service entrance, walked down the back lane and, striving for invisibility in the shadows, strode briskly to the nearby Plantation Hotel where he climbed into a taxi. The drive to the hospital took only fifteen minutes in the pre-dawn traffic.

***

Khlot met him at the broadly arched front entrance to the hospital and led him past the reception desk and down a corridor where, unlike the Western practice of keeping morgues hidden from public view by burying them deep within the windowless bowels of the buildings that house them, the mortuary existed on a prominent ground-floor wing of the hospital, well lit by overhead fluorescent light fixtures. Early morning daylight had just begun to flood through high windows. The attendant was clad, not in a stiff white jacket, but in a brightly colored sport shirt and khaki trousers. A dozen canvas, army-style cots were arranged in two rows of six in the over-chilled room. Only one cot bore a body, covered by a brightly colored bamboo mat.

The attendant led Trutch and the policeman to the cot and lifted the mat. Although he knew what to expect, Trutch still felt a reflexive jolt when he gazed upon the pale and waxen face of Andrew Quang, unseeing eyes open wide.

Trutch murmured, "Yes. It's him. It's Andrew Quang."

Khlot said gruffly, "We have a few further questions for you, Mr. Trutch. But perhaps you'd like a moment or two alone with the … victim. We can meet in the hallway, then go for a coffee to discuss this."

"Yes. Thank you. Please give me a few minutes."

His scalp tingled as he looked down at Andrew's remains. Another fine young man brought down in the prime of life by his overzealous passion to right the wrongs in this world. Another young man, like those soldiers in his command so many years ago whose loyalty to him had caused their deaths. Guilt, grief, sadness and fatigue washed over him. He longed to be away from the pain of the cold, sterile morgue and in the warm haven of Catherine's arms.

Catherine. A disquieting thought took shape. Given all the malignity surrounding this child trafficking business, was Catherine in peril in Saigon? If they, whoever *they* were, would kill Andrew because he was nosing around would they stop at one death? Captain Minh was obviously a corrupt cop on the take, capable of selling anyone out for a buck. So what exactly should be read into his interrogation of Catherine? Was he a part of this web of evil on whose fringes he now found himself? He needed to get on the phone later today and tell Catherine to get herself onto a plane back to the States. Except Catherine wouldn't respond to that kind of assertiveness. He'd strongly encourage her to get home.

Then another thought struck him. If they succeeded in finding and rescuing

Lien, how damaged would she be? He hadn't allowed himself to think that Lien could be physically or emotionally bent beyond repair, but now, as he stared again at Andrew's face, he realized just how malevolent this nest of vipers could be. There is no moral belief system in this place, he thought. It's as though the evil inflicted on the country by Pol Pot and his Khmer Rouge forty years ago lives on in its former victims and their descendants.

He signaled the attendant, who had occupied himself with paperwork on the opposite side of the large room, and the man ushered Trutch out to the hallway, where Colonel Khlot waited alone.

"The hospital canteen is this way, Mr. Trutch. Let's have a coffee."

Still dazed, but with his mind now also scrambling through concerns, Trutch accompanied him down a set of stairs to the windowless basement cafeteria.

Khlot poured them each a coffee and then steered Trutch to a table. He sat across from him and said, "The victim had his hotel room key in his pocket. From the front desk, we were able to develop the fact that he checked in two days ago after arriving from Ho Chi Minh City. He was in the company of you and an Australian woman named Judith Grinder. We were able to determine that you are a retired US Army officer and that Ms. Grinder runs an NGO in Saigon. She is the wife of the Australian Consul General in that city. Can you tell me why the three of you have come to Phnom Penh together and why the victim was in Svay Pak last night in the company of two young American men?"

"Yes. Recently I have become interested in the problem of child trafficking. Both Andrew and Judith also work in this area. The two of them are aware that many Vietnamese children wind up here as sexual slaves. We traveled here together to try to get more of an understanding of the problem."

"May I ask just why, as an American, you are so interested in this subject?"

"Because, Colonel, it pisses me off. I think anybody who exploits innocent children for sexual purposes is an animal. And any culture that condones it is nothing short of bestial."

Colonel Khlot affected a smug smile. "Hmm. So what do you think Andrew Quang and two American university students were doing in Svay Pak? Were they looking for ... how you say ... *bestial* pleasure?"

"No. I suspect they were just trying to get an understanding of the depravity that goes on in Svay Pak."

"Mr. Trutch, I realize that many of you Westerners judge prostitution harshly. But I'd like to suggest to you that this practice is older than the references to it in your Bible. Prostitution has been a way for women to earn a living for centuries. It has also been, especially in this country, a way for men to have their physical needs met, for centuries. You are wrong to judge our culture just because it is different than yours."

"You misunderstood me, Colonel Khlot. I do not presume to have a judgment about prostitution. It's child exploitation — it's the rape and enslavement of little children — that I find reprehensible and indefensible."

"Things are not always as they seem to the Westerner in this country. We do not always see things as black or white, left or right. You cannot begin to understand our culture unless you have experienced what we have experienced as a people."

"I don't buy that bullshit. Our cultures may be different but we're all members of the human race. We may come from divergent societies but we should have our humanity in common. The sexual exploitation of children, whether for pleasure or for financial gain, is an unconscionable departure from everything that is human."

"You use many big English words. But they do not justify your desire to interfere in our way of life. This is still our country. We have our laws, and you should already know that child trafficking is against the law here. But the manner in which we enforce our laws is our own business and not yours. Now, I have another question for you." Khlot glanced down at a sheet of paper.

With another oily smile, he said, "The two young American men who were with Andrew Quang last night tell us he was looking for a specific child in Svay Pak. He gave them each a picture of her. Do you know anything about that?"

Trutch hesitated. There was no way to answer that question without falling into a trap. If he was honest with this guy, it could lessen the chances of finding Lien. On the other hand, getting caught in a lie could be counterproductive.

Finally, Trutch said, "No. I have no idea," but too late he realized that by avoiding the question for a few seconds, he had already revealed his hand.

***

Bill Anderson's raspy voice came through the phone like an out-of-tune sousaphone. "Pete, I understand things are turning to rat shit over there for you. How you doin' buddy?"

"I could be better, but who've you been talking to? What've you heard?"

"It's been a couple of weeks since I heard from you, so I phoned your room in the Continental Hotel and got Catherine. She told me what's going on. Sounds to me like you're in a snake pit, my friend. I mean … Jesus … it's the shits to hear about your young friend getting offed. Watch your ass, will you?"

"Yeah, losing Andrew was an agonizing blow. I've just come from IDing his body. It feels exactly the way it did when we lost soldiers all those years ago — a mixture of grief, anger, guilt, sadness. And yes, I'll watch my ass. But I'm more determined than ever to find Lien. It's the highest tribute I could pay to Andrew."

"His death really hit you hard, then."

Trutch was silent for a moment. "They're all hard. You remember that. You cope with the grief by focusing on the job at hand. That's what I need to do."

"Well, just don't go single-handedly charging up any hills. You're obviously up against some mean fuckers. What a nightmare."

"It's nightmarish, all right. Like something between Dante's Inferno and a horror movie. This whole child enslavement scene is evil, Bill. It's horrible. A lot of bad actors — cops, criminals, judges, politicians, petty thugs — all exploiting very real children. It's an ugly landscape."

"And going back was the right thing to do?

"Absolutely. I've met a number of good, decent people — humanitarians who are fighting to combat this scourge. They're an inspiration to me. I think I can return the support they've given me. Certainly if we find and rescue Lien, I'll want to continue helping them in some way."

"Apart from all this, are you finding anything to like about being back in Southeast Asia?"

"The women are still gorgeous in this part of the world."

"You licentious old fart. You're one lucky bugger to still have Catherine. Don't risk losing her."

"Wasn't it you who used to say, 'It doesn't matter where you get your appetite as long as you take your meals at home?"

"We all said shit like that when we were younger, all the macho posturing over beer and nachos. All I'm saying, buddy, is if I had a woman like Catherine, I wouldn't do anything to wrong her."

"And I won't either. But every time I see an attractive young woman over here I'm reminded of Dream and it eats at me. I was a cad to both of them, Catherine and Dream, and it's haunting me. I had a two-month fling with Dream and then just flew off into the sunset, leaving her pregnant — even if we didn't really know it at the time. But the result was the same — I left her vulnerable to the punishment she ultimately received."

"What else could you have done, buddy? You couldn't very well take her back to the States and say, 'Catherine, look what followed me home.'"

"Yeah, well. But now that I know she was raped and died in prison … God, the guilt I feel."

"Shit, man. You were young and randy, and dealing with shit no one should have to, especially at that age. You can't blame yourself for having hormones."

"But I can blame myself for walking away. I think I hurt her badly."

"Sounds like this trip's taking a toll. You're introspective, maudlin even. I hope you don't get too syrupy to have a scotch with your buddies once you're home."

"No problem there. Let's just say I'm discovering I have a soft side."

CHAPTER TWENTY-SEVEN

The cavernous customs hall of Los Angeles International Airport was utilitarian and sterile, its hundreds of people faceless to Customs and Border Protection Officer Thomas Lowen until they reached his station as individuals. Lowen had been at this job for 19 years and, although the work was often monotonous, he considered the pay not bad and the benefits excellent. He was beginning to think about retirement. With his anticipated federal pension and a nice low-stress part-time job, perhaps clerking in a grocery store, he and Beth would have it made, and they could enjoy their 22-foot travel trailer for longer and more frequent getaways up and down the California coast.

Like most well-trained customs and immigration officers, he was a careful observer of nonverbal behavior and a wary listener. He knew every ruse and sham in the book and had an uncanny ability to spot the tiniest, most minute nuances of attempted deception. Despite the monotony of his duties, his well-honed vigilance and consequent success rate at identifying liars and smugglers was legendary among his colleagues. Over coffee and donuts one officer had declared, "Man, if I had a crap detector like Lowen's, I wouldn't be working for CBP. I'd be up in Las Vegas gettin' filthy rich by calling bluffs. What's the key to your success, Lowen?"

"I guess it just takes a bull shitter to know a bull shitter," he had replied with "Aw shucks" modesty.

Lowen had just returned to his wicket in the primary screening area from a coffee break. It had been a routine morning of scanning passports, checking faces and making cryptic marks on declaration cards and traveler entry forms. Now, fully charged after a morning hit of caffeine, he looked out at the long cattle-like queues of travelers just off two jumbo jets, one from Hong Kong and the other from Singapore.

The fourth traveler in line was a scrofulous-looking Caucasian man wearing camouflage cargo pants and a red t-shirt with an image of Che Guevera on the front. He presented an American passport and rubbed the stubble on his chin. He was completely bald above the ears, but around the edges of his head he had scraggly gray hair reaching to his shoulders.

Thomas Lowen asked, "Where have you been, Mr. Bates?" as he scanned the man's passport into the computer system.

"Cambodia and Singapore."

Lowen studied the computer screen for a few seconds, then held the passport up and looked closely at the traveler's face, perhaps for a bit longer than he would normally. Finally, he stamped the passport, made a couple of marks with a red felt tip pen on Mr. Bates' declaration card and handed the documents back to him. "Okay. Welcome home. Collect your luggage at the carousel and present this card to the officer at the door."

Mr. Bates waited at the crowded carousel for fifteen minutes before claiming his two pieces of luggage, an older model American Tourister suitcase and a navy blue sports duffle. The officer standing at the exit of the customs hall glanced at his declaration card and said, "Sir, you've been selected for a secondary inspection. Follow me, please."

***

For the second morning in a row, the phone in Trutch's room announced an incoming call with a scratchy clatter. Just out of the shower and toweling off, he thought it might be Catherine. He snatched the cordless phone off the night stand and spoke into the receiver with an enthusiastic, "Good Morning."

"Colonel Trutch, it's Brad Cassidy at the embassy. Can you get over here in about thirty minutes? I think we have an important lead."

Twenty-five minutes later, Cassidy, Trutch and a female imagery interpreter sat before a computer screen in Cassidy's office. "This won't be easy to watch," Cassidy observed. "It's one clip in a series of videos on a flash drive seized by Homeland Security in Los Angeles. The perp is some dude named Bates who sang like a bird when told he was about to be charged with possessing and trafficking child pornography." He paused to glance at a sheet of lined yellow paper. "Get this: Gerome Bates is a defrocked physician from Texas. A pediatrician, for Chrissakes. Anyway, he told the FBI investigators in LA that this particular scene was shot in a brothel in Svay Pak."

The imagery interpreter flicked a remote. Instantly a color image of an Asian girl, no more than about 12, appeared on the screen. The video clip showed her nude, lying on her back, and fingering her genitals with two hands.

Trutch took a close look at the expression on her face and concluded that her actions were performed under coercion — not for pleasure.

The interpreter froze the video on a close-up of the girl's face and said, "Look at her eyes, Mr. Trutch. She looks as though she has some Caucasian blood."

Trutch felt nauseated, "Are you suggesting …?"

"Yes sir. We've enhanced this image and our analysts have compared it to the picture you provided Mr. Cassidy of your granddaughter. We think it's her."

Trutch choked back a bit of bile. "But do you know exactly where this is?"

"This Bates asshole provided enough detail to pinpoint the building that houses the brothel. We've had it under surveillance for a day and although there's a lot of coming and going, our resources haven't seen any underage girls on the premises. But that's not surprising and it doesn't mean they're not there. The proprietors, a couple named Mau and Nakry, would keep them as virtual sex slaves, locked in their quarters when they're not working."

"What's next? Will you organize a raid?"

"I'm sure you understand, Colonel Trutch, we can't raid this place ourselves. All we can do is go to our counterparts in the Cambodian National Police with evidence that might persuade *them* to conduct a raid. But we need to do this in such a way that they're not tempted to forewarn the perpetrators in exchange for a bribe. I can't tell you how many times we've influenced the authorities to raid these places only for them to report the next morning that they found the premises empty."

"Call me Pete, please. Can the police be persuaded to conduct a raid without knowing the location until they're already underway in their vehicles?"

"That has worked once that I know of. One of the NGOs developed intelligence pointing to a brothel using under-aged children. The managing director, an American and a devout Christian, went to a Cambodian police captain whom he knew to be a Christian as well. He persuaded him that busting this brothel was exactly what God wanted them to do. Of course, he also reminded the captain of his mandate as a law enforcement official. So the raid went down with only the American knowing the specific location of the target until the last minute."

"And the results?"

"Jackpot. The proprietor and two of her pimps were arrested. Four girls were rescued and turned over to the Ministry of Education, Youth and Sport — MoEYS for short — who in turn delivered them to a shelter run by another Christian NGO here in PP. That was a year ago. Three of the girls are still in rehabilitation — intensive counseling, group therapy, basic skills training, general education and so forth. The eldest girl, a 17-year-old, left the shelter on her own and went back to hooking."

"Jesus, why would she do that?"

"The most common motive is addiction. As sex slaves, the girls become dependent on methamphetamines."

Trutch nodded.

"Unfortunately, the postscript to this story is that the perps spent not one night in jail and never faced a judge. The mama-san had lined other police pockets, so all three of them were back on the street within hours, and she had a stable full of new girls within a matter of days."

Trutch grunted and rested his chin in the palm of his hand. Hampered by the local climate of corruption and sluggish bureaucratic inertia, the rescue he had envisioned wouldn't be easy. Quang's death had rattled him, but the only way to avenge that tragedy was to get on with the mission. He felt caught in an insidious cesspool, where both cops and criminals bobbed and floated like turds, while he was forced to watch from the sidelines.

"Does anyone ever undertake to rescue some of these kids without the involvement of the local cops?" he asked Cassidy.

"It's sometimes done. But an NGO that has evidence will usually attempt to use moral suasion first. They'll take the facts they've collected to the police and say something like, 'Look, here is the evidence. Here is your law. Let us help you enforce it.' As an aside, the argument can usually be ramped up if there's a Western predator, or predators, involved — especially an American. Some of the aid we provide to this government can be linked to their cooperation in executing warrants. They also know that we'll extradite US citizens accused of pedophilia, so they don't have to bother with a trial themselves."

"But what about NGOs or concerned persons doing a rescue without police involvement?"

"Although it's morally justified, it still amounts to kidnapping and can be very dangerous, so it's not advisable. That said, if the circumstances are truly dire, an NGO may take matters into their own hands. But before you go off on your own, let me tell you about a little scheme I'm cooking up.

"I need to think this through and run it past some other folks here in the embassy, but I'm aware of a CNN news team in Thailand. They're working on a documentary about the political turbulence that has been going on in that country for the past six years. Now this is what I'm proposing…"

CHAPTER TWENTY-EIGHT

Just looking at the breakfast made Catherine sick. There was so much of it. Not that it looked or smelled unappetizing. Far from it. Even the steam from the rice soup had a fragrant nutty odor. And she knew those little glutinous packets of softened rice paper would be delicious, filled with whatever. She was enjoying the food in Vietnam, even when she couldn't identify the ingredients, and any other time the variety of dishes would have delighted her, but not this morning.

Since Pete's call last night, when he told her about identifying Andrew's body and the interrogation by Colonel Khlot, every sound made her jittery. Her sleep, when she finally got to sleep, was filled with nightmares. Andrew's murder put the whole trip in a shocking new light. And then Pete had added to the tension by reacting vehemently to the tale of her encounter with Captain Minh. Now, as much as she hoped for a relaxing, stress-free day, her recollection of the conversation had her nerves in knots.

"What did he want?" Pete had asked. "What did you tell him? What on earth did you do to attract his attention in the first place?" He hadn't shouted at her, but she hadn't heard that authoritarian, army officer voice in years. "I don't want you to leave the Continental until I get back there," he said.

"And when will that be, Colonel Trutch? I'm not about to sit locked in my room while you're off chasing criminals." She had surprised herself with that, all strident and bristling. He was, after all, only expressing his concern. But given how tired she was, his tone had been scary and disorienting.

"I'm so sorry I've dragged you into this, sweetie," he said, before she could apologize. "It's bigger and uglier than I imagined."

"But Pete, you didn't drag me into this. I came of my own accord. Remember? I honestly thought I could be useful. I even thought that we might have a few days to enjoy ourselves. When do you think you'll be back in Saigon?"

"Things are so uncertain," he said, all the tension and grief of the last few days evident in his voice. "I know we're getting close to Lien, but we're hamstrung by police inertia. To know she's that close and be unable to act torments me. I didn't know that I could care so intensely about someone I've never met. My heart aches for both her and Ngoc. I'll dash back to Saigon if you need me to. You know that. Or, if you're too frightened, you could just fly home."

"I'll think about it. But something tells me that I'm here for a reason. The other day at the pagoda and finding Dream's grave were almost spiritual experiences for me. I've been thinking about how fragile life is, and I'm so fortunate, so privileged. There must be something I can do to ease the pain for Ngoc and Lien, and for you too. This must be quite a burden for you."

"No kidding. The last few days I've been plagued with misgivings. I've been questioning my behavior and my expectations. No sleep, little food and too much adrenaline for an old guy. It's all taking its toll. I can hardly wait for it all to be over and get back to the sanity of Seattle, but I have to see this through. I hope you understand."

She had reassured him that she did understand. But now, as she stood feeling woozy, staring at the bountiful breakfast table, the food all looked decidedly distasteful. Fleetingly, she thought it was also obscene, given the simplicity of the meal at the pagoda yesterday.

"It's a bit overwhelming isn't it?"

Catherine turned to see who owned that Australian accent, and discovered a smiling face below masses of red curls, the woman's plate heaped with fruit, a Danish pastry and a cup of yogurt.

"It takes me a few days to ease off and not be a glutton," the Aussie said.

"I think all I can manage is a coffee at the moment," Catherine said, her voice wan as she meandered away to the beverages table. Armed with a coffee, she sat and stared at the wallpaper while she sipped it and attempted to decompress.

"Would you like some company?" the Australian asked. "I'm not a tourist, so I won't be grilling you about what attraction you're going to today, or how long you're staying. I'd love to know what news you have from home and if the elections are pleasing you."

"Oh gosh, I'm American. And as far as I know there are no elections at the moment." Despite her glum frame of mind, Catherine laughed. "I don't think I've been mistaken for an Aussie before. But I'm in a fog this morning. I won't be much company."

"That's OK," the woman said, and plunked her huge breakfast plate down. She lowered herself into the chair opposite Catherine. "I'm Alison, from Brisbane, and I'm in Ho Chi Minh City to audit some of the operations here for my boss back home. Queasy tummy this morning? I have every known cure stashed in my suitcase. I come prepared for all digestive emergencies."

Catherine looked up from her coffee cup, prepared to be annoyed at the intrusion. Instead, on seeing the warm empathy on Alison's face, she felt a tear sliding down her cheek.

"Oops," said Alison. "It really is a bad day, isn't it? I'm sorry for barging in. Shall I drift off or would you like to talk? I can listen, despite my overactive tongue."

"I do feel rather alone," Catherine confessed. "I'm so overwhelmed with this country and our reasons for being here. My husband's in Cambodia at the moment, in Phnom Penh. And I'm here trying to make the best of it in this mad city."

"Should we start with those reasons for being in Vietnam? In my years of travel here, I think I've heard them all. My work for a philanthropist has cast me into circumstances that I couldn't even imagine before I signed on as his field agent."

An hour later, after another cup of coffee, Catherine finally ran out of words.

"The sex trade and the threat to young, poor Vietnamese girls is something that I'm aware of," Alison revealed. "My boss is a veteran who made buckets of money after he left the service. He retired eight years ago, but he never forgot the devastation he witnessed here, so he has decided to invest his time and money in helping. My job is to monitor the projects. Say, would you like to come with me today? I'll be checking out things at an orphanage. Sounds like you could use a diversion."

"Oh, no, thanks for the offer, but I don't want to get in the way. I had a scary day on the road the day before yesterday, when we went to a pagoda and looked for Dream's grave."

"I understand, believe me. But I have a very good driver and a safe air-conditioned car. I'd enjoy the companionship. Besides, the children at the orphanage are starving for attention. You could get a kid-fix while I bury my nose in administrivia."

"That does sound like a welcome diversion from all this tension. How soon should I be ready?"

"Meet me in the lobby in 20 minutes. And bring a change of clothes in case I get snarled up in something and we have to stay overnight." She produced a business card and chuckled. "Here, you'd better have this, so you know I'm who I say I am."

***

Catherine made a quick attempt to reach Pete by phone and failed. Instead, she left a message about her planned outing, and then threw a few things in her small backpack. With her passport and medications in her purse, she settled into the back seat of a large SUV, the interior both luxurious and cool.

Alison sank into the leather upholstery beside her and buried her nose in a bundle of documents, while Catherine stared out the window at the sights — block after block of consumerism. Appliance stores, computer stores, cell phone stores and furniture shops stood like a dike containing the miasma of carbon monoxide through which they drove. Hopefully, another day in the countryside would be therapeutic.

She snapped out of her reverie as she realized that she had no idea where she was going. Alison was now also gazing out the window, so Catherine broke the silence in the car to ask, "Could you tell me a little more about the orphanage we're visiting? How did your boss get involved? And I didn't even ask where it is!"

"We're on Highway 15, headed for Dau Tieng," Alison answered. "About eight years ago, Ed, my boss, first stopped there on his way to Tay Ninh. At that time, more than 150 children lived there, but the place was severely underfunded. The locals gave what they could, and some dedicated women from the village helped as volunteers, but they had a huge shortfall and the babies just kept coming."

"But why? Are these all children of unwed mothers?"

"Not all. The area, like so many places in post-war Vietnam, had been devastated, first by the war and then by the severe rules and collectivization by the Communist government. Everyone was hungry. Parents couldn't feed their children and girls and children with disabilities were considered a burden."

Catherine shook her head in dismay. "So your boss, Ed, decided right then to give financial aid?"

"Right. It's been six years now. Last year we invested in a new classroom and special equipment for disabled children. I can hardly wait to see it in operation."

"I'm looking forward to it, too. It will be good to see the results of some well-directed aid. Besides, it's nice to be away from Saigon and off Captain Minh's radar for the day."

"Who?" Alison asked with a start. With a look of alarm, she swung her head toward Catherine.

"Captain Minh. He's the cop that bugged me in the hotel the other day. He seems to want to know too much about Pete and me, although he did give Pete the lead that took him to Cambodia. Why, the look of shock?"

"My God, Catherine. I know of this Captain Minh. He's a bad one — always willing to sell people out for a few dollars. I don't mean to frighten you, but it's rumored that people have died violently because of his duplicity."

"Oh dear Jesus." Catherine thought about Andrew Quang's death. Was Minh responsible? "Alison, I need a phone."

"Here. Use my cell. By all means call your husband and alert him."

CHAPTER TWENTY-NINE

At 10:05 p.m., Trutch stood beside Brad Cassidy under the corrugated metal overhang of a sidewalk coffee stand. The hot night air was thick enough to taste and the steamy rain drumming on the roof overhead sounded like a cavalry charge. A blinding flash of lightning exposed sky the color of eggplant, briefly illuminating the grated metal gate of the building across the muddy road — the target. Trutch worried a coin in his pocket. So far in this quest he had experienced three pieces of luck — finding Uncle Vu, learning from Minh that Lien was in Cambodia and seeing the videotape evidence that had led them here. Trutch's long military and business experience made him wary of too much luck.

Two days ago, when Cassidy had briefed Trutch on the planned raid, he was only guardedly optimistic that it could be brought to fruition. Keeping the target location secret until the last minute was dicey with so many bad cops and the ever-present temptation of payoffs. Brad had managed to persuade Brigadier General Banak, the deputy director of the Anti-Human Trafficking and Juvenile Protection Department of the Cambodian National Police, that there would be favorable publicity for the police if they planned and executed a secret raid of a specific brothel in Svay Pak. After all, CNN had a global reach. The anti-trafficking police, doing their job efficiently and effectively, would be featured on the world stage thanks to satellite uplinks and global television audiences, always hungry for action-packed stories.

But this was Southeast Asia and one could never be certain of anyone. After all General Banak's predecessor, the former deputy director, was himself convicted of involvement in trafficking in 2006 and sentenced to five years in prison. And Captain Minh's dishonesty, all the more undeniable since Catherine's phone call from somewhere near Dau Tieng three hours ago, had raised more questions, which he would have to think about later. Here and now, the action was about to start.

Three police vehicles approached, their muscular engines growling, high intensity headlights boring through the gloomy downpour like laser beams.

Twenty-five years of military conditioning kicked in and long dormant impulses triggered an adrenaline rush. This felt good. He was in on the action again.

Doors flew open. Booted feet hit the ground. Twelve helmeted policemen brandishing flashlights and riot batons charged through the gate, crossed the small courtyard and exploded into the two-story building. Immediately behind the three police trucks an SUV pulled up and two CNN newsmen jumped out, laden with portable camera equipment. They followed the cops into the building.

"Let's go," Cassidy shouted, as they raced across the mucky road. "We can follow them on their sweep but be careful. This can be dangerous. Taking product away from a brothel owner is like taking cocaine away from a drug dealer."

As Trutch and Cassidy entered the small courtyard, the panic and chaos inside ramped up to the level of terror. Female voices shrieked, male policemen barked orders and warnings. Other male voices, perhaps those of pimps or customers, yelled defiantly.

He and Cassidy wheeled though the door and into the tiny front room. Trutch caught a fleeting glimpse of overturned cheap plastic furniture. Broken bottles and glasses littered the floor. Several middle-aged men attempted to hide their faces from the probing TV cameras. Two young girls cowered in one corner wailing, their hands covering their eyes.

The cops worked their way down the thin corridor, charging through beaded curtains into the working rooms where more girls howled. Men attempted to cover both their faces and their nudity. A few cursed at the cops and the prying camera of the CNN crew.

Trutch followed the camera crew, watching intently for Lien while attempting to reassure the panicky young girls. "It's okay. It's okay,' he said repeatedly. When he took their hands to reassure them, they shrank from his touch. They had no idea what was happening. To them he was just another older Western man, a threat. He was one more john, here to hurt them. He managed to take two girls by the hands and lead them back to the front room, away from the melee, where he seated them on an overturned settee. "You'll be okay. You'll be okay," he whispered to them, then he ran back down the corridor hoping to find Lien.

As the cops moved along the corridor, some charged up the stairs toward the girls' quarters and some down to the basement toward Mau's torture chamber.

Trutch remained on the main floor corridor with Cassidy, listening to meaty thumps as fists and riot batons smacked into flesh. There were more screams, both young female and older male. From behind him he heard the unmistakable blast of a pistol shot followed by a loud crash of breaking glass and shattering wood.

"Back this way," shouted Cassidy. "That came from a front room above."

The two of them spun around, darted through the tiny front room and up the spiral staircase to the second floor. The tiny room was filled with smoke, its only window shattered. The body of a policeman lay on the floor near the small kitchenette, a crimson puddle spreading around his head and shoulders. Trutch took in the scene and concluded the assailant, or assailants, had gone through the window after shooting the policeman. Maybe they had been in the act of escaping through the window, perhaps with some of the girls, when the cop arrived on the second floor and ordered them to halt.

A middle-aged woman stood at the doorway to a small bedroom staring defiantly at them. "I am Nakry," she said in broken English. "I own this house and business. You cannot do this."

Trutch took two steps to reach the woman. He grabbed her wrist and twisted it behind her back. "Where is the girl called Lotus?" he demanded. She was silent. His face twisted into a knot of fury while he further wrenched her arm into a hammerlock. "Where is Lotus? Where is Lien?" She turned her head and spat defiantly into his face. He released her from the hammerlock and backhanded her across the cheek. "Where is she? Where is she? You tell me."

Cassidy grabbed Trutch by the arm. "Jesus, man. Cool it. She's not going to tell you, even if she knows."

The raid ended as abruptly as it had started. Six young girls were wrapped in blankets and placed in the front room, where they huddled in a corner, while Nakry and several adult males were led to the police vehicles.

As one senior police officer began an initial interrogation of the terrified girls, Trutch noted their vacant, dazed looks. Several were trembling. Two wore scanty underwear under the blankets, while the others were clad in skimpy, cheap dresses. Their skin, having not seen sunshine or fresh air in some time, was sallow. When he realized Lien was not among them, Trutch's shoulders sagged. The adrenaline which had fueled his excitement and energy no longer coursed through his body. Instead, he felt overwhelmed with fatigue.

Cassidy explained to Trutch that the girls too would be driven downtown. They, as well as the adults apprehended, would be interviewed in an attempt to sort out who was who. A lengthy, deliberate process would determine the perps, the johns and those who had got away. "Come on. Let's go downtown. We won't be allowed to sit in on the interviews, but we can badger the cops to give us the lowdown once they've finished sorting things out."

CHAPTER THIRTY

Trutch remained silent and sullen as they traveled the 10 kilometers back to the central business district.

Cassidy drove. "I know you're upset that Lien wasn't there, Pete. But on the positive side, six girls have been sprung from sex slavery. It's likely that the cops will hand all six of them over to MoEYS and from there they will go into aftercare, rehabilitation. We should feel good that some lives may have been saved tonight."

"I guess so," said Trutch. "But I feel like I have two strikes against me. Andrew Quang is dead and Lien has disappeared. I spoke with Andrew's parents in Australia this morning. That wasn't an easy conversation. Now I'll have to tell Ngoc that we came up empty in an attempt to rescue his daughter."

"Yeah. It's a big disappointment."

Neither man spoke for the next 10 minutes. The somnolent effect of the tires humming on the wet pavement and the hypnotic swooshing of the window wipers lulled Trutch into a trance-like state. He emerged from his torpor only as the downtown area came into view through a hazy prism of heavy rain, where neon and fluorescent lights reflected off a layer of clouds to give the lower sky the texture of greenish vapor.

Trutch turned toward Cassidy, whose face was illuminated by the amber glow of dashboard lights. "In spite of the shitty results, I have to compliment you on a brilliant plan. Using the promise of CNN publicity as an inducement for the police to act was a stroke of genius."

"Actually, I can't take credit for it. This was a replication of an NBC Nightline segment shot here in Svay Pak during a raid 15 years ago. That footage created a huge wave of outrage, even before the social media craze. Follow-on global media attention and diplomatic pressure resulted in things improving in Svay Pak for a short time. But it didn't take long, once the world moved on to more topical news, for business to get back to usual." He glanced sideways at Trutch.

"The social milieu in Svay Pak is cyclical and volatile. Occasional showcase crackdowns and raids by the police and armed forces, alternating with extortion by the same agencies, cause the brothel owners to suffer from time to time. So they develop devious means and shady alliances in order to survive. Many of the mama sans and pimps are in patronage relationships with government officials and judges, so they rarely get arrested. When they do, they're usually back in business in a matter of days. I have no doubt tonight's event will play out the same way. The best we can hope for is that six girls get into rehab."

"I suppose that's something. Still, this evening feels like a big setback for me."

Cassidy merely nodded.

A few minutes later, Trutch found his voice again. "Some cities in the States have attempted to clean up prostitution by arresting the johns as well as the operators. The theory is that the stigma of arrest, along with a range of negative publicity for the stalwart citizens caught *in flagrante*, will be a deterrent for others."

"It won't work here. Arrests, convictions and the frequent deportation of *foreign* predators are a device used to relieve some of the pressure exerted by the international community. But the majority of the pedophiles who make up the demand for child prostitution are locals and almost never prosecuted. This practice is too deeply ingrained in the culture. It's considered acceptable male behavior. What's more, the police, the military and many government officials are not only involved in profit taking from this business, but they're customers as well. I'm afraid this problem is fed by a complex system of corruption and greed, and by social norms and definitions of acceptable behavior that differ greatly from our own."

"Yeah. Three days ago when I identified Andrew's body, I was told, in so many words, by a police colonel named Khlot that I have no right to judge the Cambodian male's morality."

"Ha. Yes. And Khlot's one of the good guys. Cooperative, usually willing to help us. But he's still a Cambodian, set in his beliefs and no doubt also reaping the benefits, both business and pleasure, of the prostitution game."

They were driving south on Sisowath Quay along the dark and roily waters of the Tonle Sap River. "I didn't have a chance to speak to the two young men who were with Andrew when he was shot," said Trutch. "Do you know what their situation is?"

"Yes, they were questioned by the Cambodian police, but not detained.

One of our consular people met with them at the police station. They were shaken up and wanted to get back to the States as soon as they could. Our folks helped them obtain tickets for early the next day. They were probably at the airport by the time you went to the mortuary to ID Andrew's body. We have their contact information, in case you wish to reach them at some point."

"Yes, I would. And I'm sure Andrew's parents would want to speak with them as well. I'll pass the contact information onto them." His mood had almost imperceptibly migrated from despondency back to determination. "We *will* find Lien."

"Yes, and here's the police station, coming up on the right. Now comes the tricky part. Finding a parking place."

***

Inside the station, Trutch and Cassidy were made to wait for three hours in a small office. It had stopped raining and a few early hints of dawn shone through the only window in the room when at last a Cambodian policeman, with numerous brassy adornments on his uniform, came out to speak with them. Brad introduced him to Trutch as Brigadier General Banak. Tall and officious-looking, Banak shook hands with Trutch and then seated himself and smiled broadly at the two Americans.

"All six of the girls are underaged prostitutes," he said, still smiling solicitously. "Naturally, they're traumatized, but they've been helpful. They're speaking with two of our female officers. A social worker from the Ministry of Education, Youth and Sport has joined in on the interview. The five men we brought in, all Cambodians, are customers. Needless to say they're embarrassed. But proving in court that they actually had sex with these underage girls would be next to impossible. Therefore they will be released."

Once again, bile churned in Trutch's stomach. He closed and opened both fists, but said nothing.

The general continued. "The mature woman is named Nakry and she owns the house and the business. We'll discuss with the prosecutors and the judiciary whether she should ... uh ... be charged with anything. A decision must be made as to whether there is enough evidence to charge her." Trutch and Cassidy exchanged glances. "Two men escaped through the upstairs window after ruthlessly killing our young member. One of them is named Mau. He is Nakry's partner. The other is a man called Luong, a trafficker. We want these men."

Trutch spoke. "Have the girls spoken of other girls who may have been there? I'm interested in knowing about one who goes by the name Lotus."

"This girl, Lotus, is also named Lien," Cassidy chimed in. "She's Mr. Trutch's granddaughter."

Banak glanced down at his notes. "There are actually two girls missing according to the others. One has been missing without explanation for several days. Her name is Thanh. The other one *was* called Lotus. She was last seen by the other girls late yesterday afternoon, several hours before the raid."

Trutch's exhaustion melted away. He leaned forward in his chair. "Can I speak to these girls? I need to know more about my granddaughter."

"That wouldn't be a good idea, Mr. Trutch. The girls are too wary right now. They'd be scared of another man coming in to see them. But if you'd care to wait a while longer, I'll see if our female members can find out anything more about the one called Lotus."

An hour and a half later, Banak again entered the small office. "All we were able to learn about Lotus was that she came to Cambodia about six weeks ago along with another 13-year-old who goes by Diamond. Diamond is exceedingly traumatized, almost incoherent. She said only that two men brought them from a hotel in Saigon in the back of a dirty truck. That's all we have."

***

Trutch opened the minibar and selected one of the tiny two-ounce bottles of scotch, which he poured over ice cubes. It had been an emotional night. How totally his daily life had changed in the matter of a few short weeks since he had opened that letter in his kitchen on Queen Anne Hill. He now had a son he'd only recently met and a granddaughter. Because of them, he had stepped into a gritty world. Immersed in this web of trafficking and unspeakable child abuse, he'd met corrupt cops, impotent government officials and well-meaning but under-resourced do-gooders. He had been emotionally moved by the courage of Ngoc and by the goodness and helpfulness of Andrew, who had taken on the cause of rescuing Lien as though she were his own blood. And Catherine — even though he'd kept his affair with Dream secret for four decades, Catherine was committed to helping him, both determined to learn what had become of Dream and supportive of his efforts to find Lien.

He pictured Andrew's corpse in the morgue and wondered if Catherine or Judith Grinder were now in harm's way from supporting his nosing around in the underbelly of Southeast Asian life.

Four weeks earlier, he had been a semi-retired executive enjoying a good life — the fruits of many years' worth of hard work — with a good woman at his side in a peaceful and progressive city in the United States. Now, here he sat in one of the world's most impoverished countries, where four short decades ago a madman ordered the execution of three million countrymen because of ideology. Now children were chattels and people died in the street at the hands of their own police merely for expressing themselves.

Could any single person, or even a well-organized NGO, make a difference in a country where police and government officials were corrupt? Perhaps not in a big way. Child trafficking, police brutality and autocracy all seemed to be tied together in one big invasive disease — like cancer. But people like Judith Grinder and Chakra Dith were making a difference one girl at a time, at least in the realm of child trafficking. That did something to arrest a small part of the malignancy, at least, and provided something to build on. For now, he cared primarily about finding Lien, but what about later when her situation was resolved? Could he make a difference?

CHAPTER THIRTY-ONE

The orphanage in Dau Tieng, a pagoda-like building of white stucco that gleamed picturesquely, topped by a red-tiled roof, looked like just the place to find peace of mind, and Catherine's first look at the grounds convinced her that this was the tonic she needed. The tiled courtyard was ablaze with flowers growing in huge pots and a large pond where lotus flowers bloomed and languid golden koi glided. She desperately needed this reprieve from her apprehension about Captain Minh and her continuing worries about Pete's safety.

"Oh my gosh," she said when she entered the nursery, a wrinkle of surprise forming on her forehead. "It's so tranquil. Just beautiful. And they're all so sweet. It brings tears to my eyes."

Behind them, a peasant woman swept the already spotless stairs. Inside, a clutch of children toddled about, all dressed smartly, the girls in little dresses with Peter Pan collars, the boys in blue shorts and white t-shirts. Babies and toddlers sprawled everywhere, segregated by age, the infants asleep, rolled like sausages in their blankets, the crawlers in one "cage" and toddlers staggering around in another. Attendants busily ministered to each group, feeding, changing diapers, playing and refereeing, the vast room divided into areas, with cribs lining the walls, and fenced and matted floor space in between.

My God it was crowded, Catherine thought.

"You must try not to weep," said Alison. "We Westerners understand tears of joy, tears when we're overwhelmed, different tears. Here, tears often mean just plain sorrow and can be misinterpreted. Vietnamese are proud. If we cry, they could read that as pity or censure. Your tears could stem from your appreciation of the enormity of what they're doing, but the caregivers don't know that. It's tricky terrain for even the most skilled interpreter, so best avoided."

For twenty years, Co Minh Hanh, the director, had been taking in abandoned children in an effort to give them a loving home, Alison had explained. With almost 30 children in the room, what she had accomplished seemed miraculous to Catherine.

She didn't want to cry. She wanted to help. What were those privileged, dotcom mothers in Seattle thinking, she wondered, when they obsessed about attachment parenting, or enrolling their little urchins in the right preschools, or spending $500 on strollers the size of aircraft carriers? What if, instead, there was some way to create better awareness and divert that excess energy into more positive assistance in the Third World? She clambered over the little fence into the cage of infants and rolled up her sleeves.

Thirty minutes into the job of cuddling and comforting, Catherine stepped out of the enclosure, stretched and wandered to the window. Outside, a small girl with a big stick tried to herd some wayward ducks back into the flock she was steering toward the opposite side of the road. How little she looked — no more than seven or eight, Catherine guessed. Dirty face, dirty clothes and bare feet. What was she doing alone on the road? Why was she not in school?

But the adroit tyke soon had all the ducks obediently in the far ditch as she shepherded them along.

Then Catherine stepped suddenly back from the window and drew a sharp breath. She stood sideways behind the window frame to watch as three young men in cheap polyester slacks and white open-collared shirts sat astride motionless motorbikes. They talked animatedly and gestured toward the orphanage.

Oh my God, cops, Catherine thought. They had a look she now recognized. She felt the blood drain from her face and immediately sank into a folding metal chair.

A young nursery attendant ran over to her and knelt. Gently, she took Catherine's hand with both of hers. "Are you okay, Miss Catherine? What the matter?"

Catherine took several deep breaths to slow her pulse rate. "I will be. I'm fine. Maybe I just need some water."

As the attendant scurried off to fetch a bottle of water, Catherine rose and, hidden from view, peered through the window again. The men were gone.

Now she imagined them crashing through the nursery door to seize her. Any second now they would come, and she couldn't let that happen in front of all these children. She made her way across the room full of toddlers and infants and gripped the door handle with trembling hands. She stepped into the covered breezeway.

The men did not come for her.

As her heart rate slowed and her color returned to normal, a surge of anger toward Pete gripped her. He had not only buggered off to Cambodia and left her in harm's way, but he had yelled at her on the phone when she told him of her interrogation by Captain Minh. That bastard. How could he be so selfish and insensitive?

She took a breath. And then another. Wait. Wasn't what he was doing selfless rather than selfish? Attempting to help his granddaughter was a good thing to do. And didn't she tell him so herself as he was leaving Seattle? The real problem was that this country had knocked her sideways. She needed to slow down, take a few more deep breaths and try to think rationally. Pete was a good man. It might take time, but she'd get over the hurt that his long ago betrayal had caused. She ran a hand through her hair, opened the door again, and returned to her duties in the nursery.

***

An hour later, still somewhat shaken but composed, Catherine entered the dining room and sat next to Alison and close to Co Minh Hanh, who sat at the head of the table.

"Busy morning?" asked Alison.

"Ups and downs."

"You look a little rattled. Kids get to you?"

"Oh, I'm just frazzled. Too much emotional energy for my age, I guess."

Co Minh Hanh gestured towards the many dishes of steaming food on the table, indicating that they should eat.

Uncertain, Catherine waited to judge the protocol, not wanting to appear rude or overeager.

But within seconds the older woman, smiling and nodding, put a variety of food into Catherine's bowl.

Catherine began sampling. Each morsel was delicately flavored — curried vegetables, rice, noodles, tofu and spring rolls. She helped herself to a couple of small pancakes to hold the crispy greens, along with nuoc mam and soy for dipping.

"Oh shit," Alison whispered.

Catherine looked up to see the three men from the motorbikes entering the dining room. Her heart seized. She dropped a chopstick, which clanged when it struck the side of a glass and then rattled as it hit the floor. Once again, she felt herself paling as both fear and anger washed over her.

"Excuse me," Alison said, and she leapt up from her chair. Rapid Vietnamese and faltering English flew between the players. Slowly Co Minh Hanh rose from her chair and ushered the group into her office.

Catherine stayed at the table, as her appetite once again evaporated. Why had they not invited her to the office? Were they discussing her? Alison knew only a few of the details of the saga that had been unfolding for her and Pete. Maybe she shouldn't have trusted her.

Unsure whether to stay or hide, she returned to the nursery. She knew with certainty that the young woman with whom she had silently worked all morning would like a lunch break.

That is where Alison found her about an hour later.

"Sorry," she said. "What a mess."

Catherine's heart did a flip-flop. "No, I'm sorry to drag you into this pickle. I had no idea that the cops would follow me here."

Alison bleated with laughter. "Oh God," she said. "I should have explained. Those guys aren't cops. They're officials from the Commune. Officious paper pushers. They have nothing better to do than harass people who are trying to make things better. A discrepancy in the documentation that Co Minh Hanh submitted for this quarter triggered some confusion. They just came here for a clarification."

Catherine stared at her. Then she laughed. "Damn. This country has me reeling." She couldn't stop her giggles. "You can't tell the good guys from the bad guys. You don't know who to trust."

Of course, her husband was also off crusading around Cambodia like a star in his own movie, she thought. Or like the hero in a Nelson DeMille novel. No wonder her world had become so upside-down in the short span of six or seven weeks. If they both came out of this alive, she would have a serious come-to-Jesus meeting with that man.

CHAPTER THIRTY-TWO

As the gray truck rolled into the border city of Poipet, Luong asked Mau, "Where do you want me to go? I don't know this city."

"My cousin Phirum lives near the railway station. We'll go there first. He knows Thai border guards who can move the girl to Bangkok." He paused to look pensively out the side window from his perch on the passenger side. "His wife will clean her up, make her more presentable. Then we'll call on the border people. She's not a virgin but she still looks young and tender. We should get about $500 for her."

"What's my share?"

"Forty percent."

"I own the truck, take the risks of driving. I'll need to pay my expenses back to Vietnam. I want 60 percent – $300."

"We can't do that. She's still my property. We'll have to share some with Phirum."

We'll see about that, Luong thought. If Mau wanted to pay his cousin it could come out of his share. If he argued about that, the cousin was expendable. With little persuasion, he'd put a bullet in both their heads.

A small thump from behind them in the cargo compartment caused Luong to check the side-mounted rearview mirror, where he saw several vendors from the market flood into the street and hover over a supine figure. He slammed on the brakes. "Damn it, the girl!" he shouted.

Mau craned his neck to check his own side mirror and saw the crowd bending over the girl. "You fool. I thought you secured her with duct tape."

"Of course I secured her. She must have had help getting loose. Maybe someone got aboard and helped her while we were stopped in Battambang."

Several men from the market had begun moving toward the cab of the vehicle.

Mau said, "We'll have to leave her," just as Luong smashed the gas pedal to the floor. They sped off down the rutted road past Poipet's chaotic, trash-strewn strip mall.

They drove several kilometers down Highway 5, away from Poipet, and then Luong pulled the truck onto a dirt track and stopped the engine.

"You're an idiot," Mau said. "You couldn't have taped her properly. I might've lost my investment because of you."

"I taped her fine. Did you check her yourself?"

"Of course not, I expected you to handle it."

"And you know I do it right, that's why you don't check."

"Just shut up, you idiot. I need to decide how to fix your fuck up. And you say you want more than 40 percent. I should be giving you 10 percent." Mau turned to stare out at the rice paddy, as if formulating his next barrage of insults.

Luong reached around to the small of his back and gripped the plastic handle of his pistol. He didn't need any shit from this asshole. He pointed the gun at Mau's chest. "You do nothing but insult me, but who does all your dirty work for you, eh? You want to call me an idiot? You fuck with me, you get my gun up your ass. Who's the idiot now, huh?"

Mau's expression shifted rapidly from blank anger to surprise to fear. "Wait. Listen. Blowing me away won't solve the problem. You won't get the girl without me. Let's both calm down and figure out how to get her back."

"All right." Luong lowered the pistol. "That's better. And I want 60 percent."

Mau's lip curled with scorn and he opened his mouth to speak.

Luong raised the gun again.

"OK, OK. Sixty percent. Fine."

Luong stuffed the pistol into his waistband and opened his door. "I'll look in the back to see if she left any clues about who helped her."

In the cargo compartment they found a wad of twisted duct tape stuck to the edge of the bench seat on the left side. "Well," said Mau, "she must have used her hands to get the duct tape off her ankles. Her wrists were probably still bound."

"So what now?" Luong asked. "Got any ideas?"

"Not really. I need to think."

"Well, I have an idea," Luong said, feeling a little smug. "Let's go visit your cousin. He'd know this armpit of a town. He should be able to help us find Lotus."

"Good thought. But if we find her and sell her to the border people, we'll have to cut him in."

Luong acknowledged this with a nod, but he had no intention of splitting the money with *anyone* if they managed to recover the girl and sell her. He adjusted the gun in back of his waistband.

***

Sister Chenda Sobunvy was meditating in her ascetic, cell-like quarters at Wat Sreah Trach, in the squalid city of Poipet. In late September, to the annoyance of many monks, she had traveled 370 kilometers from a nunnery in Udong to lend her voice to the small, largely ineffective movement to stop the trafficking of young women through the porous border of Poipet into Thailand. Traditionally, women in the wats cooked and cleaned for the monks, but now a handful of those nuns who knew the dharma had installed themselves among the young novice monks, to teach them the nuances of the eightfold path. Moreover, this small alliance of older nuns sought to improve the lives of girls and young women in the male-dominated countryside.

A light tap on Chenda's door interrupted her meditation, and she leapt up from her lotus pose on the hard-packed dirt floor as two middle-aged nuns carried in the limp form of a young girl, emaciated and covered in bruises. The poor child reeked of perspiration and urine. "Lie her on the cot," Chenda told them. "Who is she?" She bent over to examine her face. One eye was badly swollen, the surrounding flesh the color of a ripe plum. The other eye appeared uninjured but was closed.

"She was lying on the ground in the public market," said one of the nuns. "The vendors said she had fallen, or jumped, from the back of a truck. Her wrists were tied with gray tape. They had just moved her from the roadway into the market stall and cut away the tape when we came. We brought her here because it's closer than the hospital and she may be safer here from whoever has been hurting her."

Chenda touched the back of her hand to the girl's forehead, then with two fingers of her other hand, located her carotid pulse. "Her heartbeat is strong but she's in shock and is badly dehydrated. Bring hot water, towels and cold tea. Let's get her cleaned up and rehydrated." She leaned closer to the girl's face. "Can you hear me, dear? Can you tell me who you are?"

The undamaged eye opened. The girl emitted a small, startled cry as she took in the strange surroundings. "Can you hear me?" Chenda tried again. The girl weakly uttered a couple of strange syllables. Although it had been little more than a whisper, Chenda thought that it was Vietnamese and switched to that language. "Can you tell me your name?"

The response was weak, "Lien."

"That's good, Lien. We are bringing water and tea. Later some food."

"Where am I?"

"You are in the town of Poipet on the border between Cambodia and Thailand. My name is Sister Chenda. Can you tell me where you're from and how you got here?"

Lien didn't respond. She had fallen into the sanctuary of sleep.

In all likelihood, Lien was a trafficking victim, Chenda thought. They would keep her safe until she was in better health and then take her to a shelter in Phnom Penh. As soon as the other nuns were back to watch over her, she'd go tell wise old Brother Khong Kea. They'd need his cooperation.

CHAPTER THIRTY-THREE

At 8:15 a.m. Colonel Khlot burst through the doorway of Brigadier General Banak's office like a raging bull. "What do you mean, raiding Nakry's establishment in Svay Pak?" he bellowed. "Surely you know I have a business arrangement with her." He reached the senior officer's teak desk in two long strides and, with a single vicious swing of his forearm, swept the lacquer ware in-basket and crystal ashtray onto the tile floor. "Why wasn't I consulted before you made this foolish decision?"

Unruffled, General Banak leaned back in his leather chair and sipped his tea. "I run the Anti-Human Trafficking and Juvenile Protection Directorate, Colonel. I have no obligation to coordinate our operational plans with other departments unless I, or my immediate superior, determines there is a need to do so. Now, I suggest you have a seat and calm down. I'll explain what we have. After that, you will send one of your people up here to clean up this mess," he gestured toward the broken ashtray and other debris scattered as a result of Khlot's temper tantrum.

Still livid, Khlot sat heavily in one of two rattan armchairs in front of Banak's desk. He struggled to control his rage, which he knew was inappropriate and possibly career limiting. After a few deep breaths, his pulse slowed and his facial color returned to normal. "Sorry, General. I was out of line. It's just that we both know that Nakry, and others like her, have a relationship with members of the police, military and even the judiciary. We obtain valuable information about criminal activity from them in return for looking the other way some of the time."

"Yes. Valuable information, *plus* fringe benefits, I'm sure."

A vein in Khlot's temple pulsed at the barb about fringe benefits, but he remained silent.

"Listen," Banak said, "I know that our enforcement must be tempered. Their business does have a certain economic value. So let me assure you that, in all likelihood, Nakry will be home by this evening and back in business within a few days. She won't be seriously hurt. We've managed to rescue a few underage girls and that looks good to those who criticize our law enforcement practices. On the other hand, one of our officers is dead. Quite probably killed by Nakry's partner, Mau, and an accomplice whom we understand from Nakry is a trafficker named Luong. When we get our hands on them, we won't go easy."

Khlot stared past Banak's left shoulder and out the enormous plate glass window toward the Royal Palace and beyond, where big billowing cumulus clouds painted a backdrop for the richly carved prangs and curly roof edges. He moved his gaze back to Banak.

"Where is Nakry now, General? I'd like to speak with her."

"She's in an interrogation room on the fourth floor. I'll have someone take you up there to see her as soon as this mess is cleaned up." He smiled.

"How about the girls? How many were rescued?"

"Six are now in the hands of MoEYs. Two were missing. One had been apparently missing for several days before the raid and one is believed to have been taken by Mau when he escaped."

"Do you have a list of their names?"

"Yes. Somewhere in that mess of papers you have strewn across the floor. Without digging into the mess and finding the list I can't tell you names of the ones who are with MoEYs, but I remember the names of the two who are missing. Thanh and Lotus."

For a fleeting second, Khlot's eyebrows darted up, a subtlety not lost on Banak. "Those names are familiar to you, Colonel?"

"I've met the one called Lotus."

"Indeed." Now Banak's eyebrows arched. "She's the one apparently taken by Mau. Coincidentally an older American, accompanied by Mr. Cassidy from the US Embassy, was here last night asking about the one called Lotus. He claims to be her grandfather."

"What was his name?"

"Trutch."

Khlot hoisted his brows again. "I've met him. He was connected to that young Aussie who was shot dead on the street in Svay Pak a few days ago. Now I understand their interest in the village."

"Well, here's something you don't know. A colleague in Saigon, by the name of Captain Minh called me yesterday. He wanted to tip me off that this Trutch is nosing around and could be the cause of some embarrassment for the police if he finds what he's looking for. He thinks that Trutch should meet with some kind of accident. That was about six hours before I met Mr. Trutch, so I welcomed his visit. I was able to size him up firsthand."

"And what do you think, sir?"

"He's smart, he's aggressive and he's determined, but he's no threat to me personally. He could, however, cause great embarrassment for our ministry, should he discover that any policemen are involved in trafficking. He's cozy with Cassidy, the FBI man in Phnom Penh who, in turn, seems to know how to use the press. And embarrassment to the ministry could result in scapegoating of any policemen who may be profiting from, or otherwise enjoying the fruits of trafficking."

"I assume you've alerted the Border Department to be alert for Mau and Luong? They'll probably head for Thailand with their victim. And on the premise that Trutch may also go up there, have you told them to watch for him?"

"Of course not. As I told you, he'd merely be an embarrassment to us, and then only if he had evidence of police complicity in trafficking. I don't think he's looking for that. He just wants to find his granddaughter. Do you have cause to worry about him, Colonel?"

"I don't want to see the Cambodian National Police embarrassed, sir."

***

Khlot brushed a spec of lint off his shirt and examined his shoulders for dandruff before he entered the 4th floor interrogation room. In the windowless room, it took a second or two for Khlot's eyes to adjust to the dim light from the single caged bulb on the ceiling.

Nakry sat in a straight chair at a small wooden table, her gaze fixed on Khlot. Still in street clothes, she looked disheveled, but her folded hands rested on the tabletop.

"So, how did Mau and Luong manage to grab Lotus and make off with her?" Khlot asked, without greeting or preamble.

"Lotus was working upstairs in my apartment. Mau and Luong were having a meeting at the table when the police burst in the front door. Escaping was stupid. Mau should have surrendered. He'd be free in a few hours along with me."

"He's in big trouble now. A cop was killed as they escaped."

"I know."

"They're watching for them at the Thai border. Tomorrow, I'll go up there myself."

"What for? I doubt if the border cops need your help. Are you that interested in Lotus's welfare? You've never been so attached to any of my girls before."

Khlot considered his own motives. He was married to a beautiful and dutiful wife and had two spoiled teenaged boys. Yet, despite a satisfactory marriage and family life, he had always had an appetite for young girls. His first sexual experience, at age 17, was with a 12-year-old in a Svay Pak brothel. He had paid exorbitant prices to deflower several virgins since, but something about Lotus's naivety was especially appealing to him. Maybe because she spoke no Khmer she seemed more vulnerable and he felt more dominant. But in a perverted way, he also felt a sense of paternalism.

"I don't want to see her bought and sold several times and ruthlessly exploited in Thailand. I would feel the same about any of your girls. I realize that you can't relate to that sentiment. To you they're just commodities. It's all about money."

"You haven't done too badly in that department yourself."

He didn't hear her. His mind was on the several tasks that needed attention before he could travel to the border tomorrow. Most importantly, he needed to decide whether or not anything should be done about Trutch.

CHAPTER THIRTY-FOUR

The afternoon sky at Phnom Penh International Airport had darkened with roiling pewter clouds, the torrential rain typical of the southwest monsoon that runs from May to October. Trutch stood on the wet, glistening tarmac beside Judith Grinder and a male representative of the Australian embassy; he struggled to prevent the spindly umbrella he shared with Judith from inverting in the gusting wind. The Australian stood under his own sturdy golfer's umbrella. Together, they watched the long metal transfer case containing Andrew Quang's remains as it was conveyed into the belly of a Singapore Airlines A-330.

"You've spoken with his parents?" asked Judith.

Trutch, preoccupied with the question of what to do next in the search for Lien, stared blankly for a moment. "Yes. Twice. They'll be at the Sydney Airport when the body arrives." Then, apropos of nothing, he said, "It's a long journey, more than 14 hours once it leaves the ground here."

"He was a fine young man. I imagine his parents are distraught."

"They're taking it hard."

Judith turned her head in the direction of the terminal and just as the casket disappeared into the cargo compartment of the huge bird, she nodded toward a solitary figure standing beneath a passenger Jetway, who also watched the casket as it rolled into the plane. "Do you know who that is?" she asked.

Trutch looked in the same direction and struggled to obtain a clear image of the man through the sheets of rain. A strobe light on a taxiing aircraft triggered a brief glint of metal on the man's hat. "It looks like Khlot," he said.

"It is. I know him," agreed the man from the Australian embassy.

"And who is Khlot?" Judith asked.

"A colonel with the Cambodian National Police. He's the one who asked me to go to the hospital to identify Andrew's body. He also used the opportunity to interrogate me. He wanted to know what Andrew and two friends were doing in Svay Pak the night he was killed and what interests us in Svay Pak."

The cargo doors closed. When the Jetway rolled back and the engines of the A-330 started, they turned and walked through the downpour and into the cargo handling area of the airport.

"Well, must get back to the office. Toodles." The embassy man offered first Trutch and then Judith his right hand, and then he headed toward a stairwell up to the main departures section of the terminal.

Trutch moved to follow, but Judith grabbed him by the sleeve. "Wait. Before we get into that crowded terminal where we can't hear ourselves think, what did you tell Colonel Khlot?"

"I told him that we're interested in the human trafficking issue from a human rights perspective, that we're activists opposed to child exploitation. I don't think he believed me."

"Probably not. But listen, now that we have a modicum of privacy ..."

A tug towing three luggage jitneys roared up and drowned out her words. The two men on the machine dismounted and began throwing bags on a carousel.

Judith steered him to a remote corner further removed from the action. "As I started to say, I obtained new information this morning. A possible lead as to where Lien is now."

Trutch's face went blank. "Tell me."

"I think we should be circumspect about what we do with this information. Last night I had a call from Chakra Dith at the Phnom Penh Women's Shelter. Do you remember who she is?"

"Of course. She's the founding director." Trutch leaned forward and gripped both her shoulders. "Tell me about the lead."

"Chakra was contacted by a Buddhist nun called Chenda Sobunvy, who is currently working in a wat in the border town of Poipet. Apparently she has a young girl in her temporary care who's been abused. This girl managed to jump from the back of a moving truck to escape her tormenters. As soon as she is well enough, Chenda wants to move her to the PPWC for rehabilitation. Her name is Lien."

"Jesus. How can we get to this Poipet place? Will you get us a car and driver?"

"Not so fast, Pete. Your friend Colonel Khlot is approaching."

Ten meters away, Colonel Khlot crisped up the creases in his trousers by pinching and tugging at them, and then he strode purposefully toward Trutch and Judith. "Good afternoon, Mr. Trutch. Ah, and you would be Ms. Grinder."

Simultaneously, Judith said, "Correct," and Trutch said, "Howdy," in a crap-I-can't-be-bothered-with-you tone of voice.

"You don't seem pleased to see me, Mr. Trutch."

"I'm busy. What do you want?"`

"Yes. I imagine you're frantic about finding your granddaughter."

Trutch said nothing.

"So. You were telling the truth when you said that child trafficking "pisses you off" — I believe that's how you put it. But you weren't telling me the *whole* truth — that it pisses you off because your granddaughter is a victim. Well, now I have a truth for you, Mr. Trutch. Do not take it upon yourself to find her. Do not interfere with our law enforcement practices and, as I told you the last time we met, do not presume to judge our culture."

Trutch unconsciously touched the scar on his left cheek. His body went through a slow burn as he struggled to keep his voice under control. "I understand that I am in your country and that I should play by your rules. But as you have just observed, this whole seamy business has become personal to me, for two reasons. First because my granddaughter is a victim of this … sewer of exploitation, a part of what you so grandiloquently call your *culture*. And secondly because Andrew Quang, a good man, was wasted by the rats that inhabit this sewer."

"I'm beginning to like you, Mr. Trutch. It would be a shame if you were to get hurt."

"Is that a threat?"

"It's just practical advice. Watch your back."

Trutch bristled, but kept his mouth shut. Was it only six weeks ago that he heard almost those same words from Bill Anderson? *If you go over there to play detective, you'd better watch your ass.*

Khlot turned abruptly and Trutch and Judith watched in silence as he strode away. He crossed the cargo handling area, exited through an open bay door onto the tarmac and got into a waiting police vehicle.

"Well," Judith said. "That was friendly."

"Yeah. He's beginning to like me."

In response, Judith shot him a wry grin. "We'd better go somewhere and talk about the next steps, Pete. I don't think it's advisable to rush to Poipet without thinking it through."

"At this point, I doubt if Khlot knows about Lien being in the wat. He probably thinks she's still in the hands of these animals Mau and Luong. So I don't think that was a specific threat for me not to travel to Poipet. I suspect, however, that Mau and Luong will be aggressive about trying to find and recover her, and apparently Poipet is not a large city."

"It's somewhere in the neighborhood of 70,000 souls."

"All right. I'm eager to get there as soon as possible. But you're right. We need to put some forethought into the next steps. I'll call Brad Cassidy. If I find him still in his office, I'll pick his brain for thoughts. In the meantime, why don't you call Chakra and ask her to contact the nun — Chenda? She should be cautious about keeping Lien hidden and protected. Still, we should try to go up there tonight. How long a drive is it?"

"About six and a half hours. I understand your sense of urgency, so I'll arrange for a car and driver to be standing by at the Blue Lime. We can taxi back there and make our phone calls enroute."

***

Trutch easily reached Cassidy.

"My advice," Cassidy said, "is get to Poipet as soon as you can, but wait until first light to depart. Highway 5 can be treacherous at night. Lots of tired truck drivers heading to and from the border. You're also likely to run into many drunken motorbikers and even a few criminals lurking about looking for opportunities."

CHAPTER THIRTY-FIVE

Lien gradually emerged from a troubled sleep to feel something damp and cool on her face. She was able to open her left eye and could see the dim outlines of two women through a halo of weak, flickering candlelight. The room was dark beyond the corona of pale light. One of the women gently wiped her face and forehead with a dampened cloth. She spoke softly, "Do you remember my name? I'm Sister Chenda. We'll take care of you. You're safe here."

Muzzy, not yet fully conscious, Lien weakly pushed at the hand stroking her face. Her yama-addled mind could not yet accept that people wanted to help her. Her innocence and child-like trust of kindly adults had dissolved eight weeks earlier. At one level, the voice that had spoken to her was soft and tender. But the cocoon of numbness and indifference within which Lien had learned to live now isolated her from Chenda's compassion as easily as it did the cruelty that had been visited upon her daily.

The next morning she awoke coiled into a tight ball in a corner of the small cot. The swelling in her right eye had begun to recede. But her stomach and intestines quivered with nausea. She had already vomited what little was in her stomach during the night. Now she straightened out, rolled onto her side and heaved again, but only bile and saliva drizzled down her chin. Her throat and tongue felt bitter and burning, like vinegar and hot sauce. She could make out Chenda hovering above her but could not make sense of the words she spoke.

The awareness of safety gradually crept into her mind. Where was she, she wondered, that these women wanted to help her? But even as she struggled to become more conscious of her new surroundings, everything seemed to float around her as though weightless. She wanted to ask the nuns if they would help her to her feet. Instead, she mumbled in a barely audible voice, "Can I have yama?"

"This is a wat, Lien. We don't have drugs here. Besides, yama won't help you recover your strength. We'll bring you some food later this morning. Your body needs nourishment. I think it has been a long time since you have had either fresh fruit or protein."

Slowly, Lien gained some perspective and clarity. "Will my Papa come for me?" Her thoughts now centered on her Papa. She tried to picture him in her mind but the image was blurred.

"We hope we can get you home to your family. But first you must get stronger. You need healthful food and fresh air and sunshine."

"I want to see my Papa."

"We want that too, but it may take some time. Can you tell me your papa's name and where he lives? We'll contact him and let him know that you're safe."

"His name is ... Ngoc." She grasped the tiny Buddha on the chain around her neck. "We live in the village of Tuy Phuoc."

"Tuy Phuoc sounds like a Vietnamese village. Can you tell me which province it is in or which city it's near?"

"I can't remember the province. My teacher, Co Loan, would be unhappy with me. We go to the city of Quy Nhon for the market. Oh. My grandmother is Quy. She was in the hospital in Quy Nhon."

"That's good, Lien. Now you lie back and rest some more. I'll have the sisters bring you chicken soup and maybe noodles. Later, we'll get you up on your feet and into the garden for some air."

***

Brother Kong Kea emerged from his meditations and rose from the Padmasana posture. For 45 minutes he had remained in the pose, contemplating the problem of what to do about the young girl in Chenda's cell. He stretched his elderly limbs and ambled to the tiny cell that housed his cot and little else. From a shoebox stored under his bed he withdrew a long stemmed pipe and a plastic packet and began the ritualistic preparation of his pipe. First, the old monk lit an oil lamp sitting on an upturned wooden box beside his bed. He removed a hard lump about the size of a candy bar from the plastic bag and with his thumb and forefinger broke off a peanut-sized piece. Sweat glistened on his shaved head as he shaped the piece with his fingers and impaled it on the end of a straightened paper clip.

His anticipation grew as he heated the small piece of opium over the burning lamp until it became soft and hot; then he smeared it around inside the pipe's ceramic bowl. Kong lay down on his left side and heated the pipe itself over the lamp. Then he placed the end of the long bamboo stem between his lips and inhaled a wonderful lungful of smoke. The smoke tasted like flowers on his palette and produced an immediate, overwhelming sense of wellbeing.

He thought of the nun Chenda and of two others who had arrived three weeks ago. A Khmer Theravada Buddhist wat was no place for women. He believed that Cambodia's few nuns should remain in the two or three wats that traditionally housed them. And certainly Chenda had no business sheltering a young girl, more than likely a *srey kouc* — a broken coconut — in this wat.

His door sat ajar, and in the wedge of light beyond it, the other monks passed by. When the deep reverberant tone of the gong in the main shrine announced mid-morning chanting, he took one last, long, luxurious drag on the pipe. He sat up and slipped into his sandals. How he loved the melodic ritual: the deep intonations of his fellow monks, the blending of soprano voices of the prepubescent novices. As he rose to join his brothers at the great gilded image of Buddha, the answer came to him.

***

Two kilometers south of Wat Sreah Trach, and across National Highway 5 on a dusty street behind the railway station, 48-year-old Phirum sat watching the traffic, in front of the grimy façade of his stucco and sheet metal house. Glancing up at the piece of blue sky visible between the buildings and the tangled webs of overhead utility wires, he wished for a little afternoon rain to cool the air and staunch the puffs of dust stirred up by the steady stream of motorbikes, tuk tuks and light trucks, but there was not a cloud to be seen. He lifted the bottom of his greasy orange singlet up from his potbelly and used it to wipe the perspiration away from his forehead.

His gaze returned to the sweet amber tea in his smudgy glass. A shiny black fly had settled onto the rim and waved its antennae. Phirum swished it off with his free hand, then leaned back and lit a cigarette. A pair of mongrels copulated in the dust across the road. His cousin Mau had looked almost as mangy when he appeared briefly the night before, after an absence of almost four years. But Phirum had agreed to help him with his current problem.

Word traveled swiftly in Poipet's loose network of traffickers, pimps and thugs. He had already made a few calls to put the little bitch's description onto the grapevine. It would only be a matter of time before a lead developed. He could then help Mau and his accomplice recover the girl and get her through the border into Thailand. With his share of the money he would buy a new motorbike. He coughed up a glob of phlegm, then noisily spat into the dust at his feet.

Out of the corner of his eye, a splash of orange moved amid the otherwise drab traffic along the litter-strewn street. The decrepit old monk, Brother Khong Kea, laboriously pedaled his bicycle in Phirum's direction. Soon Phirum would have the information he sought — and all for the price of a few ounces of opium.

CHAPTER THIRTY-SIX

Trutch's thoughts raced through possibilities and complications as he and Judith sped toward Poipet. The roadway ahead was still shrouded in darkness, but behind them, to the east, a tangerine dawn blossomed. Even with their early departure, they wouldn't arrive until mid-morning, and he worried that the two thugs, Mau and Luong, would find Lien before he and Judith could get there. They had killed a policeman; that meant they were armed. What were their capabilities? Their limitations? He had no way of knowing, and not knowing their vehicle make and model was another serious handicap.

Disregarding Brad Cassidy's advice, they had left Phnom Penh at 4 a.m., at least two hours before first light, determined to get to Poipet early in the day. But would that be soon enough?

The highway had been all theirs for the first hour, but now traffic built on the two-lane roadway. Many heavy trucks rolled in each direction and periodically a sluggish farm vehicle or cart pulled by a water buffalo slowed them to a crawl.

The driver, a swarthy Cambodian who spoke Khmer, passable Vietnamese and limited English, turned and spoke over his right shoulder. "Do you need break? Happy stop?"

Judith looked enquiringly at Trutch who shook his head. Then to the driver "We're okay for now, Shank."

"Shank?" Trutch asked.

"His name is Chankara, but he likes to be called Shank. Thinks it's macho. We use him whenever we're in Cambodia."

Shank glanced over his shoulder, his smile of acknowledgment more a smirk as he nodded at Trutch.

Minutes later, Shank pulled a cellphone from his shirt pocket, pushed a couple of numbers, and then whispered something in Vietnamese into the phone.

Trutch listened, briefly wondering if had called a girlfriend or his wife, and why he had spoken in Vietnamese instead of Khmer. It didn't matter, he supposed, as long as the man concentrated on getting to Poipet as soon as possible.

An hour later as choked traffic slowed their progress even further, Trutch silently cursed his aging prostate and announced, "Okay. I could use a quick pit stop now."

"Me too," said Judith. "There won't be any restrooms here, so we'll have to do as the Cambodians do and use the side of the road. There's no such thing as modesty out here."

Shank pulled the car well off the road and rolled it to a dusty stop. To afford Judith some privacy as she started around the rear of the vehicle, Trutch went to the front where he found Shank with his equipment already hanging out of his trousers and in full stream. Just past him, beyond the verge, on a small sign crudely nailed to a wooden post, Trutch thought he recognized a sinister warning. He moved closer and confirmed his fear — an inverted equilateral triangle, faded red in color with a yellow band around the three sides.

He shouted to Judith and pointed at the post, "Don't leave the edge of the roadway."

The top of the sign contained symbols in Khmer script, meaningless to Trutch, but the bottom contained a clear warning in English:

DANGER!! MINES!!!

Back in the vehicle, Judith asked, "Would there really be mines out there, this close to the highway?"

"That's the legacy of many years of warfare. Much of Southeast Asia — Vietnam, Cambodia and Laos — still has vast tracts of unexploded ordnance. The gift that keeps on giving."

Ahead of them the road appeared snarled with vehicles of all descriptions: trucks, buses, carts, motorbikes, SUVs and sedans. Shank braked, and unlike the other drivers in the fray, maintained a safe distance from the vehicle ahead. Both hands gripping the wheel, he piloted around a logjam of trucks by driving on the right-hand shoulder. Other vehicles swerved recklessly into the left lane in a mad race to pass the slower trucks before they met an oncoming bus.

Their vehicle had just pulled back onto the roadway when Trutch heard a thumping from the right rear. The car buffeted and rocked as though driving on boulders.

"Shank, you have a flat tire."

"I know, I know. I stop ahead — wider place."

Trutch glanced at his watch as Shank braked and stopped. He said to Judith, "In the military we called it Murphy's Law."

"I know about Murphy's Law. It's axiomatic in organizational screw-ups: whatever can possibly go wrong, will. So always plan for it."

"Murphy was an optimist. That's why I insisted we leave so early. You can always count on things going differently than expected."

Shank opened the trunk and then closed it again and returned to the driver's seat "No spare tire. I call for help."

Trutch's face heated up. "Jesus, Shank. How the hell could you even think of getting on the highway without checking your vehicle first? This is indefensibly stupid. Every minute could count."

Judith clutched his upper arm. "Shh, Pete. If you yell at him, he'll lose face. We've got no choice but to let things play out. See? He's already on the phone."

Trutch stepped out onto the wide gravel threshold and began pacing. The roadside was littered with detritus thrown from passing vehicles: cans, bottles, plastic bags, Styrofoam cups and bowls, even a torn and soiled child's diaper.

He glanced over at Shank, who stood on the other side of the car. Only a moment ago, Shank had called for help and closed his phone. Now he spoke rapidly and furtively into it, again in Vietnamese. When he noticed Trutch watching, he turned abruptly to face the other way.

Trutch walked around the front of the car and said, "What the hell was that call about? That's the second surreptitious call you've made in Vietnamese. Why? You finished the call for assistance a few minutes ago."

"I have Vietnamese girlfriend. She live in Phnom Penh. I call her."

"I'm not so sure about that." Trutch yanked open the rear door and slid in next to Judith, who was looking at a Google Earth image of Poipet on her smartphone. "Just how trustworthy is our Mr. Shank? My gut's telling me something's not right."

"Well, he's always been reliable. I think he's honest and above board."

"I don't. I believe he's deliberately stalling and reporting our progress to someone."

At the front of the vehicle, Shank put the phone to his ear again, apparently answering an incoming call. He listened for a few seconds and then approached the rear window and said, "Service car come 90 minutes. Mebbe sooner."

Trutch exploded. "This is bullshit. We can't sit on our thumbs for 90 minutes. Shank, you'd better make it happen a whole lot sooner or you're going to be dog meat. Do you understand?"

Judith grabbed Trutch's arm again. "Pete, don't. Let me talk to him." She slid out of the car and led Shank to the front of the vehicle.

Trutch remained in the car, fuming, as Judith spoke with Shank. He couldn't hear her words, but her body language and gestures struck him as both assertive and persuasive, particularly when Shank pulled out his phone again.

Judith returned to the back seat. "Okay. I think we've got it sorted. Our ETA is now 35 minutes."

"What the hell did you say to him?"

"I asked him to persuade the roadside assistance people that this was a life or death emergency and that we need the assistance sooner."

"I'm surprised that worked."

"Well, I think telling him there'd be an extra $100 in it for him clinched the deal. Also for the roadside assistance people. You can afford that can't you, Colonel Trutch?"

Trutch considered her appreciatively. "I have to say, I'm glad you persuaded me that you should come along on this mission. I apologize for reacting negatively back in Saigon."

She accepted his apology with a wry smile. "Never underestimate the clout of an assertive woman."

CHAPTER THIRTY-SEVEN

Warm rays of sunshine streamed onto Lien's face. Underfoot, the earth surrounding the wat felt warm on the soles of her feet. All around her, flowers bloomed. Unseen birds chortled from the trees, and insects clacked and hummed as they moved from stem to stem.

She stood amid the flowers and hungrily inhaled the fresh, fragrant air. Her chest lifted and expanded as she breathed in. For ten seconds she felt exultant, until the dreadful experiences of the past six weeks resurfaced and her eyes darted about nervously. She trembled slightly as Sister Chenda led her through the garden with a gentle grip on her upper arm. Lien managed a cautious smile as she turned toward the nun and asked, "Will I go home soon?"

"Not yet, Dear. Later today some kind people will take you to a place where you can rest and heal for a while."

"Where is this place? Who will take me?"

"It's in Phnom Penh. The people coming are …"

"NO!" Her knees buckled and she crumbled onto the paving stones. "I won't go there. I want to go home." She pushed her back against one of the large concrete planters, drew her knees up and hugged them to her chest. In her mind, she could see and feel, once again, the basement room in the brothel. Through the hazy notions she heard a scream. It was her own. A fuzzy image of Mau, with his electric stick, swayed before her.

Sister Chenda knelt on the pavement and wrapped both arms around Lien, holding her tightly to her bosom. She rocked her gently. "It's okay, child. Everything is okay. We'll get you to a place where kind women will take care of you until you are ready to go back to Tuy Phuoc."

Lien quaked, her temporary euphoria gone. "I need yama," she rasped.

"Just breathe deeply, Lien. Breathe. Try to take big breaths."

Still shaking hard, she continued to take rapid, shallow breaths, her thoughts muddled and tangled. Where was Papa? Where was this place they wanted to take her? Where was she now? In the margins of her consciousness she saw the rice paddy outside her house, her school, a fleeting sensation of herself and her friend Ha pedaling home from school — familiar things. She wanted them. Her gaze fell on a fragment of a coconut husk lying near one of the planters. She looked into the nun's face. "I am broken. Like that coconut, I am broken."

"You'll be okay, child. Please know that. Good people will take care of you. Now, try to take some deep breaths."

Somehow Chenda's words soothed her. Lien relaxed enough to inhale deeply.

Chenda lifted Lien's chin and looked closely at her tear-streaked face. "Would you like to go over to the shrine and light some incense with me? Perhaps we can meditate together until lunchtime."

Lien nodded.

They rose together and walked through the garden to the central pavilion of the wat, where the large Buddha sat amid offerings of joss sticks, flowers, fruit and rice cakes. A saffron forest of young monks sat prayerfully in the lotus position before the icon, their shaved heads glistening. Chenda and Lien knelt on a bamboo mat toward the rear of the large open-walled room. They were silent. Chenda held Lien's hand. Lien kept her eyes on the monks.

After a few moments of silence one monk stood and walked to the side of the altar. He approached the *bonsho,* a large suspended bronze bell. With its sloped shoulders and flat base, the bell mimicked the sitting Buddha, next to which it hung. The monk gripped a horizontal wooden beam, suspended from the rafters by heavy ropes. He swung the beam rearward, then forward so that it struck the bonsho.

At the resounding clang, Lien's shoulders twitched convulsively. But the random thoughts swirling through her mind slowed and the long mellow reverberation of the gong lulled her into a sense of calm. The resonance lasted for nearly a minute before it ebbed and faded.

The monks began their sonorous chant, and rich baritone notes filled the space as their mantra rose and fell in rhythmic cadence, joined by the soprano sounds of a novice. From one side of the pavilion, an older monk entered and took up his position at the front of the congregants. This most venerable of monks picked up a microphone from the altar and with his cracking, aged voice chanted the mantra in a higher pitch and a contrasting tone. His amplified mantra enhanced the others, harmonizing but not overpowering, even with the microphone.

Lien knelt, eyes tightly closed and one hand folded into Chenda's. For the first time in weeks, she consciously felt at peace.

Thirty minutes later the monks rose. Each went forward to light a handful of joss sticks from a candle burning on the altar. Then, in turn, they held the burning incense aloft between their prayerful hands and bowed reverently in the direction of the statue of the Buddha. They placed their little bouquets of smoking incense sticks into pots of sand next to the altar and turned to file out.

***

As the monks left the pavilion and walked into the garden, they abandoned their silence and bantered and jostled one another with adolescent humor.

Brother Khong Kea replaced the microphone on the altar, turned and limped toward the rear of the pavilion. Unseen by Chenda or Lien, he reached into a fold of his robe and removed a cell phone. He pushed three buttons, paused, then whispered briefly into it.

CHAPTER THIRTY-EIGHT

Luong sat on a red plastic stool against the wall in the small house near the railway station with Mau and Mau's cousin. Seeking a more comfortable position, he shifted his weight from one cheek to the other as he listened to Phirum speak.

"The girl is at Wat Sreah Trach, a temple not far from here. It's near the casino district," Phirum said. "My contact in the Thai border police is on duty between 6 p.m. and midnight," Phirum said. "So timing is important."

"What about traffic at the border?" Luong asked.

"It's heavy until about 9 p.m. We should snatch the girl about 15 minutes before our crossing time and go straight to the border. I suggest we aim for 11 p.m. to cross."

"Do you know where in the pagoda complex Lotus is?" Mau asked.

"No. But probably in one of the small sleeping rooms."

"Then we must arrive earlier than 15 minutes ahead of time to search for her," Luong said. "Darkness will not help us either."

"We should get there by a few minutes after 10. The gates will be locked by then, but they're flimsy. We can drive the truck right through them."

Luong's phone interrupted with an impatient buzzing. "Hallo," he said.

"Luong *oi*," said Captain Minh. "So. I understand that Quang has been dealt with."

"Yes," answered Luong. "He's no longer a worry."

"What about Trutch?"

"Haven't seen him. There was a problem at the brothel — a police raid. I'm now in Poipet. We're delivering one of the girls across the border to Thailand tonight. It's the one called Lotus, Trutch's supposed granddaughter."

"You left something out. I'm aware that at the moment you're not in possession of the girl."

"What? How did you know?"

"Surely you don't think you're my only source in Cambodia? I'm kept well

202

informed. I've also learned that Trutch is onto you. He's on his way to Poipet right now, in a car with the Grinder woman. I just heard from his driver."

"We're planning to snatch the girl from the wat tonight."

"He'll be there before then. He's no more than one hour from Poipet now. You'll have to act soon."

"All right, we'll get her. But we'll have to hide somewhere for a few hours. We need to wait for a certain Thai border policeman to be on duty."

"I'm sure you'll find a place. If Trutch finds you, you must dispose of him. He's becoming a nuisance."

Luong stood and put the phone in his pocket as Mau and Phirum both looked expectantly at him. "We have to move soon," he said. "The American named Trutch is on his way."

Phirum's phone rang then. He put it to his ear and listened for a moment. He grunted and switched it off. "That was the old monk. The bitch is on the grounds of the pagoda with her minder *now*. Let's go."

CHAPTER THIRTY-NINE

While they awaited the service car, Trutch studied the screen of Judith's smartphone and panned around the Google Earth image of Poipet using the touchpad. As he zoomed in on a segment of the city adjacent to the border, he asked, "What's this area? From the aerial photo it appears more modern and clean than the rest of the city. It doesn't seem to fit."

Glancing at the screen, Judith commented, "That's the casino district. It's a place where Thai nationals can go to gamble. Gambling is illegal in Thailand, so they go here to ..."

"It's within about two blocks of the wat," Trutch interrupted. He moved his finger over to the temple complex. "If the bad guys recapture Lien could they cut through the casino district to go directly into Thailand?"

"I don't think so. It's fenced all the way around. The only people who can enter from the Cambodian side are employees of the casinos."

"How is that controlled? Are there vehicle barriers at the gate?"

"I don't know. Let me ask Shank."

"Never mind. How about the wat? How many entrances are there?"

Judith leaned over the screen. "I've actually never been there. Maybe Shank knows." She lowered her window. "Shank, can you come here for a minute?"

Shank ground out his cigarette beneath his foot and leaned down to look through the left rear window. "Yes, Madam."

Trutch considered Shank with disgust, and asked sternly, "How many entrances and exits to this compound?"

Shank poked a finger at the screen. "Here main entrance. Parking here. One more small gate on north side, I think for grocery and delivery. Mebbe more, but I don't know."

So there were gates on the south and north side and it appeared that the east and west sides were butted right up against other buildings, Trutch thought. That wasn't particularly good. It would be a piece of cake for Luong and Mau to get into this place if they knew Lien was there. He zoomed out from the pagoda to obtain a smaller-scale view of the entire city, a veritable warren of streets and alleys. Shit, he thought. There were any number of routes a vehicle could use to dash from the pagoda to the main Thai border crossing just south of the Casino Zone. He checked his watch and barked at Shank. "Have you heard from that service car?"

"Service car come soon. Mebbe five more minutes."

Trutch opened the right-side door and slid out. He paced back and forth along the shoulder of the highway, briefly entertaining, and then rejecting, the idea of sticking out his thumb to passing traffic.

Ten agonizing minutes later, the service vehicle, a Toyota pickup truck, arrived. Trutch unconsciously chewed on the inside of his lower lip. He fingered the scar on his cheek as the two attendants fussed over changing the tire. He glanced at his watch every few seconds. Finally, concluding that he couldn't influence the speed at which the Cambodians worked, he turned away and stared out over the rice paddies.

Judith touched his arm. "They're finished, Pete. Let's go."

Trutch sat on the edge of his seat and glanced at his watch every five minutes during the hour it took them to reach the eastern outskirts of Poipet. He constantly fingered the scar on his cheek; a nerve near his temple jumped rhythmically. Route 5 had become clotted in both directions with heavy truck traffic, apparently traveling to and from the Thai border.

His watch now showed two o'clock, over four hours past his initial target time to arrive at the pagoda. And they still had several kilometers to go before they would turn off Highway 5 and make their way through the labyrinthine streets and alleys to the temple. He could think of little to do, other than fret. Surely Luong and Mau would be looking for Lien aggressively, if they hadn't already found her.

After another 15 minutes of bumper-to-bumper, stop-and-go traffic, Trutch spotted, ahead of them by about a kilometer, the large gate-like structure which represents Cambodia's entry portal from Thailand. The gate was partially occluded by multiple lines of trucks and tuk tuks approaching the border, but its upper reaches were plainly visible, vaguely reminiscent of Berlin's Brandenburg Gate, but much uglier.

"That's obviously the border ahead," he said. "Isn't our turn here somewhere?"

"Right here," Shank said, and he turned the vehicle sharply to the right, off the highway and onto a narrow street.

Now, surprisingly, traffic thinned and the 4X4 moved faster. Shank accelerated and piloted the vehicle skillfully toward the pagoda.

"About ten more minutes I think," Judith said.

Trutch checked his watch again and grunted as the vehicle bounced along the unevenly paved roadway.

CHAPTER FORTY

Chenda rose from her knees in the meditation room and silently urged Lien to rise with her, keeping a warm grip on her hand. "Come. Let us light incense."

Passive and obedient, Lien accompanied her to the altar, where they each went through the ritual of lighting incense and bowing toward the statue and then resumed their kneeling positions.

Lien's rhythmic breathing lifted her from painful reality and softness cloaked her heart. The terror of Svay Pak and the trip to Poipet as a captive had dimmed enough that she could intermittently relax.

By the time she and Sister Chenda rose 20 minutes later, she felt the succor of meditation. "I've never meditated before," she said. "I like the calm and peace. Can we do it again later?"

"Yes. This afternoon. That would be good for you," Chenda said.

They stepped from the pavilion and strolled through the garden. Content with the comforting contact, Lien allowed her limp hand to stay in Chenda's firm grip.

"We'll have lunch now, Lien. How about some nice steamed vegetables and maybe some broth?"

Lien looked around at the masonry beds of colorful flowers and at the verdant potted topiary, noticing how the warm breeze caused the flowers and greenery to frolic in their planters and urns. "Can we stay in the garden a while longer?" she asked.

"Of course. Lunch will be ready for us when we're ready for it."

They walked farther along the edge of the grounds where only faint traffic noises passed over the high brick wall and its tangle of red bougainvillea. A bluish-green haze had blotted out the sun, higher in the sky now, and a dense blanket of humidity hung over the pagoda and surrounding city.

Twenty meters ahead of them, the wall moved. A wide wooden door opened inwardly, pushed by a man who stepped through the opening, his glance darting around the courtyard until it fell upon Lien.

Lien screamed and froze where she stood. "It's Luong!" she shrieked.

At the same moment, a gray truck drove in through the gate and stopped. Mau jumped out of the passenger side, followed by another man.

Lien screamed again and ran back toward the shrine, the pathway and shrubs a slow-motion blur. The sound of her own breathing filled her ears as she stretched her legs to their full length. It wasn't enough.

Luong caught up with her and grabbed her wrist. He swung her around and flung her onto the paving stones.

The stones cut into her arms and cheek as she landed. Unable to push herself up because of the heavy weight that pinned her to the ground, she thrashed her head from side to side, hoping for something to sink her teeth into. With nothing to grab onto, she went limp.

Luong twisted her arm into a hammerlock and dragged her to her feet.

Chenda ran up and pounded Luong on the back of his neck and shoulders. "Let her go. You let her go."

Mau and the other man arrived, both of them panting.

"Phirum," Luong said, "Get rid of her."

Phirum struck a blow to Chenda's back that sent her to her knees on the pavement. Mau pushed her aside and grabbed Lien's other arm. "Let's get her into the truck quickly," he said. Then to Lien, "You little cunt." A burst of foul breath and spittle spewed into her face.

Lien screamed and writhed between them. She refused to walk and used her weight to slow them as they half-pushed and half-dragged her toward the back of the truck. "Help me. Help me," she shrieked to the stupefied and incredulous monks who had begun gathering in the courtyard.

Luong and Mau lifted her into the truck and pushed her face-first onto the floor. She tasted dirt and grit as she opened her mouth and yowled in pain. Her left arm, still pinned behind her, throbbed. She felt the dead weight of one of the men when he sat on her shoulders.

As the truck moved in reverse, she turned her head to the side just enough to vomit. She tried to cough but the weight pressing on her upper body prevented that. She retched again and then gagged.

Outside, a gunshot sounded and a cold chill settled on her spine.

She felt a bump as the truck struck something and the vehicle jerked to the left. Then she sensed that they turned further to the left and shifted into a forward gear. The rumbling vehicle got underway, rapidly shifting gears as it accelerated.

CHAPTER FORTY-ONE

The 4X4 wended its way down a street bordered by a conglomeration of shanties and hovels with corrugated tin roofs. Trutch thought they must be nearing the pagoda and wiped sweaty but unshaking hands on his trousers. His heart rate also remained steady. For the hundredth time he went through a calculated assessment of the possibilities. They may find Lien safely within the wat and they may not. The distance from the temple to the border crossing into Thailand was less than a klick, so if Luong and Mau had recaptured her while Trutch was on the long road from Phnom Penh, they would most likely have proceeded directly to the crossing with her. Images of what they would find at the pagoda raced through his mind as he willed himself to stay focused on the here and now. He needed to concentrate on the situation as it unfolded so that he could respond properly to whatever might develop.

"Almost there," Shank said.

Trutch's pulse quickened. He took several deep breaths and stared intensely at the roadway ahead, anticipating his first glimpse of the wat, wondering if they had made it on time.

The street jogged 35 degrees to the right. As Shank steered into the curve he said, "There."

The wat bore no resemblance to the traditional picture Trutch had been carrying in his head for the past 12 hours. Instead, a gray brick wall rose to about eight feet, splotched in places with mold stains. Several building tops within the compound stood apart from one with a tall pointed spire, but all appeared equally bland. "It's not nearly as grand as I had imagined," he said. "Can we drive all the way around it once before we go in?"

"I think so. I'll try."

They drove slowly past the front entrance. The large sliding gate stood open and Trutch craned his neck to peer into the grounds. A single building dominated the space immediately behind the paved entry and courtyard. It looked much taller than its single story, owing to the tall prang at the center of the roof and the ornate curly ends on either side. Behind either end of the main building, other structures were less ornate than the main building which likely housed the main shrine and several other rooms. The front façade sat atop a half dozen wide steps and was decorated with bas-relief images. Trutch couldn't see any people, but a yellow temple dog lay at the base of the steps.

"Seems quiet," he said.

Judith glanced at her watch. "It's past 2 p.m. The monks have probably finished their afternoon chanting and will be resting, or taking tea with a light meal."

They turned left at the end of the front wall, about 100 meters past the entrance, and drove along the north wall. From this vantage point, it was apparent that the grounds were well treed. Beautiful red bougainvillea vines clung to the top of the wall.

They turned left again and crept along the rear wall of the complex. Midway down the length of the wall, a gate stood open for a gray truck that slowly backed out. A man walked backward behind the truck, and was using hand and arm signals to guide the driver through the narrow gate.

As they drew closer, a surge of adrenaline electrified Trutch as he recognized the same evil-looking man into whose eyes he had stared as they passed this same vehicle in Svay Pak. "Shank. Pull up close behind him. Block him." He opened the rear door and leapt out.

Shank maneuvered the SUV to within centimeters of the man, forcing him to stop walking and the truck to stop backing. Trutch swung the car door shut. He opened his mouth to shout something at the man, but then closed it. His instincts told him to approach silently.

The man's hand moved to the small of his back and came back around to the front holding a gun.

Trutch saw this movement as if it were a slow-motion replay of a sporting event. He lunged toward the man, thinking he could knock the gun arm aside. Just as he recognized the weapon as a 9 mm Glock, it spat a tongue of flame. A deafening roar sounded and an impact on the right side of his rib cage felt like a blow from a swinging baseball bat.

The man shouted something to the truck driver, who revved the truck's engine and lurched backward to ram the SUV in the front left fender, pushing it out of the way.

Trutch fell onto his knees, his hand pressed to his side.

CHAPTER FORTY-TWO

Still on his knees, Trutch pressed his left hand against the rapidly expanding bloodstain on the right side of his shirt. With his thumb he found the bullet hole in the fabric, then he tore the shirt open. He felt around the wound with his left forefinger, trying to assess the damage. Blood seeped between his fingers, and as he probed into the open flesh he felt a jab of pain. The wound didn't feel deep, more like a shallow trench about three inches long. A flesh wound. The bullet had grazed him. Plenty of blood, but probably no real damage.

Judith ran up to him. "Are you badly hurt? Shank, let's get him into the wat."

"No. It's nothing. Help me to my feet. Let's go after those guys."

"Pete. They're obviously armed and dangerous. Besides, we don't know if they have Lien or not. Let's see if she's in the pagoda."

Before they could move, Sister Chenda ran up to them.

She asked in English, "Have you come for Lien? They took her. Those men in the truck. They beat her and took her and … Oh, you're hurt. You've been shot. Let's see to that wound."

"No. It's nothing. How many men were there? Did they say anything? Where they're going? Anything like that?"

"I don't think so. It happened so fast. I think there were three of them. We must dress that wound. You're bleeding badly."

Shank, looking serious and shaken, had already fetched the first aid kit from the vehicle and pulled out a large sterile dressing. While Judith and Chenda peeled back the shreds of Trutch's shirt, he applied the dressing to the wound and pressed firmly. "I don't find tape in the kit. Just the dressings and smaller Band-Aids."

"To hell with it. Let's go. We've got to stop those guys before they reach the border." Trutch tried to pull loose from Judith and Chenda, both of whom now held him by the shoulders.

"Just wait," Chenda said. "You can't go on bleeding like a beheaded chicken." She released her grip on his shoulder and ripped a wide strip off her gray robe, and then several more. "By the way, I'm Sister Chenda. We've been caring for Lien. She's very brave."

"All right. Thank you, Sister. But please hurry. Get those strips secured and we'll be off. Shank, you jump back behind the wheel and be ready to take off the second these two finish with me." He tried to sound authoritative, but he felt weak and dizzy.

CHAPTER FORTY-THREE

Luong sat in the passenger seat while Phirum drove. Mau sat in back to keep the girl quiet.

"We can't go straight to the border," Luong said. "Your contact's not on duty for several hours yet."

"We can hide in my house for a few hours," Phirum said. "We'll conceal the truck behind the train station."

Luong knew his bullet had connected and that Trutch was down, but it didn't have the look of a killing shot. Trutch had dropped to his knees. That was as much as Luong had seen before he jumped back into the truck and sped away. But was Trutch sufficiently disabled to stop the search, or did he merely have a flesh wound? This man Trutch was a resolute and determined foe. If he was physically able to continue the pursuit, he would. "Okay, Phirum. Your house."

Phirum steered left onto National Highway 5 heading southeast away from the border. Ahead, the garbage-strewn highway opened up, clear of traffic. Luong checked the side mirror. At the border to their rear, the road was clogged.

They passed a three-story building under construction; rickety bamboo scaffolding clung to its unfinished walls and several barefoot workers clung to the scaffolding. Brick rubble, from whatever had previously stood in its place, littered the foot of the new building and reddish dust mingled with the already smoggy air. The old yellow railway station, unused for years, its stucco dilapidated and crumbling, appeared on their right. Several street vendors sat or squatted in front of it, tending hibachi grills or building sandwiches from the contents of battered old Styrofoam coolers.

The scene reminded Luong that he hadn't eaten in some time. His stomach rumbled. He frowned as the vehicle turned right into the reeking neighborhood south of the highway.

Most of the houses, including Phirum's, where they now arrived, were disheveled affairs constructed of stucco, rusty corrugated sheet metal and canvas. Half-naked kids played in the dusty road and yellow mongrels rooted around piles of trash. This was Cambodia's armpit, Luong thought, even worse than the Saigon slums where he had grown up.

Phirum drew the vehicle to a stop and said, "My house."

Luong knocked his fist several times against the panel behind his head. "Mau. Get her out and into Phirum's shithole of a house." Then to Phirum, "Hope your woman can make us some food." He opened his door. "We'll go in. Take the truck and hide it."

***

The truck had been rolling for about ten minutes. With her eyes tightly closed, Lien coughed, gagged and struggled for breath, each moment an agony. Then the vehicle stopped and the tailgate clanked down. At last Mau rose and took his weight off her shoulders.

He said, "Move, bitch."

Lien winced under his grip as he propelled her out the back of the vehicle. She tumbled onto the dusty road and opened her eyes. Where was she now? She remained on her knees behind the truck and furtively glanced around. A few people sat outside the dilapidated houses, sheds and lean-tos. Two men sat at a roadside table, drinking coffee and playing cards. A woman squatted on the littered ground picking nits from a child's hair. Just beyond the buildings, the road ended.

The people all wore indifferent expressions. She saw no place to escape, no doors to run through screaming for help.

She flinched and tried vainly to pull free from Mau's grip, gazing again toward the end of the road where it turned into a path that led through a field, lightly pimpled with low bushes.

She averted her eyes so Mau wouldn't notice that the path had caught her attention. Maybe she could run down that path and — who knows? — find a place to hide, find someone who could help her.

But Mau tightened his clutch on her bicep and thrust her toward the house.

She struggled again as he pushed her through the open door, a thin metal panel that hung desperately on a single hinge, and bore her into what must be the main room.

There were no windows, and apart from the open doorway the only light, blue and silvery, came from a TV resting atop the lone table. The television aired a talking head in a suit, blathering away in Khmer. A platform bed occupied half of the room. Luong perched on the edge of it.

A short, podgy woman took a curious peek at Lien and then opened a half-sized refrigerator on the other side of the room. She withdrew three bottles of beer and gave one each to Luong and Mau. She set the third on the table next to the TV.

Mau swilled a prodigious swallow of beer and then forced Lien to squat on the floor. He turned to the woman and growled something in Khmer.

The woman responded with venom in the same language.

Lien couldn't understand what either one said, but the woman pointed to her chest and said, "Chaya, Chaya," in the middle of her diatribe. So her name was Chaya. Would she have some empathy and female compassion or was she as heartless as the men?

The answer came immediately when Chaya shot Lien a cold glance and then went into another room. She returned with a loose bundle of worn and weathered rope, squatted and securely tied Lien's hands together and bound her ankles. Chaya pushed Lien into a sitting position on the floor in front of the bed.

Phirum came in through the door and loudly declared something.

Lien understood two words, "truck" and "hours." She fathomed that this meant the truck was hidden and that in a number of hours they would move again. Where would they take her? Was she to be sold again? She shivered at the thought and nausea welled up in her throat.

Chaya passed Phirum the third bottle. "Phirum. Bier."

At first, Phirum looked every bit as threatening as the other two. Lien studied his face, looking for opportunity. Was he any different than the other two? Did he have any kindness within him?

Then he said, in Vietnamese, "Let's have some sport with her while we're waiting for the time to pass." He put his hand on his fly and looked toward her cowering on the floor.

Lien squirmed toward a corner of the squalid room and looked to Chaya, seeking sympathy, or at least shelter, from this new menace. When Chaya avoided her silent pleas by looking sideways, her countenance stony and indifferent, Lien wormed the rest of the way into the corner and cowered, her bound hands covering her face, her legs drawn tightly up against her buttocks, knees locked together.

Phirum hauled out his stiffening member and waggled it in front of Lien's face until Luong shouted out, "Put it away, you idiot. If we're to sell her on the other side of the border, she cannot be any further damaged." Then to Chaya, he said, "Can you clean her up? Make her more attractive to the Thais?"

While Phirum zipped up his trousers and skulked off to nurse his beer in another corner of the room, Chaya said, "I will make her up. Fix her up good."

Luong held Lien's head and Mau restrained her squirming body while Chaya spread pancake makeup on her face and applied lipstick. She whimpered as Chaya roughly drove two small gold studs through the piercings in her ears.

Perhaps half an hour later, Chaya stood back to look at her and said, "She's somewhat presentable. I covered her bruises with pancake, and the gloss makes her lips look better."

Luong then gripped Lien's stone Buddha in a tight fist and jerked on it until the flimsy chain broke.

She wailed in Vietnamese, "No. Please, it's my Grandmother Quy's."

Luong hurled it onto the dirt floor and stomped on it with the heel of his sandal. "No cheap trinkets," he said, also in Vietnamese.

Lien's lower lip quivered, and then stiffened with resolve. The amulet had been her solace during the horrible two months she had endured, but it was only a thing. She could wear the image in her heart, just as she did her father's and grandmother's spirits. They could not take that away.

CHAPTER FORTY-FOUR

Shank drove straight toward the border on the most direct route, the one the thugs who had Lien would most likely have taken.

With sticky fingers, Trutch pressed hard on the dressing on his side, where blood seeped through and ran in rivulets down to his hip. He winced in pain as the vehicle jounced over a rough stretch of road just outside the complex of casinos.

Judith glanced at him with concern. "Pete, your wound is bleeding through the bandages. We need to get you some medical attention."

"Negative. This is as close as I've been to Lien. I'm not stopping for another Band-Aid." But he flinched when they hit the next bump.

"You won't do her any good if you pass out from blood loss," Judith gently admonished him. Then to Shank, in a voice that rasped with concern, "Is there a hospital in this city?"

"A new one. Poipet Referral Hospital. It's a few kilometers east of here."

"Pete. I really think we should take you there."

"No dice," he said, swaying slightly, agony in his voice. "Shank, get us to the crossing."

They hit the traffic circle in front of the Cambodian immigration building on the border. Shank went a quarter way around the roundabout and then stopped on the shoulder within 200 meters of the gaudy portico that welcomed travelers into Cambodia. 100 meters beyond, red and white barber poles marked the Thai border. Several Cambodian National Police vehicles were parked haphazardly around the Cambodia side of the crossing, and uniformed policemen milled about, but the gray delivery truck was nowhere in sight. Colonel Khlot, however, stood arms akimbo, talking with two border policemen.

Trutch leaned toward the front seat and pointed, "Shank, see if you can get closer to that brassy looking cop. I want to talk to him." Clearly in pain now, his words came out heavy and breathy.

Shank eased forward about ten meters. Khlot noticed them and strode over. He bent and peered through the rear window. "Well, Mr. Trutch. Did you come up here for some R&R? Do you fancy gambling?"

"Listen," Trutch said clearly, then wheezed slightly, "My granddaughter was taken again, minutes ago, from the pagoda back there." He turned his head sharply to the left, signaling the direction of the temple. "The kidnappers are driving a gray truck. Its left rear panel will be damaged. They smashed into us."

"And it looks like you've been shot. Better get to hospital, Mr. Trutch. We have this crossing well covered and the one to the south as well. They won't get past our screen and into Thailand. We want that fellow Luong as badly as we want to free your granddaughter from harm."

Trutch sagged into the seat. "There are three of them. They're armed. Please be careful. If there's shooting, don't let my granddaughter be harmed."

"We know they're armed, Mr. Trutch. You've been shot. And they killed a policeman in Svay Pak. Don't worry. Now that we have your description of the truck, we'll put out a province-wide bulletin on them. And we have the border under surveillance. We don't want your granddaughter hurt either, especially me. I have children." An expression of genuine concern softened his features. "You should get to hospital. Your color is bad." He turned and snatched a radio microphone from the dashboard of one of the police vehicles.

***

Minutes later, Shank drove up to Poipet Referral Hospital's emergency entrance, where several attendants rushed to the vehicle. Carefully, they lifted Trutch out and placed him on a gurney. They wheeled him in through swinging doors and parked him in the emergency department, a four-bed closet. Glass-fronted and locked, a stainless steel cabinet hovering on one wall contained resuscitation equipment and a variety of instruments, bandages and medications. Several IV poles stood like sentinels along the same wall, their suspended bottles resembling hanging victims. Aside from these few items and the beds, there was little else to the facility.

Trutch had difficulty focusing in the brightly lit room, but he managed to read the label on one of the bottles. What the hell is Ringer's Lactate? he wondered, thinking it sounded like something on the agenda of a wet nurse.

His thoughts were interrupted when a young man's face appeared directly over his own. "I'm Dr. Tam. You've lost a lot of blood. We're going to give you a unit of whole blood, intravenously. Fortunately, you're type AB, the universal recipient. While that's going on, I'll debride and drain the wound. Then we'll suture it and re-dress it tightly. I'm going to use a local anesthetic, so you'll feel a couple of stings."

"Okay, Doc. How soon can I be out of here?"

"You should stay overnight, but I understand your situation. We'll try to have you on your feet in about four hours."

"Shit. That long?"

"At least," said the medic. "Do you know when you last had a tetanus shot?"

"About three years ago, I think."

"Okay. They're good for ten years."

Trutch lay back, resigned. He grunted with the effort of even that small movement and didn't bother to argue or struggle. He needed to regain his strength to carry on.

A young nurse found a vein and neatly inserted the catheter that would deliver new blood to his partially depleted system. Even through his pain, he couldn't help but note that she wore a push-up bra that accentuated her breasts, firm, neatly rounded mounds.

Trutch closed his eyes.

Judith leaned over his gurney, "Your friend Colonel Khlot has been in touch with us by cell phone. There have been no sightings of the gray van or Lien so far, but there are many border police and national policemen on high alert. He assures us they can't get across the border."

"Thanks. I feel so useless lying here with a needle in my arm and some dude fiddling around my side with scissors and needles."

"They'll have you on your feet in no time. Would you like me to call Catherine and bring her up to speed?"

"Oh God, no. She'd be worried sick. Just do what you can to get us out of here."

CHAPTER FORTY-FIVE

At 9:30 p.m., Lien again sat on the hard wooden bench in the back of the truck, her hands still bound. Mau sat opposite, staring malevolently at her. Over the engine noises, the faint sound of voices issued from the cab. She thought Phirum might be talking on a cell phone, using that foreign Khmer tongue.

She now felt certain she was about to be sold again and delivered into another world of degradation and horror. If she was to escape, it must be within the next few minutes. But how? If the vehicle slowed or stopped, could she again leap out the back? Her legs were unbound, but she would still have to open the canvas curtain over the tailgate. That would be difficult with her hands tied, but she had managed it before. But this time, she had Mau to contend with. He wouldn't just look the other way while she attempted to clamber out over the tailgate.

The vehicle swerved sharply first to the right and then to the left. Unable to grip the bench, her body teetered and swayed. She almost toppled over twice but recovered at the last moment each time. Mau snickered. This must be a roundabout. She knew of two at home in Quy Nhon.

The vehicle accelerated sharply and she slid toward the tailgate. Seconds later, the driver slammed on the brakes and she was thrown forward into the bulkhead. Mau, too, pitched into the dividing wall and then fell onto the floor. Lien's head hit the wall hard. Dazed, her vision blurred for a second or two. But Mau was down. Was this the time to bolt?

She rose on trembling legs and moved toward the curtain over the tailgate. Shouts sounded from outside the vehicle. Then both of the cab doors opened. More shouting. Then gunshots, many of them.

CHAPTER FORTY-SIX

Poipet was engulfed in darkness. Over Dr. Tam's mild protests, Trutch insisted on being discharged and received a small ziplock bag of analgesics. With Judith, he crossed the grass and gravel parking area to the SUV and climbed in.

"Head for the border," he said to Shank. "We'll check in with Colonel Khlot."

They approached the roundabout from the east, in light traffic. Floodlights bathed the entire crossing area and Cambodian National Police vehicles still sat poised near the immigration building.

Shank said, "There!" He pointed to Luong's gray truck as it emerged from the other side of the circle and sped toward the border.

Trutch shouted, "Go, go, go!"

On the Thai side of the border, 150 meters ahead of the truck, a border policeman pumped his arm in a signal for the truck to proceed.

Shank sped through the circle and aimed the vehicle toward the border, no longer driving so much as pointing the vehicle, like a missile homing in on a target.

Several national policemen spotted the speeding truck and ran toward the roadway, weapons drawn. The Thai border guard continued to wave furiously.

Seconds before the truck would have left Cambodian territory, two police vehicles lunged, tires spinning, from either side of the roadway. In a cloud of dust, they blocked the road.

The gray truck braked hard and slid to a halt. Policemen ran toward it brandishing their weapons.

Both truck doors opened, and the two men scrambled out.

Luong raised his pistol and took aim at a policeman.

He went down in a fierce fusillade of gunfire.

Phirum shot his hands into the air over his head.

Shank stopped the SUV ten meters behind the truck.

"No," Trutch rasped, as he watched the scene unfold through the windshield. "No shooting. Don't fire." He sat frozen to his seat, his throat open and dry.

By the time he got the words out, the shooting had stopped. Luong lay crumpled on the ground, his hand still gripping the Glock.

Two policemen yanked open the rear curtain and dropped the tailgate. Two others stood by with AK-47 rifles at the ready. One of the cops reached in and helped a girl to the ground. She stood quaking as they pulled Mau from the rear of the truck and dumped him on the ground to cuff his hands behind his back.

Lien wobbled a bit on her feet and listed to one side, her expression that of a soldier who had seen too much combat.

The thousand-yard stare, Trutch thought. So, this was his granddaughter. She looked so tender, so terrified. He reached for the door handle.

From the back seat, Judith gripped his shoulder. "Don't. Right now you could be just another pedophile to her. She's traumatized."

In spite of her caution, Trutch opened the door and stepped out. As he moved toward Lien, Colonel Khlot approached her from the opposite direction.

Lien rushed to the colonel. She embraced him around his waist, and sobbing without constraint, lay her head on his chest.

Khlot looked around at the police and at Trutch, his expression one of awkward embarrassment. He made eye contact with Trutch, held it for a second or two, and then amid a stream of electrified chatter sputtering from police radios, he shrugged and pulled Lien close.

CHAPTER FORTY-SEVEN

Thirty minutes into the flight from Tan Son Nhat International Airport to Taipei — the first leg of their trip back to Seattle — towering clouds, muscular and threatening, appeared outside Catherine's window. A chime sounded and the seatbelt sign came on. The captain's voice announced that there could be "moderately bumpy air" ahead.

Catherine tugged on her seatbelt as the aircraft bounced slightly in the roily air. She turned to Pete, reclining in his business class seat, eyes closed, oblivious to the lightning and ominous cloud formations. Cautiously, with tenderness, she reached for his hand. It had been nearly two months since his revelation of unfaithfulness. That had been a bombshell, she thought, to say nothing of his terrifying romp around Vietnam and Cambodia over the past few weeks.

Her own experiences in Vietnam had far exceeded the boundaries of her day-to-day life, and she had never before experienced such high levels of fear and adrenaline. This had changed her somehow, although she wasn't yet sure how, exactly. For the past eight weeks their world had been turned upside down. Did they even know each other any more?

She squeezed his hand. "Pete, are you awake? We've hardly had a chance to speak to each other since you got back from Cambodia. We need to talk."

"Of course. I'm so tired I feel like putty. I've been running on empty for days now. But maybe talking will energize me again. Where do you want to start?"

She preferred to start with something somewhat benign rather than plunge right into a deep-water discussion about their relationship. "With you. You've been through hell the past couple of months. How do you plan to decompress once we're home?"

"Initially I don't want to do anything except hang around the house with you. I want to try to recapture the life we had before that letter arrived just before Labor Day."

The aircraft shuddered and Catherine cinched her seat belt tighter. Still not quite ready to broach the subject of their marriage, she dodged the issue. "Then what? If I know you like I think I do, you're already mapping out some actions you want to leap into because of all that's happened in the past two months."

"Well, yes. I've thought of several things I'd like to do."

"Like what?"

"I want to go down to LA and shake the hand of a customs agent by the name of Thomas Lowen. Brad Cassidy, the FBI man in Phnom Penh, told me that they learned of Lien's whereabouts in Svay Pak because this Lowen guy was suspicious of one particular passenger. I'll do my best to see that he's officially commended for helping save the life of a thirteen-year-old girl. The man deserves a medal."

"I'll go with you. I'd like to visit Mrs. Nguyen, the woman who launched me onto my quest for Dream in Xuan Loc."

"I'd love it if you came along. Do you want to continue on from LA to Australia? I'd also like to deliver my condolences, in person, to Andrew Quang's family. He was another hero in finding Lien."

"Yes. You should do that, and I'll go with you."

"Jeez. This is bumpy, isn't it?" Now Trutch tightened his seatbelt, too, as the quivering intensified in the unstable air.

"Terrible," Catherine said. "What about Lien? Do you think you'll have a relationship with her? How are you feeling now that you've got her in rehab?"

"It's been a crazy four days hasn't it? But yes, I want a relationship with her. I feel like I bonded with her even before I laid eyes on her. And then when she turned and hugged Colonel Khlot ..." his eyes clouded. "I thought we'd lost her. I couldn't believe how she clung to that scumbag pedophile. But I realize now that she believed he'd saved her."

"Probably. And you must realize, too, that even though she was at the center of your thoughts for two months, she'd never laid eyes on you before. She had no idea who you were and likely didn't even notice you when she was pulled from the back of that truck. Colonel Khlot would have been the only familiar face for her in that terrible moment."

"A face I wanted to smash. Screw their 'cultural norms.' They're corrosive and just plain wrong. Thank God she's safely in Saigon now."

"Yes. What's the long-term outlook there?" Catherine asked. "Did Judith say?"

"She'll need at least two years of rehab to be desensitized to her experiences. Even then, she'll have nightmares and flashbacks for years. She may always distrust men, and we can only wait and see how her health is affected. They were injecting her with contraceptives that might prevent her breasts and uterus from developing normally, but that's not certain yet. And she may be susceptible to feelings of anger and frustration for years, perhaps her lifetime. She might become aggressive, or pessimistic or too fragile. We'll just have to wait and see."

The aircraft pitched and yawed a little more vigorously and in a row of seats somewhere behind them a child rattled off a chain of loose, phlegmy coughs. The middle-aged woman across the aisle from Trutch placed a medical mask over her mouth and nose.

"Well, thank God she tested negative for HIV," Catherine said. "And at least Ngoc can visit her regularly."

"Thanks to you, Catherine. I'm so proud of you for making that happen. The last few days have been so unsettled, I don't know how you found time to locate an assisted- living facility for him in Ho Chi Minh City."

"Do you think there's a chance they'll all stay in Saigon after Lien's well?"

"Who knows? My guess is not. They're country people. I'm just hoping that they can get the necessary home help, so Lien and Ngoc can live together as a family again."

"We can afford to help with that. I'd like to."

"That's good of you," Trutch said. "You've been amazing through all of this."

"Well. Was Poipet any less depressing than Svay Pak?" she asked, still trying to delay getting to the real issue.

"I'll put it this way. I don't think it's entirely coincidental that Poipet sounds like toilet."

They suspended their conversation as the flight attendant offered each of them a pillow and blanket and checked that their seat belts were secure.

When she had moved on down the aisle, Trutch took a careful sip of the rich, steamy coffee from his sloshing mug. "Ahh. I love Vietnamese coffee."

Catherine clutched Trutch's hand tightly. "Pete, Look at me please. I need to talk about us — you and me."

He turned and their eyes met. "I know. I just don't know where to begin. While I'm relieved that this whole fiasco is over and that Lien is safe, I'm also exhausted and on edge. I know that I have some explaining to do and the words are just not coming easily."

"Oh Pete, just speak from your heart. I've begged you so often to do just that."

"I know that you have, but I have to confess I'm not sure I know what that means. I'm always open and honest with you. If you don't already think I speak from the heart, maybe I don't have a 'heart' in the same sense that you do. "

"You've just demonstrated my dear, sweet man that you most definitely have a heart. Leaping on an airplane and flying to Asia to rescue a granddaughter you hadn't met or heard of is not the action of a heartless guy. But, because you're a man of few words, those of us who love you are often confused and hurt. What I'd really like is for you to speak of your *feelings* — not just your conclusions and impressions. And I'd like you to listen deeply when I try to share my feelings with you."

"But I think I do."

"Pete. Often when I'm trying to tell you how I feel about something, your response is to want to fix the problem … to offer a solution. That's natural to you. That's why you were successful in the army and as a businessman. But that's not responding from the heart. Coming to Vietnam, and for you Cambodia, was the right thing to do. No question. And I think that, in time, I'll get over your affair with Dream. But through all of this I've realized something profound about our marriage."

The plane plummeted several hundred feet as it hit a pocket of turbulent air. Coffee sloshed onto their tray tables. Several passengers screamed. Despite herself, Catherine gasped and grabbed again for Pete's hand. The plane regained the lost altitude just as rapidly, but jounced and yawed severely. The pilot asked the crew to take their seats. His voice struck Catherine as somewhat overly calm and controlled.

Her heart pounded. She'd better say what she had to say before the bloody airplane crashed into the Pacific and she and Pete still had this gulf between them.

"Something profound?" Pete asked, putting his lips close to Catherine's ear as the aircraft continued to quake and shudder violently.

"I saw clearly how wrong I've been all these years." She turned, her words harsher than her intent, her voice bouncing as badly as the airplane.

Pete's face registered fear. "Wrong about what?"

"We've had a good life together, and I don't regret much of it. But there's always been, at some deep level, a distance, an unspoken gulf. I always thought, because we didn't talk about it, that you were disappointed in me because I was barren. Now I wonder if that distance was because of Dream."

Pete took her hand. "Catherine, no. I've never sensed any distance between us and if it seemed to you that I was distant at times ... then I'm so sorry. I think I may get lulled into thinking that you can read my mind after all these years. I promise you that it wasn't Dream. She's been stored away in the deepest recess of my mind for many years."

"Are you sure?"

"Absolutely, sweetheart. And listen, I've learned a lot about myself over these last two months. It was a mistake to keep that affair bottled up for four decades. But I've also learned not to take our marriage for granted. At times I've been complacent and I need to work on that." He smiled at her and added, "And I'll need your help to learn to speak from the heart."

"Then we have a lot of work to do." Catherine said.

EPILOGUE

Since Lien's rescue, she had blossomed into a mature and poised young woman, tall for a 16-year-old. Three years in rehab had rebuilt her self-esteem, though her eyes occasionally mirrored sadness. Some nights she still suffered nightmares, and at times she panicked at the nearness of an unknown man.

Now, wearing the white ao dai of a high school girl, her luxuriant black hair gathered into a ponytail that hung to just below her waist, Lien stood erect and confident beside her father's wheelchair, her hand resting affectionately on his shoulder.

Trutch, looking a little haggard from jet lag, stood in front of the two, chatting amiably with them and Duc, Judith Grinder's investigator. Just this morning, he and Catherine had completed the 20-hour journey from Seattle to Ho Chi Minh City, their sixth in the last three years, and had immediately gone on to the cemetery near Xuan Loc, where they had come to honor Dream. In halting Vietnamese, he asked Lien, "How is your friend Diamond?"

In response, Lien looked puzzled.

Trutch smiled apologetically. "Sorry, and that's after completing all four levels of the Rosetta Stone course in Vietnamese."

Ngoc laughed and repeated the question in more accurately enunciated Vietnamese for Lien.

"I'm sorry to say, Grandfather, that she left the rehabilitation center and returned to Phnom Penh. She's a prostitute there."

Ngoc translated.

Tears welled up in Trutch's eyes when Lien called him 'Grandfather.' "That's unfortunate," he said. "I'm sorry to hear that."

In response to his tears, Lien reached for his hand and squeezed it.

"We all did our best for Diamond," Duc said. "Once they moved from Phnom Penh to Saigon, Judith and I visited the girls in the rehab center weekly. Diamond was severely damaged. And hopelessly addicted. She had to be on methadone to hold off her craving for yama. The specialists in the center

228

warned us that she would likely not re-integrate. But we kept our hopes up."

Twenty meters away, across the unkempt field of headstones, Catherine and Judith stood talking with a saffron-robed monk and a man in blue coveralls. Catherine slipped the man in coveralls a $20 bill and shook his hand. Then she called to the others, "Would everyone come over here please? I'd like to show you something."

"Hang on," Trutch said, as he pushed Ngoc's wheelchair over the rocky turf.

Duc and Lien followed, trailing a few steps behind Trutch until, at Catherine's direction, the group gathered in a semicircle before the monk. She distributed joss sticks, and they each lit one and clutched it.

The monk then placed his palms together in the prayerful position and chanted a short mantra. When he finished, he stepped aside and with a swish of his robes revealed a new headstone made of elegant black marble. Catherine had arranged the engraving:

Nguyễn Thị Tuyết 29 tuổi
Con Trai 1 ngày tuổi
"DREAM"

Both Trutch and Ngoc smiled broadly. "That's *outstanding*," Trutch said. His eyes brimmed for a second time as he moved to Catherine's side and hugged her. Into her hair he murmured, "You're a beautiful, thoughtful woman

A short distance back, unseen by Trutch's group, a man in a green uniform held a burning joss stick aloft between his palms and bowed reverently three times. He used the incense to light a cigarette and then plunged the stick into a planter. With a final deferential glance toward the group, Captain Minh turned and strode to his SUV for the drive back to Saigon.

ABOUT THE AUTHOR

R. Bruce Logan is a retired US Army officer. He served two one-year tours of duty in Vietnam during the '60s and early '70s. Since 2006, he and his wife, Elaine Head, have engaged in humanitarian work among the marginalized in Vietnam. Together they have written an award winning memoir, *Back to Vietnam: Tours of the Heart*, published in 2013, which describes their experiences in Vietnam. When not in Hoi An, Vietnam, which has become their second home, they live on Salt Spring Island in British Columbia.

ACKNOWLEDGEMENTS

Writing a piece of fiction is a complicated and tricky undertaking, particularly when one attempts it for the first time in his 70s. Fortunately, I've been surrounded by a number of bright and helpful people during the two years I've been working on this manuscript, not the least of which is my dear wife, Elaine. Without her gentle encouragement, her timely suggestions, her editorial talent and her sometimes scathing critiques, I would still be wallowing in a miasma of wimpy verbs, corny similes and mixed metaphors. My writing mentor, Pearl Luke, is a stellar technician of words and sentences, an exemplary coach and a steadfast friend. She deserves much of the credit for any measure of success I achieve with this work. I'm grateful to the following people who served as beta readers and provided me with helpful comments on early drafts of the manuscript: Gail McKechnie, Roger Upton, David Logan, Linda Hutchison-Burn, Chance Chambers, Jennifer Peterson Stockstill, Letitia Lane, Wendy Eggertson and Shelley Wigglesworth. Brian McConaghy, founder of the Ratanak Foundation in Vancouver, BC, was kind enough to sit patiently with Elaine and me to answer our questions about the structure of the trafficking and slavery network in Cambodia and to advise us on typical scenarios for raids on brothels in Svay Pak. Chad Smith, a volunteer for Agape International Missions in Svay Pak conducted us on a tour of the former brothels in that village. Don Brewster, founder of Agape International Missions, which has rescued over 200 enslaved girls in Cambodia, helped to greatly expand our understanding of the scope of the problem. Murray Reiss, of Salt Spring Island, is an outstanding copyeditor who devoted hours to relocating misplaced commas and repairing grammatical transgressions. Last, but certainly not least, I wish to acknowledge my "niece" Nguyen Minh Nguyet (Selene) who painstakingly waded through the manuscript to ensure that my spelling and usage of Vietnamese words and phrases was accurate. My profound thanks to all these people.

AUTHOR'S NOTE

This is a work of fiction. The plot, storyline and scenes are all the product of my imagination. The theme of child trafficking, however, is based on factual data gleaned from academic literature and journalism, careful investigation on the Internet, interviews and field visits to both Vietnam and Cambodia. The characters are also fictitious, although some of their stories mirror those of persons I have met and have either come to know or have interviewed.

The village of Svay Pak is real. It lies 11 kilometers north of the capital city of Phnom Penh on the bank of the Tonle Sap River. At one time, more than six brothels operated in this small village, specializing in trafficked children. The events set in Svay Pak, and my character Lien's horrifying experiences there, accurately represent the nefarious activity that occurred on a daily basis in Svay Pak.

I am happy to report that as of this writing (2015), no active brothels remain in Svay Pak. Thanks in large measure to the efforts of Don Brewster and his wife Bridgette, the situation has improved measurably in the past few years. This dedicated couple, along with a stable of international volunteers and local talent, is committed to prevention, rescue and rehabilitation. Owing to their visionary gift, coupled with hard work, economic alternatives to trafficking and slavery are developing within the community.

But many other Svay Paks exist in Southeast Asia, where the sexual exploitation of children continues to flourish. In fact, child prostitution has become less visible and less concentrated in geographic enclaves as a result of technology and mobility. A predator visiting Phnom Penh, or any of several other cities in Cambodia, Thailand or Malaysia, need only make a phone call or send a text message to have an underage prostitute delivered to his hotel room.
Child trafficking for the purpose of sexual exploitation is a global issue of catastrophic proportions. The predators and thugs who achieve gratification and profit from this practice make me feel shame for my gender. Profits from this book will be donated to several foundations working hard to combat this problem.

Purchase other Black Rose Writing titles at www.blackrosewriting.com/books

and use promo code PRINT to receive a 20% discount.

BLACK ROSE
writing™

CPSIA information can be obtained
at www.ICGtesting.com
Printed in the USA
LVOW12s0408210416

484588LV00001B/51/P

9 781612 966908